S0-BAE-063

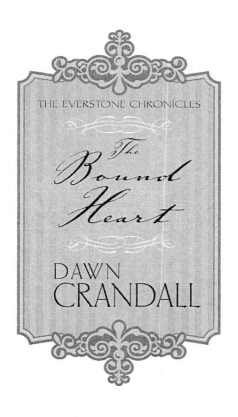

THE EVERSTONE CHRONICLES

The
Bound
Heart

DAWN
CRANDALL

NOV 1 1 2015

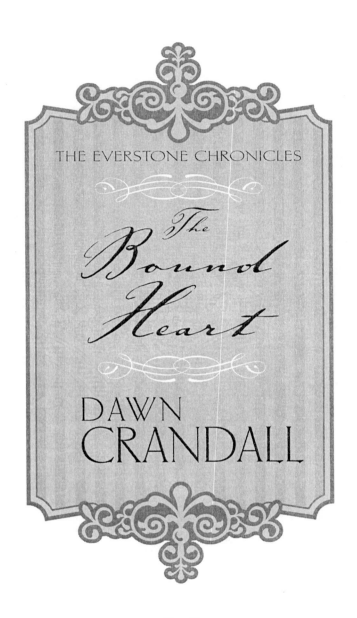

THE EVERSTONE CHRONICLES

The Bound Heart

DAWN CRANDALL

WHITAKER
HOUSE

Publisher's Note:
This novel is a work of fiction. References to real events, organizations, or places are used in a fictional context. Any resemblances to actual persons, living or dead, are entirely coincidental.

All Scripture quotations are taken from the King James Version of the Holy Bible.

THE BOUND HEART
The Everstone Chronicles ~ Book Two

dawncrandallwritesfirst@gmail.com
www.facebook.com/dawncrandallwritesfirst
www.twitter.com/dawnwritesfirst/@dawnwritesfirst
www.pinterest.com/dawnwritesfirst

ISBN: 978-1-62911-659-4
eBook ISBN: 978-1-62911-230-5
Printed in the United States of America
© 2014 by Dawn Crandall

Whitaker House
1030 Hunt Valley Circle
New Kensington, PA 15068
www.whitakerhouse.com

No part of this book may be reproduced or transmitted in any form or by any means, electronic or mechanical—including photocopying, recording, or by any information storage and retrieval system—without permission in writing from the publisher. Please direct your inquiries to permissionseditor@whitakerhouse.com.

This book has been digitally produced in a standard specification in order to ensure its availability.

PROLOGUE

The Cave

"All human happiness and misery take the form of action."
—Aristotle

June 19, 1885 · Mount Desert Island
Bar Harbor, Maine

Come on, Meredyth," Vance Everstone urged with a smile.

"Only if you go first," I called down as I sat upon a large boulder, positioned higher than his broad six-foot frame.

Vance suddenly seemed so grown up as he gazed at me with that crooked grin. In that moment, I had the first inkling of what it might be like to have Vance Everstone fall in love with me. I had loved him, had waited for him to love me—for years while I'd been at boarding school, and then as I'd suffered through my first season while he'd finished his last year at Harvard.

I wasn't truly afraid of going into the cave or of anything that might be inside those familiar caverns. They were accessible only during low tide along the coastline of my family's summer cottage on Mount Desert Island. However, Vance didn't know anything about my fears or the lack thereof. All he knew, as evidenced in his eyes, was that I had changed in the last year.

And I *had* changed. I would soon turn nineteen, and I'd finally grown up enough for Vance Everstone to notice me. I was finally more than just my brothers' little sister.

We'd known each other since the day I was born. Every summer, our families would sail from Boston to Bar Harbor to enjoy the cooler weather. And for as long as I could remember, the boys had ruled the summers: the three Everstone brothers, my three older brothers, and Lawry Hampton, whose family lived in the house between the Everstones and the Summercourts.

This left me with only Estella Everstone, who had just turned fifteen, and Ainsley Hampton, who was only twelve. It was apparent, at least to Vance, why I would want to seek out his company that day. He was the most intriguing person in the whole bunch, and he knew it well.

Vance's only response to my declaration was a hooded look, added to the assertive gaze he'd already been giving me. I knew he could see my wet and sandy bare feet, as well as my ankles. The very same ankles he'd seen above those bare feet my entire life.

Instead of tucking my feet beneath my petticoats, I lifted them an inch higher. I extended my right foot, moving it this way and that, and laughed. "What dirty feet I have!"

He took a step closer to the high rock I sat upon and grabbed my foot, gently brushing off the sand. Then he did the same for my left.

The touch of his hands on my skin made me uncomfortable, but instead of shying away from the feeling, I wanted more. It became almost addictive.

When he finished brushing off the caked-on sand, he placed his hands firmly upon my ankles and positioned my feet against his chest, particles of sand getting all over his white shirt. He stood there, holding my ankles, staring at me with a new look in his eyes. One I'd never seen before.

I didn't know what it meant, but I wanted to find out.

He suddenly let go of my ankles and stepped back. I wasn't prepared for this, and I slid down the gently sloped rock, landing upon my feet directly before him.

His deep brown eyes took me in, and he repeated his question: "I dare you to go into the cave, all the way to the back—where it's deepest and darkest."

It was the same request, the same exact phrase we'd always taunted each other with, ever since we were children, playing together on those very rocks. However, with no one else present, it sounded like a completely different kind of question.

With a brand-new, soaring self-confidence, I stood my ground. "I'm not going in there alone."

It took him a few seconds of deliberating to decide whether to remain standing only inches from me or to do as I'd requested.

"Mere." He almost choked on my name. He surprised me by taking my hand and leading me into the familiar crevice of the tall, mountainous rocks. It really wasn't that dark in the caves during the morning hours, and so we could see as we followed the rough, uneven floor of the cave until it narrowed—and that was where we stopped.

"When did you get so beautiful?" In the time it had taken for him to lead me to this place, my confidence had doubled, if not tripled. I loved the way I felt with his eyes on me.

Knowing that I'd produced that look created a new power within that I hadn't known I possessed until that moment. I stepped closer, testing it.

"I must say, this old dress makes you appear rather...uncivilized." Vance fingered the tattered ruffles of my torn-up, ratty dress and then my collarbone just above them. Emboldened, I took his other hand and placed it at my waist. Since I wore a corset under my dress, I really didn't think I would be that affected by this touch—but that was before both his hands were sliding up and down the material of the bodice.

Watching Vance's face as he apparently enjoyed himself pushed my new feelings along and made me wonder, if he liked touching my feet and my waist, what else would he enjoy?

I soon found out. His fingers grazed my arms, traveling upward, past my collarbone again, then tunneled through my hair at the back of my neck, setting my long tresses free.

"Vance." His name upon my lips darkened the desire on his face. I had yet to touch him after years of wanting to, and I was deliriously happy to find I could now make him want me.

My hands were behind me, pressed against the rough wall, out of the way. For all my bold thoughts, I didn't know if he would welcome my doing the same things to him…or if I dared. This was all too new, and while he was enjoying my newfound beauty, which I had presented to him willingly, I wasn't sure if I had the courage to enjoy him in the same ways.

It was simply enough to enjoy him with my eyes.

"Meredyth, where are your hands?" he breathed.

I pulled them out from behind me, palms up, between us, splaying my fingers for him to see.

"What are you doing with them?"

"Nothing."

"I noticed," he said with a smile. He took hold of them and caressed my palms with his lips, then moved on to my wrists, which made my blood boil.

Without another thought, I put my arms around his neck, drew his face to mine, and kissed his lips. It was a tentative, almost innocent, first kiss, but when I realized how ardently he kissed me back, my boldness grew once again. I pressed myself to him, clutching his neck. I let him delve deeper and deeper into that kiss until it was all I knew.

Finally, Vance Everstone wanted me. Surely, he loved me.

I sank into the kiss, relishing the power of the emotions I'd evoked from him, kissing him back with equal desire. He pressed me against the hard, jagged wall. The force of the rocks in my back, and his groping hands as he grabbed at my skirts, brought me to my senses.

"Vance." I pushed at him with my fists.

His ragged breath passed my ear as he kissed my neck, not slowing in his exploration of my skin.

The balance of control had suddenly shifted, and my confidence turned to distress.

I tried to break free from his kiss, from his ever-searching grasps of my skirt. "Vance!"

He didn't listen; he only continued to kiss me more urgently. I didn't know how to stop him. I'd set this in motion without having the power to stop it. Shame replaced my earlier courage as the course of my actions became all too clear. I'd led him to that cave—to me—never knowing where my actions were headed.

Until it was too late.

ONE

Lawry Hampton

"There is no surprise more magical than the surprise of being loved."
—Charles Langbridge Morgan

Wednesday, January 21, 1891 · Back Bay
Boston, Massachusetts

No matter how well practiced I was, I couldn't help but stare.

There was something about Lawry Hampton that kept drawing my attention. The last time I'd seen him was at the park near the docks of Bar Harbor as my family and I had departed for Boston at the end of summer.

He'd seemed different when he'd returned from his hiatus to Washington State in February, almost a year ago. But who didn't change some in two years? However, it was the change that had occurred within the last four months that gave me pause. He seemed altered after spending so many months at his father's law firm in Bar Harbor again. He seemed far more determined to do something.

Everything about him seemed different, save for those reserved yet unyielding blue eyes that had a way of searching a person through and through, those eyes that always seemed to discover the truth of any matter.

No matter how things seemed.

Before I knew it, dinner had come to a close, and Lawry stood from his seat at the other end of the room and walked directly toward my end of the table. Surely, he was crossing to speak with my brother, except that I realized Garrett had already made his way out to the hall with Lawry's youngest sister, Ainsley, on his arm, along with everyone else from the party.

That meant only one thing: Lawry wanted to see me and me only.

"Meredyth." He offered me his hand, his face lit by the familiar boyish grin I remembered so well.

I took his hand and stood. I didn't know why I hadn't until that moment. Everyone else had.

"Lawry." All I could do was smile.

"It's good—it's so very good to see you again," he said, as if struggling for words.

He appeared much taller, though it was impossible for him to have grown an inch above his height, which I knew to be at least six feet, at the age of nine and twenty. He had always towered over me. His famous Abernathy nose, with the slight bump along the bridge, was level with my eyes, just like always.

"Ainsley and I have become marvelous friends since she's come to stay with your aunt Claudine." I gripped his arm possessively. "I can tell you, Lawry, I like her a hundred times more than all the other debutantes who came out this year."

He guided me down the hall toward the drawing room, where most of our party was already congregated. Garrett and Ainsley walked ahead of us. I remained silent, trying to catch what they said to each other, but I couldn't make it out. I gave up trying when they entered the drawing room. Ainsley Hampton proved difficult to read, at least when it came to Garrett.

Lawry held me back while the rest of the party settled in to listen to Ainsley's friend Hazel Detlefsen play the old box grand piano at the far end of the room.

"Meredyth, have you ever wondered just what I was doing in Washington those two years I was away with Nathan?"

I thought his question rather odd, until I realized that neither he nor Nathan had ever actually explained the reasons the two of them had been gone.

"Washington? I don't even know what you've been doing in Bar Harbor for the last few months. You're away so often, it seems. I feel I hardly know you anymore."

He stared at me with those rich, ocean-blue eyes. I could tell they were taking in every unspoken cue. "Yes, that's my fault, I admit."

"Weren't you and Nathan simply exploring the West Coast?" I looked into the drawing room from where we stood in the hall and noticed that Garrett no longer sat next to Ainsley. "Or were you doing research for a case for your father?"

I turned back to him to find he'd glanced away, down the hall. "Research. Yes, that was why I initially went west. But I did more than that."

I feared what he planned to tell me. He seemed reluctant, almost apprehensive. Was he really that anxious to tell me what he'd been doing? Was it something terrible he was afraid to admit? I couldn't believe it of him. Not Lawry Hampton.

"What did you do?" I dared to ask.

"I founded an orphanage...in Seattle."

"Lawrence Edward Hampton!" I tried to whisper, but it still came out a little louder than it should have. "Are you serious? Is that the truth?"

He laughed. "I know it's odd, isn't it?" His gaze found mine again and held it. "I don't even know what made me do such a thing. Somehow, I was compelled to act, and it seemed like a good idea at the time."

"A good idea? You must have changed countless lives!" I squeezed his arm with mine. "Are there many orphans in Seattle?"

"As many as are here in Boston." The hard muscles of his upper arm flexed under my fingers. "Especially after the fire that obliterated much of downtown the summer before last, their parents either are deceased or simply cannot afford to feed them. In any case, there are many children running wild, looking for food, and whatever else they can find."

"Wild orphaned children…." The thought appalled me, but I tried to conceal my shock. The orphans I knew weren't at all wild but rather were well-behaved little girls. "And now they have somewhere to go, somewhere to live, someone to feed them, to care for them…all because of you."

"Yes." He turned from me, his handsome face flushed with color. His profile was still striking, even as he neared the age of thirty.

I had a hard time dragging my eyes away, even though I dreaded the thought of him seeing my admiration and the sudden attraction I felt toward him. But he didn't end up turning back my way at all. It was almost as if he were too embarrassed to face me again.

"Lawry?" With the slightest of movements, I reached for his clean-shaven jaw and gently drew his face toward me. His eyes immediately sought mine, and I was struck by the seriousness of his countenance.

"Am I the only one you've told…besides Nathan?"

"I've wanted to tell you, Meredyth, for the longest time. I knew you'd understand."

He pricked my heart with his words, and I wished I deserved them.

"I'm glad you told me, Lawry. Especially since it means so much to you."

Lawry Hampton, Master of Surprises. Had I ever really known him at all?

"I'll see if I can sneak you back to the study a little later to show you the photographs I took before I left. I've hidden the ones of the orphanage all this time. You know, so I wouldn't have to answer everyone's questions."

"You baffle me." I met his eyes again. The look he gave me told me that I baffled him just as much, although the reason why was beyond me. Anyone else would have been just as surprised at his news. I felt incredibly honored that he'd chosen me to entrust with such information. Was his long-held secret the reason he'd acted peculiar all spring, and why he seemed different now?

"How long have you really wanted to tell me these things?"

"Oh, I don't know. Since boarding the train in Washington last February." He smiled ever so slightly.

At the sight of his crooked smirk, something in my chest warmed, and I had an overwhelming desire to weep. I forced myself to think of Vance Everstone…and my *almost* engagement.

"Almost a year, then? Why have you waited until now?" I pressed.

"Go ahead. Call me a coward."

Lawry Hampton was a lot of things, but a coward was not one of them.

"You still baffle me," I said instead.

"Good." And with that little word, he stepped into the drawing room and escorted me to the seat next to his sister.

⌒

True to his word, Lawry finagled a way for the two of us to escape the drawing room while Ainsley played a piece on the piano for the rest of the guests.

I followed him down the hall and into the immaculate two-level study. "Did my brother explain to you why he's decided to stay stateside this spring instead of joining Anton Partenheimer on his trip to Europe?" I asked. "Garrett has spoken for years about going with him."

"I have a feeling it has something to do with Ainsley. He seemed rather enthralled with her at dinner, but don't tell her that. I don't want her to know." Lawry walked to the opposite side of the room.

"Truly? Little Ainsley?" I walked around the large library table and strolled through the room, browsing the shelves of old books I'd seen a million times before. I'd spent a lot of time in that room over the years with Lawry and his closest friends, Nathan Everstone, Jayson Crawford Castleman, and my three older brothers. "Why wouldn't you want her to know? This is Garrett we're speaking of."

"Exactly. Everyone knows your brothers would rather play with hearts than settle down." Lawry walked the perimeter of the room and met me where I stood in front of my favorite section of books.

I studied him, still trying to figure out what it was about him that was so different. I'd always known Lawry was a *good* man, but how had I failed to grasp just how attractive he was? His tall, lean physique was cut to perfection in his formal evening wear.

I glanced at my cream-colored silk gown. Did he like how I looked? How my dress complemented my bright ginger hair? Did he appreciate anything about my appearance? I really was much too tall and too thin. "Willowy" was the word my mother always used to describe me—willowy, like my father.

After perusing the bookcases—while I perused him—Lawry selected a book from an upper shelf and cocked an eyebrow when he caught my lingering stare. I really couldn't tell if it was because of something I'd said or done...or something to do with Ainsley.

"I don't think she likes his attention," he said.

"But who wouldn't want Garrett's attention?" I took the small book from him, running my hand over the rough brown leather cover.

"She simply doesn't seem like the type of girl who would keep his interest for very long. She's so young and inexperienced. You know how your brothers like to flirt." Lawry stood before me, as if waiting for me to open the book.

"I believe Garrett has matured over the years, and perhaps he doesn't know what's hit him yet." My eyes met his again as I said the words, and a strange swirling sensation coiled about my stomach.

"Perhaps you're right." Lawry's blue eyes sparked. "It's always interesting when something like that happens between friends."

I swallowed. "I think they would be a perfect match."

"I, for one, think Ainsley's perfect all on her own."

"Of course you do. She's your baby sister." Jealousy welled in my chest. How many times had I wished my brothers were more like Lawry Hampton?

"And you're Garrett's baby sister. Which means you're perfect, as well, I suppose." He cocked his head, his intense gaze lingering on my face.

"At the age of four and twenty, I can hardly be considered a baby," I insisted.

"Oh, I don't consider you a baby, believe me. What I should have said is, you're Garrett's beautiful younger sister, who is quite perfect in almost every way possible." He gave me a teasing smile that made his eyes glimmer.

"Yes, that is precisely what you should have said." I cracked the book's binding, intent on finding out just what title he'd wanted me to see so badly.

Lawry cleared his throat and stepped away. "Let me find those photographs for you." He crossed the room to the wall, opened a hidden door in the elaborate dark wood wainscoting, and brought out a small wooden chest.

In all the years I'd been snooping around that room, I'd never known the hidden door existed. Lawry was far more secretive and mysterious than I'd ever imagined.

He opened the chest and took out a pile of photographs.

I sat in the middle of the long, deep leather sofa in front of the roaring fireplace. When Lawry walked over, I expected him to sit beside me, but instead he shuffled the photographs in his hand as he paced between the sofa and the fireplace.

"What's the matter, Lawry?"

"I don't know. It's just...I'm not used to feeling like I have secrets. I don't know what I'm supposed to do."

"You mean, as benefactor of an orphanage?"

"I wasn't going to come home, Meredyth. I was set on staying there forever. I had a well-put-together plan, a life. I even considered marrying and settling down. Life is different in Seattle. It has a way of bringing out what's truly important to a person."

"You were going to stay there indefinitely?" It sounded selfish of him, but then, I remembered why he'd considered staying. He was so...giving. "Who were you going to marry? And what changed your mind?"

"As I mentioned, the fire destroyed every last belonging of many people, leaving them with nothing...especially children." He glanced from me to the photos in his hand, then returned his gaze to me. "I can tell by the look in your eyes that it doesn't make sense to you, and I don't know that it makes any more sense to me." He suddenly seemed guarded, as if afraid of what I might think of him. "I felt it was the right thing to do, that it was what God wanted me to do." He finally sat beside me, resting his elbows on his knees, still clutching the photographs. "Meredyth, I've wanted to show these to you more than anyone."

"Why?"

"Because you're one of my best friends...and you mean a great deal to me, Merit."

I grinned bashfully at the use of his old nickname for me.

"Even though we've hardly seen each other for the last few years—save for the few months we both spent in Boston last spring—no matter how long it's been, I can always count on you to welcome me back into your life with open arms."

Lawry Hampton still thought so much of me?

"But I need you to keep this a secret for now. I'm not certain how my family would take this news."

"Not even your parents know? In all the months you've been staying in Bar Harbor with them?"

"I doubt they'll understand. Life is very different outside of Bar Harbor, outside of Back Bay and Boston, even New England. There's less money, but more need of it." He handed me the small pile of photos, which I situated atop the leather-bound book.

There were maybe a dozen of them. The one on top showed what seemed to be a mansion built in the Queen Anne style, set high on a hill, with rows of weary-looking children standing in front of the wide covered porch. Flanking the children stood two women—one of them middle-aged, the other a pretty young lady—dressed in dark clothing.

"Who are these women?"

"The older one is Mrs. Flanagan. She followed her husband out to Washington, only to find he'd died from diphtheria days before her arrival. And the younger woman is Amelia Grendahl. She moved out west from Chicago years ago with her husband, who worked as a doctor in the area until succumbing to pneumonia just three weeks after she lost their first child." Lawry's eyebrows were scrunched together in frustration.

Never in my life had I heard of such misery. Those poor people—Mrs. Flanagan, Amelia, and all those orphaned children.

"Mrs. Flanagan and Amelia had both been working at a hotel in a nearby town when the establishment was sold to a man who intended to make the hotel into a saloon and a brothel. There would have been only one way for either of them to keep their job." Lawry didn't seem quite his usual free-and-easy self. I hardly recognized this side of him. "At least I was able to hire them in time to save their dignity."

I sat back against the sofa. His words stunned me into silence. Brothel. Keeping their jobs.

I knew very well what it meant, although theoretically, I wasn't supposed to. It surprised me that Lawry would speak of such things in my presence, but I was glad. It meant he considered me his equal, which was how I'd always regarded our relationship.

I was happy that Lawry had been able to found that orphanage in faraway Seattle so that these two women could keep their self-respect. Was Amelia Grendahl the young woman Lawry had considered marrying? Her appearance was the very opposite of mine. My willowy height and red hair were a complete contrast to her petite figure and light blonde curls.

I shuffled quickly through the rest of the photographs, hoping to find another picture that offered a clearer view of Amelia, but there weren't any more. Just that one.

The rest of the photos were clips of life inside the Queen Anne house. I kept going back to the first one of Mrs. Flanagan, Amelia, and all the children.

"How many orphans live there?" I asked while attempting to mentally count the heads in the photograph. When he didn't answer, I looked up.

Lawry studied me for a moment before speaking. "We'd convinced about two dozen to come live with us by the time I left last February, but there are always more. They're everywhere, living in the streets, growing up without any direction, without education, without anything, really, but the clothes on their backs."

I leaned toward Lawry and handed him the photographs.

"Meredyth, you understand, don't you?" He set them aside and covered my hand with his. "How I feel...? How this is—"

"Understand...that you want to go back?" I hoped I was wrong. I didn't like the thought of never seeing Lawry's handsome face again, of missing the camaraderie we'd always shared, and, of course, of losing him forever to some widowed stranger named Amelia Grendahl.

"And that there's more to the world than this glittering, gilded cage of wealth and society in which we've been raised. There are people suffering from more than just poverty and disease. They're living in a realm of darkness and sin—even in our own Boston."

"Then...then you're going to stay?" I asked hopefully.

"I don't know what I'm going to do. But to be honest with you, Meredyth...." His eyes searched my face as he placed his left arm at the back of the sofa beside me. Without another word, he moved in and enveloped me in his strong hold.

He held me pressed against his chest for some moments before the shock dissipated, and I relaxed into the comfort of him: my good, safe friend, Lawry.

As I melted into his warm embrace, I lifted my chin just a fraction of an inch in an effort to look up and smile. However, as my nose grazed his jaw, he leaned forward ever so slightly and pressed his lips to mine, infusing my mouth with the taste of peppermint. His arms tightened around my shoulders, but almost cautiously, as if he wasn't quite sure what he was doing.

I wasn't at all sure, myself.

Suddenly, I was having such a difficult time keeping my senses straight. All I could think was of how undeniably secure I felt because of his gentleness—and how very odd that seemed—while he kissed me.

His sculpted nose bumped into mine as he deepened the kiss; his hands were at my shoulders, his fingers lightly searching, caressing the skin from my spine to my collarbone and back again, until they were tunneled through my loosely pinned-up hair. I allowed him to continue to kiss me, all the while struggling to not seem too untoward, for I'd learned my lesson once before, and all too well.

But this kiss from Lawry seemed so very different.

"Mere—" his lips begged against mine between lingering kisses. "Meredyth, I…."

I let go of the book crushed between us, allowing my fingers to creep up his chest until my arms were around his neck, savoring the connection more than anything I could remember. He let out a heavy sigh when he realized I wasn't interested in stopping him.

The shock that this was my oldest, most favored friend leaning over me, kissing me eagerly, soon gave over to the fact that I was enjoying it very much. I never would have thought it possible that I could incite such passions from the even-keeled, levelheaded Lawry Hampton.

Before such eye-opening revelations were even finished forming in my mind, Lawry let go of me and stood to his feet, his treasured photographs scattering all over the floor between us. The safety and warmth of his embrace were quickly replaced by nothingness.

Raking his fingers through his disheveled hair, Lawry again paced before the fireplace. "I'm sorry, Meredyth. I have no idea why I allowed—" He looked disgusted with himself, and my only coherent thought was that I probably should have been disgusted with him, too.

What was it that made men want me and hate me at the same time?

First Vance. And now Lawry.

Lawry's kiss hadn't been expected, and it certainly hadn't been sought. Never in my life had the thought of kissing Lawry Hampton crossed my mind.

But it had happened. It was done. And now what? Contrary to my long-held expectations, the kiss hadn't repulsed me. Quite the opposite, actually. There was a strange new sensation that came over me: that, perhaps, we were meant for each other, Lawry Hampton and I.

But as the thought registered in my mind, I couldn't help rejecting it as preposterous. What was I thinking?

Noticing again the photographs at my feet, I took up the leather-bound book and stood from the sofa, now quite angry with myself...and with him, for making me forget myself—who I was, and what I needed to do.

I couldn't have him. I could never marry Lawry.

That much was certain.

I had to think of me—of my future.

Vance Everstone.

And my atonement.

Lawry still paced between the sofa and the fireplace. When he saw that I was also standing, he walked up to me and placed his hands on my shoulders. Oh, for all that is good and holy, was he going to kiss me again?

"Meredyth, please, you can't hold this against me." He closed his eyes. He sounded almost desperate. "I didn't mean for that to happen—"

"Yes. What were you thinking?"

He opened his eyes. He seemed agitated, very different from the Lawry I'd known for the duration of my life. "I didn't realize I was going to kiss you...and then, you—please, Meredyth, I need you to not turn on me now. I'm sorry I kissed you, but with Nathan and Amaryllis in Washington, you're the only one I have left here to understand what I'm going through."

His words reminded me of the reason we'd gone to the study in the first place.

The photographs. The orphanage.

Yes, I understood his problems. And I understood how conflicted he felt about his family's expectations of him. I even understood his bewilderment concerning me...and that kiss.

But Lawry Hampton had nothing to do with what I needed to accomplish with my life.

Vance Everstone—he was the one I needed to focus on, even if he was roaming about aimlessly on the other side of the world doing only God knew what. Marrying Vance was the only way I could make up for my gravest mistake.

I didn't need Lawry Hampton inadvertently leading me down the same path of destruction...or my leading him, which was probably a likelier scenario.

Lawry didn't deserve that.

And, more important, I didn't deserve him.

I stalked out of the room and down the hall to the drawing room. Claudine Abernathy, Garrett, and my parents were playing cards around a table, while Ainsley and Hazel were situated on a settee in the far corner of the room with their heads drawn close to each other, giggling at something.

"What have you and Lawry been doing, dear?" Mother never looked up from her cards.

Heat crept up my back as I reflected on the truth. "Lawry was telling me about his—Seattle."

"And where is he now?" Garrett shot a glance in my direction, then took a second, more thorough, look. "Is he coming back to join us?"

"I have no idea what he's doing," I replied, meaning the words in my heart so differently than anyone could have guessed.

⌒

I couldn't sleep that night. Kissing Lawry had brought back all the shame from the first time a man had wanted me so much.

Vance.

I fought the memory of Lawry's kiss and what that single act had done to weaken what had been, up until then, my well-maintained and self-composed determination to marry Vance Everstone.

I hated that I felt so bound to Vance, that there seemed to be some invisible, unbreakable thread stitching us together against our wills.

That it was against Vance's will to be bound to me was something I'd learned to accept over the years. He hadn't wanted me. Not forever, at least. And I'd tried to convince him, to persuade him, to reconsider, more times than I could count.

The sudden realization that I was tied to him against my own will was altogether new to me.

I sat up, keeping my long auburn hair spread about my shoulders as a layer of warmth, and, for a long while, stared at the shadows cast by moonlight upon the floor of my bedchamber. Then I remembered the book Lawry had handed to me in the study, before things between us had become so altered.

I'd taken it into the drawing room without a thought, and it was a wonder no one had mentioned it as I carried it all the way home.

It was only as I was walking up to my room that I had opened the cover of the book and read the title: *Leçons de Grammaire.*

I tossed back the warm, comfortable coverlet and threw my legs over the side of the bed. The cool night air didn't bother me half as much as everything sifting through my mind. I lit the small lamp on my bedside table, pulled my dressing gown about my shoulders, and stood.

Where had I thrown the book in my hurry to undress and hide under my covers, unwilling to speak to anyone for fear of bursting into tears? My reading chaise, of course. Hilda, my maid, would have placed it there, thinking I meant to read it.

How wrong she was.

I didn't want to read it. I didn't want to look at it, let alone open it.

But those things hardly mattered when I found myself standing before the plush gray velvet chaise longue, reaching down, and placing my cold fingers around the equally chilly binding.

I wouldn't open it. I wouldn't read a word. I didn't need to. It was a long-forgotten memory that haunted the book more than anything.

Lawry and I had been in the study at Hilldreth, practicing my French, using this ancient lesson book I'd happened upon. It had to have been over five years since then; right before...something else had happened.

"Lesson four." Lawry's resolute blue eyes had found mine as he'd turned the page and pointed to the first phrase at the top—meaningful and quite telling—and uttered the words with just a whisper. "Je t'aime...Meredyth."

TWO

Dr. Wellesley

"The most common form of despair is not being who you are."
—Søren Kierkegaard

I n bold block letters was the one name I dreaded seeing most of all.

LAWRENCE E. HAMPTON, ATTORNEY-AT-LAW

My family's stoic butler, Fenley, presented the calling card to me upon the silver tray, just like always. But never had one little piece of paper affected me so much.

I set down my cup of tea and took the card with shaky fingers, focusing upon the name, and what it might mean that he'd come to see me. Since kissing me, Lawry had not called at Summerton—it had been almost two weeks. And when I'd taken the initiative to call at Hilldreth to see Ainsley the day before, as I did almost every Monday afternoon, he'd come home while I was visiting and offered me a quick, awkward greeting before heading up the stairs, out of my reach.

And now, after days of trying desperately to conquer my thoughts of him, he was coming to call.

I stuffed the French lesson book in the cushions of the over-sized chair I was seated upon.

"Show him in, please, Fenley."

A few moments later, Lawry strolled into the room with his normal, casual gait. He wasn't dressed in calling attire but rather in a simple brown suit. As Fenley left the room, Lawry came bounding toward me.

"I can't stand this, Meredyth." He took my hands in his warm grasp and lifted me to my feet. "Can we forget it ever happened and go back to the way we were?"

The fact that his words brought such immense disappointment perturbed me to no end. But, really, did I not want to be Lawry's friend again? More than anything.

But could I forget that kiss? For days, I'd been under the hopeful yet delusional assumption that I had. However, seeing him again, standing close with his large hands grasping my slender ones, the familiar, stimulating woody scent of him invading my senses, I discovered that the real answer was no. I could not.

"This avoiding each other is killing me," he added, his blue eyes searching mine.

I pulled my hands from his and turned away. "Avoiding each other? I don't know what you mean. I haven't been avoiding you. I've simply been busy."

"Then let me apologize again for kissing—"

"Oh, that. Of course, Lawry," I said quickly, feeling perfectly at odds with myself. I circled about the chair I'd been sitting on, trying to keep myself as far away from him as possible.

"Splendid!"

As if it were that easily done. Surely, he could tell, no matter how I trained my tone of voice, that such an idea did not make me feel "splendid."

Lawry lowered himself onto the sofa, which was in the direction I'd been walking. "Will you go calling with me downtown today?

"Downtown? Who do we know downtown?" I asked, more than a little concerned about joining him on the sofa. I circled back around to my chair and sat.

"I'm going to see a friend of mine. You've probably heard Amaryllis speak of Dr. Grig Wellesley. He's the headmaster of the Trinity School for Girls, where she volunteered last spring."

"Yes, I've heard of Dr. Wellesley." I actually knew him very well. He was the man to whom Ainsley and I had submitted our applications in our interest to take over Amaryllis's position at the school when she'd married Nathan Everstone and moved to Washington State. "Won't people wonder what we're doing?"

"If anyone asks, we can simply say that we're interested in giving financial support to the school." He seemed to have everything already figured out quite tidily.

I, for one, had never planned on telling Lawry about my volunteering, especially now that I knew helping orphans was something dear to his heart. I didn't need him thinking we needed to combine our interests into a future together. That was not going to happen, no matter how he felt about me.

"We could drop by Hilldreth and pick up Ainsley, if you'd like." Lawry reclined at the end of the sofa. That he seemed so entirely untroubled in my presence was infuriating.

"No, I think I would rather…." What? Go with Lawry alone? No, that was a lie. But I also did not need Ainsley accidentally telling her brother about our "secret mission," as it were. "Perhaps we could invite Garrett and Ainsley to the library, instead." I knew Lawry loved going there.

Lawry sighed. "Are you really ready to play matchmaker again, Meredyth? I would have thought that after what happened to Estella, you'd stop meddling."

"Jay and Estella belong together, Lawry. He's just being a stubborn, difficult man, that's all." Fortunately, when we were focused on anyone but ourselves, conversing with Lawry seemed as natural as ever. "He could still marry her and whisk her off to whatever mission post he ends up accepting. I'm sure she would still go willingly."

"That would be akin to him asking you, Meredyth. Would you leave Back Bay to relocate to some remote start-of-a-town out West?"

His words hurt, but they rang true. Would I ever muster the courage to do such a thing? Probably not. But then again, I wasn't in love with anyone the way Estella Everstone was in love with Jayson Crawford Castleman.

"Well, would you, Mere?"

I didn't give Lawry a verbal answer. I no longer wanted to speak about what had happened, or what should happen, between Jay and Estella.

Lawry stood, took my hands once more, and lifted me from my seat. He was suddenly full of energy. "Come with me. I think it would be good for you."

"Come with you? Where? To Washing—?"

"To see Dr. Wellesley, silly."

"Oh, yes. Yes, of course." I practically stuttered over my reply. "Yes, I'll come with you."

Happy to have the semblance of my good old friend Lawry back, I would have followed him across town a million times if it would erase the memory of him kissing me. That was what I was hoping, at least.

⌒

Downtown was everything that the calm, graceful, tree-lined streets of my Back Bay were not. There were no grand mansions to be found. There were houses, and while some of them were large, they were all entirely unlike those in my neighborhood. And there were fewer trees and parks, and so many businesses—bakeries, groceries, meat markets, law firms, business offices…places I would never think of going. That was what servants were for.

The crowds, the dirt, and the chaos downtown put me on edge. Everyone seemed to be scrambling about with every movement.

The carriage finally came to a stop in front of a large brown brick house with eight large windows very symmetrically flanking the front porch. There were two dormers on the roof facing the street and a balcony above the front door. It all looked very respectable for the part of town we'd traveled to. Hanging above the door was a sign painted with the name of the establishment: "The Waterhouse Inn."

"An inn?"

"This is where Dr. Wellesley lives." Lawry helped me out of the carriage.

"But why?"

"Because he wants to, I suppose."

As my feet reached the ground, all I could do was stand and stare up at the front of the plain brick house, its gabled roof covered with the same snow that had accumulated on the streets and sidewalks overnight.

Lawry took my arm and guided me up the steps.

We walked right in the front door and came face-to-face with an elderly woman, who greeted us with a forced smile and reached out to help us with our coats. She was a tiny woman whose head barely reached my shoulders. "Welcome to The Waterhouse Inn. M' name is Mrs. Allister." She pronounced her name as if it were all one word, *Mizizallister*. "You two be needin' a room for the nigh'?"

My breath caught in my throat at such a presumptuous question. I coughed, certain the air I'd gulped had made its way down to my stomach instead of my lungs.

"No, thank you, Mrs. Allister. Perhaps some other time." Lawry cut a glance my way, smiling mischievously, and then gave her his card. "Would you give this to Dr. Wellesley?"

"Surely."

I hurriedly reached into my handbag for my own calling card and gave it to her, as well. She grabbed the card without looking at

it and held it with Lawry's in her wrinkled hand. "Come wit' me."
She turned and started walking away.

We followed her slow, wobbly gait into an empty parlor, which,
as it turned out, wasn't badly decorated, though it was rather dimly
lit. It was nothing like my mother's parlor at Summerton, of course,
but it was better than I'd expected. The walls were papered, and
there was a massive fireplace and well-appointed furniture, though
dated. A grandfather clock was ticking loudly from one corner of
the room. Lawry caught me looking around just as we heard Mrs.
Allister leading someone down the stairs. A cane thumped on each
step, filling the otherwise quiet space, as they both descended.

"Dr. We'sley, I swear, they is two of the classiest swells I ever
had step through me front door," Mrs. Allister said, probably not
realizing we could hear her.

And I really didn't doubt her statement was true. "This isn't
nearly as bad as I thought it was going to be," I whispered to Lawry.

"Glad to hear it." His answer seemed rather tight-lipped,
almost as if my comment had offended him.

Dr. Wellesley shuffled into the parlor, and Mrs. Allister immediately closed the thick olive green curtains over the doorway,
although I was sure she would remain right behind them, listening
to our every word. By the look on Dr. Wellesley's half-smiling face
as he followed my eyes, he suspected as much, too.

"Lawry Hampton," Dr. Wellesley said, excluding me, his
sharp eagle eyes measuring the situation. "I'm glad you've come.
However, I must tell you I need to be leaving soon, so this visit
will have to be a short one." His voice was gruff, which was quite
normal, no matter his mood. After shaking hands with both of us,
he gestured for us to sit on a sofa. Quite purposefully, I took a seat
in the nearest chair, still determined never again to sit upon a sofa
with Lawry.

"That's perfectly understandable," Lawry replied, smiling at
me.

Dr. Wellesley settled himself into one of the low chairs. "Is this young lady"—he looked to my calling card for good measure—"is the lovely Miss Summercourt a special friend of yours?"

Although I didn't like the way he'd added "special" into the mix of words, I was thankful that Dr. Wellesley was willing to be discreet about his familiarity with me. I directed my eyes from him back to Lawry.

"Oh, yes. Meredyth is one of my oldest, dearest friends. Meredyth, meet Dr. Grig Wellesley of Trinity Church. He manages the church's affiliations with the school."

I smiled politely. "It's nice to see you, Dr. Wellesley."

"And what has brought you downtown today, Miss Summercourt?" His brown eyes smiled, as if he thought he already knew. As if he suspected it was Lawry.

"Well...." I fumbled around for a few moments, trying to think of how to answer. What had brought us out? I had no idea, so I decided to say something incredibly vague. "Lawry...has a great interest in helping orphans."

"Yes, I know. He has been very generous in donating funds to keep the school up and running." Dr. Wellesley looked from me to Lawry, his eyes narrowing as if he were trying to solve a puzzle.

"He wanted me to...um, come with him. And Lawry is incredibly persuasive in regard to his desires." I quickly realized that my words might have been misconstrued, and suddenly I felt very warm.

Lawry grinned. "And, in turn, I've learned that Meredyth is much more persuadable than I'd ever imagined."

Oh, goodness! What on earth was Lawry referring to?

Dr. Wellesley remained silent as he studied me and then Lawry, his eyes barely visible beneath his wiry white eyebrows.

"I was more than willing to accompany Lawry downtown, you know, Dr. Wellesley, with how much I love helping the orphans and all. I mean, the idea...."

I hoped Lawry would assume I was referring to his orphans, not mine. But if he had indeed helped fund the school in the first place, my orphans were his orphans, as well.

Oh, bother.

"But you don't believe you're quite cut out to be the missionary type, do you, Meredyth?" Lawry's quick question seemed like a test.

The kind of test I was sure to fail.

"I don't know what type of person I am cut out to be, Lawry. But I do strive to be a good…whatever I am." It was too bad the only thing I was good at was being a spoiled, selfish, pampered ninny.

I knew Lawry's intent had not been to make me feel wretched about myself; but, just the same, his words cut to the very heart of the matter. I would be a very sad sort of missionary, and for some reason, the realization bothered me. Far more than it should have. Why did I care if Lawry Hampton believed I was useless to anyone who might need my help?

He was right, after all. I was utterly useless. What could I do? Decorate a bonnet for someone? Pick out a stylish muffler for a little girl to keep warm through the winter? God knew that, as much as I wanted to be of some use to Him by taking part in the music lessons at the school, I wasn't truly needed there. Everyone I associated with at the school knew that Ainsley was the true teacher of our class. I wasn't a master of anything but being a disappointment.

"Well, I need to be off soon. I'm sorry we couldn't have a longer visit. I did so enjoy seeing the two of you." Dr. Wellesley excused himself and went back up the stairs, one hollow-sounding thump at a time, leaving Lawry and me alone in the dark, dingy parlor.

"God loves you, Meredyth, and He wants to use your abilities to bless others as well as yourself," Lawry said gently. "Even if you don't feel useful, you can be. Quite easily, even."

"Yes, well, I suppose there is a fine line between being useful and feeling useful."

That was a conversation I never wanted to get into with Lawry Hampton. It was better that he see me as I saw myself. I had other things to do with my life than simply performing charitable deeds for others.

I had to take care of myself. I had to marry Vance Everstone. And I was certain my life ever afterward would be too filled with whatever Vance wanted of me to even consider what God wanted.

THREE

Wynn Rosselet

*"You can never do a kindness too soon, for you never know how soon
it will be too late."*
—Ralph Waldo Emerson

As Lawry's carriage eased away from The Waterhouse Inn,
I studied my red fox-fur scarf, holding the soft tail ends to
my cold cheeks.

What a waste of money. Even if it had been a present from my
father, who liked the way it matched my hair, it was still a frivolous
accessory. I felt guilty for having worn it to the inn. Usually when
I saw Dr. Wellesley, I was not wearing such finery.

What a liar I was becoming.

When I finally looked up, Lawry was staring at me.

"Have I said something that bothered you, Meredyth?"

"No, Lawry, it's not you. It's me. I bother myself." I faced the
window. I didn't expect him to understand.

"I think I know just how you feel." He reached for my hand as
the carriage stopped at an intersection.

I sat there in silence for a few moments, considering the idea of
baring my burdens to him, when a high-pitched scream from the
street caught our attention.

Lawry glanced out the window, concern etching every aspect
of his face. He was out of the carriage in an instant. I craned my

35

neck out the open carriage door and saw him running straight for a large bully of a boy straddling a small child with all his weight as he punched the poor thing repeatedly in the face.

I practically fell out of the carriage as I tried to get down on my own. The vehicle was, by far, the safest place for me to be, but that wasn't what I was thinking about at the time. I was thinking only about the child under attack, right there in the open street.

At the sight of Lawry coming toward him, the bully scampered away. The smaller boy stayed where he was, lying on his side in the puddle of cold slush they'd created in the snow. His face was still buried defensively in his arms, and his legs were scrunched up to his stomach.

Lawry knelt in the snow beside the raggedly dressed child while I hovered about; I was afraid of getting my dress soiled and wet. No one else seemed to have noticed the boy's distress. It broke my heart to see everyone going on with their business as usual, as if nothing amiss had happened.

Despite the fact that his coat would surely become soaked, Lawry picked up the filthy little boy and carried him to the carriage. Lawry didn't seem to care in the least what happened to himself, only that he needed to help, which was just further evidence of how far superior a person he was compared with me.

The boy didn't fight Lawry's hold, as I expected him to. But then, he probably didn't have the strength.

"He's as light as a feather."

"What are you going to do with him?" I asked as we approached the carriage. "Do you think he has a family?"

"I doubt it." Lawry stopped and repositioned the boy. He tried to catch his eye but was met only with avoidance. "Can you tell us where you live, pal? Is it nearby?"

"Don't live nowhere," was the reply through the barricade of his arms and elbows.

"You have no family whatsoever?" Lawry urged him.

The boy huddled closer to Lawry's shoulder. "Don't got none."

Lawry started toward the carriage again. "Well then."

"You can't take him to Hilldreth, Lawry." I followed in this tracks. "What would people think? What would your aunt Claudine say?" Oh, I hated that my every word, formed from my every thought, sounded so vain. Was I so completely devoid of compassion?

Ignoring my useless questions, Lawry made it to the carriage and quickly laid the boy on the front seat, then helped me in before going to speak with the driver.

I studied the boy as he lay before me, his face turned toward the back of the seat, still covered with his arms. I could see his black cropped curls sticking out from under his hat. He was still in the exact same position he'd been in on the side of the street, still striving to protect himself.

As if I was going to hurt him.

When Lawry climbed back inside the carriage, he took off his coat and spread it over the boy. Sitting beside me, he put an arm around my shoulders and squeezed, tucking me to his side.

"Where are we going to take him?" I turned to Lawry and found his striking profile only an inch from my face. He was closer than I should have allowed, but his look of concern as he stared at the crumpled little boy prevented me from protesting.

And it actually felt nice, having his strong arm around me again—

"We're going back to the inn." His attention remained on the boy.

We hadn't traveled very far from there, so it was only a matter of minutes until we stood before the brick house once more, preparing to face Mrs. Allister for the second time that day. Only now, there was a large bundle in Lawry's arms. This time, there were no calling cards or pleasantries. Lawry walked right past the woman and into the parlor.

Mrs. Allister followed us. "What's wrong? What's happened?"

"This poor child was being pounded upon by some bully right in the street a few blocks from here." I couldn't help but answer her, although I was still filled with questions myself. "Lawry just bounded out of the carriage and scared the bully off, as if he were the only one who cared."

"Most likely, he was, miss," came her snappish reply.

"Do you have a vacant room, Mrs. Allister?" Lawry asked.

"You wantin' to rent it for the nigh', the week, or the month?"

"I'll pay you double the rent if you promise you'll take care to feed and shelter this child indefinitely." Lawry didn't move; he still held the boy in his capable arms. "I'm at a loss for anything else to do. But getting him off the streets is enough for now."

I reached to touch the coarse, ragged layers of material covering his arms, which were still wrapped about his head. He didn't resist, and when I lifted his bony arm to peek at his face, I found fearful brown eyes staring back at me from under the brim of his hat. From what I could guess, he was about five or six years old.

"What's your name, li'l one?" Mrs. Allister asked, peeking around Lawry's broad shoulder.

"Wynn," the child answered with a crackly voice.

"Well, Wynn, my name is Lawry, and this is my good friend Meredyth." Lawry smiled down at me, which filled my heart with all kinds of blasted, new feelings I wished to squelch. "Oh, and this is Mrs. Allister. She'll be the one to feed you here at the inn, I suppose. Would you like that?"

Wynn gave a slight nod of his head.

"You feelin' al'ight, child?" Mrs. Allister asked. "You want somethin' to eat right away?" It was shocking how accommodating she'd become as soon as there was a child present. "You hurt?"

"Mine arms." From the look of his face, he'd done a pretty good job protecting it with those skinny arms of his. There was hardly a bruise. "An' yes'm, I'm starveling."

I turned to Mrs. Allister. "Well, if you would kindly show us the way to an available bedchamber, we'll get Wynn settled."

I followed Mrs. Allister up the stairs, trailed by Lawry carrying Wynn.

"And then perhaps a bath would be a good idea, to clean him up a bit?" Lawry added.

At those words, Wynn piped up, "But I ain't a he. I ain't!"

I looked over my shoulder and saw that Wynn had sat straight up in Lawry's arms.

"What?" Lawry asked.

I hid a giggle behind my smile. "Lawry, dear, I think what Wynn is trying to say is that she's a little girl, not a little boy."

~

Wynn, I found, was a lovely girl, once she'd been stripped of those dirty scraps of rags and thoroughly bathed.

Mrs. Allister's great-niece, Benta, went to the attic and brought down some children's clothes from two decades earlier, and voilà—even wearing only the frilly old-fashioned undergarments, Wynn looked like the little girl she'd claimed to be. Her hair, which had been tucked under her boyish cap, was long, black, and unruly. After Benta and I were through with giving her a bath, she looked absolutely stunning.

Benta had shown us to a room that was really nothing more than a large closet, with a door opening to the hall just outside Benta's bedchamber. Benta had Wynn sitting before her on the bed and was picking through her long, wet hair with a comb, undoubtedly looking for bugs.

The thought of what might be in Wynn's hair made my own scalp itch, but I remained in the room, regardless. "Wynn, I know Lawry said he's going to have you live here for as long as you need, but do you really have no one who could take you in?"

"I ain't seen Mumma since she coughed up the blood and they took 'er away and buried her."

I covered my mouth with my hand, shocked by the implications of her statement.

Wynn looked at me unabashedly, as if she'd said absolutely nothing out of the ordinary. There wasn't much space to walk in the tiny room, so I simply turned around and played with the knobs of the dresser, trying to think of where to take the conversation next.

"Where'd you live before your mother passed away?" Benta asked with her slight Irish brogue, her brown eyebrows lowered over her slate-gray eyes. She couldn't have been much older than I, but oh, what a different kind of life she lived.

"T'was a nasty board-house we lived in, where I slept at night. Mostly, I roamed free all the day long."

I knew it was probable that Wynn's birth had been the primary reason why her mother's life had been as it was, living in a shanty of a boardinghouse until she found herself dying of what surely had been consumption.

Turning around, I asked, "Wynn, did you— Do you happen to know what your mother's name was?"

"Hers was… maybe… Libby?"

"Do you know your last name?"

"I's been called Wynn Ross'let by Mumma's friends a'times."

Libby Rosselet. And if she was dead, what was to be done?

I turned to face the mirror attached to the top of the dresser and had an overwhelming desire to leave the room and run down the stairs into Lawry's arms. Taking all my troubles to him was such a comforting thought. To feel him put his arms around me again, to hear him tell me he would make everything all right for Wynn…and for me….

I closed my eyes, shutting out the idea. When I opened them again, I saw my reflection in the mirror, just the way I needed to see it. The weak, comfort-seeking, heartsick girl was gone—and would be gone forever if I had anything to do about it. In her place, I forced myself to visualize the strong, independent young woman I was determined to be. The woman I *would* be. The kind who didn't need a man's love to survive.

I turned around.

"What about your papa?" Benta asked. As she stood from the bed, she caught my eye and gave me a quick shake of her head. No bugs. *Thank heavens.*

"What's a pah-pah?" Wynn slipped off the edge of the mattress.

"A father, Wynn. Do you know anything of your father?" I was more than a little scared to hear her answer. My relationship with my own father came to mind. I'd always known that he loved me, even when I found I couldn't accept it. Didn't deserve it.

Wynn shrugged.

I studied the girl as Benta slipped a tiny dress over her head. Had her mother loved her? Ever taken care of her? She seemed quite independent for a six-year-old. Was that a trait borne from years of neglect or of mere months spent alone on the street? And what on earth had she been doing on her own since her mother died?

"Wynn, what happened at the boardinghouse once your mother was…no longer there? What happened to your mother's belongings?" I stood with my back pressed to the door, hoping to gather as many clues as I could before returning downstairs.

"Don't know. I runned away from Mr. Dunk. And finally Mrs. Dunk let me go."

Let her go, and not made her go? Had Wynn truly desired her independence? Could living on the streets of Boston really be more favorable than staying with this couple, the Dunks?

My heart was beginning to understand things I'd never dreamt possible. A little girl, all on her own, by choice. Left tragically alone and ultimately taking the chance to escape instead of staying with the only people she knew.

I thought of the orphan girls at the Trinity School for Girls. For months, Ainsley and I had gone there every Tuesday afternoon and done our "duty." Of course, between the two of us, Ainsley was worlds better at teaching. Not that it really mattered. We taught the most basic of things. Sometimes, I wondered if it was just the interaction between Ainsley and me and the girls that was needed, and not the lessons at all. For me, the most rewarding days were those when I took my violin and played for them, for it felt as if I was calling them to become something more. They would all have to grow up someday, and they would have to figure out on their own just who they were.

"Mrs. Dunk's still got our things."

Wynn seemed exceptionally aware of her circumstances, and I wondered just how long it had been since her mother's death. The fact that her mother was dead didn't seem to upset Wynn much, and that worried me.

"Was that other child—the one who ran off—one of your friends?" I asked.

"I ain't got no friends." Wynn plopped on the bed and turned to lay herself face down on the bright orange and white quilted coverlet. Turning her head to speak, she said, "Ain't no such thing."

I stepped across the small room, knelt before the bed, and extended my hand to her for the second time that day. I stroked her silky black curls and then took her tiny, rough hand in mine. I felt utterly helpless and unprepared for dealing with her, but I would try.

"Wynn, can we be your friends?"

She looked to me, and then to Benta, who stood next to the dresser. "Are you and Benta friends?"

Surely, Benta wouldn't expect me to reply affirmatively. Why, we'd just met a half hour before, not to mention that we existed on completely different levels of society. I'd never met any young woman who worked, besides the maids my parents employed at Summerton and at Summerhouse on Mount Desert Island.

That was precisely when I realized that if my parents ever found out about the morning we'd had, or what I was about to say in regard to Benta Allister, I would likely never hear the end of it. Nor would I ever be allowed to see them again.

"Yes, Wynn. Benta and I are indeed friends." And we would be—because of Wynn. "I would like very much for you to be my friend, also. Will you?"

Wynn remained quiet for a moment. She looked sheepishly at both of us, then hid her face in the coverlet, as if I'd flattered her with such a request.

Finally, Wynn sat up. "I could want some friends...like you." There were tears threatening to spill from her dark brown eyes. And when they did, I couldn't help but pull her into my arms and give her a big hug.

There was a knock at the door, and then it opened with a creak. Lawry peeked inside.

"Are you finished with her yet?" He leaned his shoulder against the doorjamb, taking special notice of my arms around Wynn. "Dinner is ready." Then he smiled at Wynn. "You want a ride down?" He spun around and crouched on the floor. "Go ahead, hop on."

The look on Wynn's face was a study in sheer joy, although the remnants of the precious tears she'd just shed were still clinging to her eyelashes.

The desire to create such joy in someone's heart, I realized, threatened to be quite contagious.

⌣⟋

As Lawry's carriage pulled away from The Waterhouse Inn for the second time that day, I glanced back to gaze at the building and saw Wynn peek through the curtains of a front window. She smiled and waved, and I did the same in return.

"Lawry, is Wynn at all like the little girls you help at your orphanage in Seattle?"

"She's precisely the kind of child I am trying to help. There are just so many of them."

Dragging my eyes from the inn, I turned to Lawry, who sat across from me. I remembered how quickly he had rushed from the carriage to rescue Wynn without a thought for himself. His heart was so...full. But why did he insist on sharing this fullness of heart with me?

"Does Dr. Wellesley know about your orphanage?"

"Not yet. I should tell him, shouldn't I?"

"Yes. And you should tell Ainsley, as well. It seems to me she would understand."

With one elbow resting against the window ledge, he slowly pulled his other hand down over his face, then looked at me again. "Ainsley has enough to worry about right now, trying to figure out her own life. While she is my sister, she's much younger than I, and...I've always felt closer to you."

"Closer than a sister, am I? Pray tell, what could that mean?" I'd wanted the question to come out as a tease, because, surely, I was more like a sister to him than anything. Instead, it sounded as if I wanted him to admit that I was more than just a friend or a sister. Which wasn't true at all...at least, it shouldn't have been.

"Meredyth, aside from Nathan, you've always been my best friend, which is infinitely better than your being my sister."

Surprisingly, his words made me feel better, not worse. Our friendship would survive the kiss. I was certain of it now.

"After dropping you at Summerton, I'm going to head back to the inn to see Dr. Wellesley again later today, to see what I can do about getting Wynn enrolled at the Trinity School for Girls. And I thought I might go shopping for some things for her," he added.

A sudden burst of laughter escaped my throat at the thought of Lawry shopping for little girls' things.

I quickly sobered at the thought of the rumors that would surely begin if the wrong person witnessed such a sight. Why, someone might think that the upstanding Lawry Hampton was involved with a paramour and had recently discovered that he was obliged to support a child born because of his own irresponsible behavior.

Which would never, ever be the case.

"Lawry, do you think that's such a good idea?" I asked, hoping to change his mind. "Perhaps I should come with you. That way, it wouldn't seem out of the ordinary. Women buy gifts for children all the time."

"Is there something scandalous about buying some clothes and a few toys for an orphaned little girl?" Lawry linked his fingers together, twisted his hands around, and stretched his arms toward me, cracking his knuckles. Was he nervous? He used to do that whenever he was anxious about something.

"Just the same, I'm going to come with you."

He shrugged. "You won't be hearing any complaints from me. Are you available tomorrow morning?"

I made a point to seem as if I were thinking through a million and one engagements in order to make room for him, when, in actuality, I had nothing planned beyond a luncheon with my mother and her whist club at eleven o'clock.

"Yes, I think I have time for you in the morning."

"I'll take as much of you as I can get. I'll pick you up at eight." He had to have known exactly what he was saying and how, but I was scared to look him in the eye to know for certain. I was afraid that if I saw what it was that caused him to say such words, there would be no escaping.

I never did have an opportunity to respond, even if I'd wanted to, for the carriage stopped in front of Summerton just then. I reached for the door handle and let myself out before Lawry had the chance to help, for taking a fall out of a carriage was the least of my concerns when Lawry Hampton was involved.

FOUR

Ainsley Hampton

"When a man has seen the woman whom he would have chosen if he had intended to marry speedily, his remaining a bachelor will usually depend on her resolution rather than on his."
—George Eliot, *Middlemarch*

Later that afternoon, I went to Hilldreth to meet with Ainsley before making our weekly trip to the Boston Inland Mission Society. Fortunately, Lawry was still out. I'd already seen entirely too much of him that day.

Claudine's carriage was already out front waiting for us, and Ainsley's maid, Agnes, was waiting in the hall.

When I entered the drawing room, I found Ainsley seated upon the sofa, and she motioned for me to do the same. "Do come in and sit, Meredyth."

"Are you not ready to leave?" We usually tried to vary our departure time on Tuesdays; that way, it wouldn't seem to any onlookers that we were going to the same location every week. Not that we'd come out and lied to Claudine or my parents, but we also hadn't told them the truth.

I really, really didn't want to run into Lawry before we got on our way to the school. What if he insisted upon coming "shopping" with us or simply decided to follow us to see where we were going?

"Nicholette Fairbanks was here earlier, sharing with me her vast new knowledge of the Everstone family." Ainsley's deep blue eyes—which matched Lawry's rather strikingly—sparkled with delight. She always did like sharing the latest news. "It's turned out that she rather likes the position she's taken in regard to the Everstones, even if she's ended up engaged to Will instead of Nathan."

"Did she have any news of Nathan and Amaryllis? It's been over a month since I've had a letter from them. Last I knew, Nathan had built Amaryllis a music school on the far end of their horse farm, and she was advertising for students." I remained standing, hoping she would rise and follow me toward the front door. She had already donned her hat, covering her coiffed light brown hair. "And really, Ainsley, can we not talk about this on our way?"

"Actually, Nicholette had more to say about Vance than anyone else."

I sat. "Vance?"

Speaking his name worsened how I already felt after such a chaotic morning with Lawry. I wasn't shocked that he would be the subject of the most interesting gossip, though. I was accustomed to hearing all about him, and everyone's speculations concerning him, at nearly every dinner, soiree, and luncheon I'd attended for years. With Vance due to inherit four million dollars on his thirtieth birthday—only a few years away—the mother of every debutante in New England was awaiting his return to the States.

"I wonder why he insists on staying in Europe," Ainsley mused.

"Vance...always does whatever he wants." *With whomever he wants.*

"That he does."

"How long has he been away now? Three years? Four?" Even to my own ears, the words seemed rehearsed. As if I hadn't counted the days.

"That's a dreadfully long time for anyone not to see his family."

"He saw his father last year. I guess that was enough of a family reunion for him."

"I would hate being away from my family for so long. I still miss Mother something terrible," she admitted, almost to herself. "But now that Daphne has decided to remarry, she's needed in Bar Harbor to plan the wedding."

"Ah, yes—your sister has found a soon-to-be husband in Captain Roderick Parker. That was surprising, was it not?"

"I knew she'd find someone else to marry by the end of the summer." Ainsley was obviously in no mood to be cheered. "She was miffed when Nathan married Amaryllis without an official engagement period. Not that she had any claim on him. I could just tell she had hopes. We all could."

"It seems she got over it quickly enough."

"It helps that she isn't terribly choosy," Ainsley replied with just a trace of disdain. I wished that I could figure her out. Why was she sore about her sister's marrying again? Daphne had to be close to thirty, and she'd been a widow for over two years.

"Can you believe Nicholette offered to have a double wedding at Rockwood?" In trying to lighten Ainsley's suddenly sullen mood, I'd said the words without any inkling that they would create just such a mood in me.

Jealousy overwhelmed me.

Nicholette and Will, as well as Daphne and her captain, would be wed simultaneously in the rustic chapel that Bram Everstone had built long ago for his first wife, along the cliff-lined stretch of coast on Mount Desert Island near Rockwood. It was in that chapel that I was surely meant to marry Vance, as well. "It must be a great comfort to have Lawry here in town, though, right? He's the best kind of brother...."

And friend...and kisser....

I took a deep breath. I needed to leave before Lawry returned home and discovered how Ainsley and I would be spending our afternoon.

"Lawry is a wonderful brother, but he's so much older than I. I'm sure he has no interest in entertaining me while I'm in town."

"Oh, but you're wrong," I insisted. "Just the other day, he told me he thought you were the perfect baby sister."

"Yes, a baby. I'm eighteen, Meredyth, and I feel as if I'm not allowed to grow up."

"Then I suggest you find a beau. That's the reason every pretty young lady comes to town, isn't it?"

"I don't believe that's the solution," Ainsley said matter-of-factly. "You see, Mother didn't want me to come. She doesn't want me to get married. I believe she fears she'll lose me the way she lost Daphne when she married Carl Langenwalter. And what if Captain Parker decides to take on another ship?"

"Daphne is hardly lost to your mother, Ainsley, and I'm certain Captain Parker's retirement from the navy will prove to be a permanent situation."

It seemed I was constantly studying Ainsley Hampton. She behaved much differently in Boston than she ever had in Bar Harbor. In all the years I'd known her, she'd been an excitable and rather vivacious spitfire of a girl, forever speaking about the eligible young gentlemen who would be coming to Bar Harbor for the summer. But now, she seemed almost desolate. Did she sincerely believe her mother didn't want her to marry only because Daphne had married that old German millionaire by the end of her first season?

"Mother would rather keep me at home forever." Ainsley bit at her lip nervously. "That's why I didn't come down sooner. Daphne came down at the age of sixteen, at Claudine's request."

"Being home for two extra years couldn't have been so bad. And you probably don't remember, but I was eighteen when I debuted, as well—my own choice." I stood and walked to the old box grand piano. We really ought to have left already, but I was just about to bring up a very important subject. "My brother Garrett seems to like you. I've noticed you've been speaking with him more often, of late."

Perhaps, just possibly, Ainsley would marry Garrett. Then she could be my sister, and I could claim her as my own forever. She could hardly be immune to his charms, as much as she clearly tried to resist them, supposedly for her mother's sake.

"You have?" Ainsley looked absolutely stunned at my words. But then she quickly schooled her features and said, "Garrett is… he's nice."

"You think my brother Garrett is merely nice?" I teased. I knew he was much more than "nice" toward any girl he was intent on flirting with.

"He is nice," she repeated decisively.

"But is that all?"

"What, do you want me to think his paying attention to me is something to take note of?" She raised her eyebrows and seemed genuinely surprised. "This is Garrett, one of *your* brothers, we're talking about. Everyone knows the Summercourt men are never serious about anyone, just like their sister. Your poor parents—I don't know how they will ever have any grandchildren if none of you ever marries."

"I'll marry someday. I'm just waiting for the right man to…." *To be in the same country as me.*

Ainsley leaned forward. "You already know who you want, don't you?"

"I thought we were talking about my brother."

"And now I'm beginning to wonder if we're not, in fact, speaking of mine."

Oh, didn't innocent little Ainsley Hampton think she was clever.

The pocket doors off the hall opened a crack, and Lawry poked his head in.

"Lawry, you're home." Ainsley stood and rushed across the room to greet him. "We were just speaking of you."

"Is that a fact?" Lawry looked pointedly at me.

My stomach dropped, and I could hardly move, let alone speak. I stood to my feet and crossed the room to join them. "We were actually speaking of brothers in general," I finally added.

"Were you two just leaving?" Lawry tipped Ainsley's hat, messing her hair in the process. "I've noticed that you both go out on Tuesday afternoons quite often. What's taking you out in such weather? It's dreadfully damp and cold today. Would you not rather put off whatever your errand may be and keep me company here, instead?"

"We're merely going to Filene's," Ainsley blurted out.

"Then perhaps I'll join you. I'm long overdue for purchasing some new handkerchiefs."

"All we do is stroll around, gawking at things we don't need," I quickly inserted. "You would surely be bored to tears by the end of the afternoon."

He looked suspiciously from me to Ainsley and then back again. "Do you think you could order some handkerchiefs for me while you're out?" He turned to his sister. "Ainsley, you know what they look like, with my initials embroidered in blue near the corner."

"Lawry, handkerchiefs are such a personal purchase…suppose we somehow make a mistake while placing the order?" I asked.

"Tell them who they're for, and they'll know what I want. I'm incredibly predictable, you know. I always want the same thing. I'm never able to change my long-standing preferences, no matter how hard I try."

Lawry had to know he was only making my life more complicated with his demands. Handkerchiefs! As if he didn't have dozens of them already.

"Certainly, we'll do that little thing for you," Ainsley assured him. Of course, she would want to do as Lawry asked.

Personally, I wasn't keen on the idea of skipping the prayer meeting we usually attended after our class was finished. Yet doing so would be necessary if we wanted to make it to Filene's to order Lawry's handkerchiefs and be back home in good time...unless we sent Agnes to Filene's while we were in class.

But, no—if Lawry asked us to do something for him, we would do it. And I didn't like the idea of anyone else ordering such a personal item for Lawry besides me. And Ainsley, of course.

"We really must be going, Ainsley, before—" I bit my lip at my idiotic blunder.

"Before what? Filene's closes their doors?" Lawry asked, taunting me directly. "It's barely past noon. I think it's safe to say you'll have time." He narrowed his eyes at me. "And why didn't you mention this outing earlier today, Mere, when we were speaking of going shopping together tomorrow morning? Now, where are you really going? If you tell me your secrets, I'll tell you more of mine."

Ainsley watched me closely but remained silent. I hated that he was forcing me to lie to him. Why couldn't he just let it be?

"Would you rather order your own handkerchiefs tomorrow, then?" I ignored Ainsley's suspicious gaze. Oh, this was all backward! I was supposed to be helping her form an attachment with my brother, not the other way around.

"Meredyth, we can order Lawry's handkerchiefs for him. It's no problem."

"We really do need to get going, dear." I grabbed Ainsley by the arm and led her to the hall, where Agnes still waited for us. "Good day, Lawry. Ainsley, do bid your brother good-bye, and let's be off."

I shoved on my coat, barely letting Ainsley bid her brother good-bye, as I'd asked. Once she, too, was dressed for the weather, I pulled her outside. Just as Agnes was about to close the door behind us, Lawry stopped her by positioning his foot in the way, followed by his whole body. Agnes gave up on her task and hurried down the steps ahead of us.

"Meredyth?" Lawry said.

Ainsley escaped my hold to join Agnes on the sidewalk, and I stopped on the icy front stoop. I drew in a deep breath of frigid air and exhaled slowly before turning around to meet Lawry's gaze. I gripped one of the cold limestone pillars with my bare hand; in my haste to get out the door, I hadn't put on my gloves.

He stepped farther out onto the stoop, into the cold. I heard the creak of the carriage door as it opened. Ainsley and Agnes had already made it down to the carriage.

"I was just having some fun with you. I didn't mean any disrespect." Little could he have known that those few, perfunctory words spelled out the story of my life. "You don't have to go to Filene's today if you don't want to." He reached out and took my bare hand in his. "I was only trying to secure an invitation to come along. But I can tell when I'm not wanted—just as I can tell when I am."

Something in me shifted uneasily at his words and at the troubled look in his blue eyes.

When he let go of my hand, I immediately turned around and raced down the steps to the carriage, where the coachman opened the door for me and helped me inside. When I took my seat, I looked out the window and saw Lawry still standing outside, despite the cold. His high opinion of me made my heart swell with pride, but I forced myself to remember that I'd just lied to him. And that he'd so easily believed me.

He always did think the very best of everyone.

FIVE

The Trinity School for Girls

"*Nothing is really work unless
you would rather be doing something else.*"
—James M. Barrie

The Boston Inland Mission Society building had a large auditorium on the main level and, upstairs, dozens of small music rooms, each with a piano left over from when the building had been used as a conservatory. Of course, even when the doors to the practice rooms were closed, anyone on the upper level could hear what was going on inside.

I hadn't brought my violin that day, which was fortunate, in light of our unexpected encounter with Lawry on our way out the door. How would I have explained my reasons for taking a violin shopping?

While Ainsley took the group of younger girls upstairs to the practice rooms, I remained downstairs in the classroom with the older ones. Usually, I was the one to take each group upstairs to practice while Ainsley taught a short lesson to the other group. But today, she wanted to hear firsthand how everyone's piano playing was coming along.

I had the four older girls arrange their chairs in a circle, and as I sat with them, I realized I hardly knew any of their names. Oh, I'd heard them all before; Ainsley knew every one of them by name.

They had always appeared very much the same, wearing the same mud-brown dresses and white aprons, with their hair pulled back into tight buns at the bases of their neck. However, since meeting Wynn Rosselet that morning, I had begun to see each one with new eyes. I hadn't been praying for these girls as I should have been—not nearly as much as I'd been praying for Lawry's orphans in Seattle and for the two women who took care of them.

For a moment, as the four eldest girls stared at me, I decided this would be the perfect opportunity to get to know them better. "Okay, ladies. We're going to do something different this afternoon while the younger girls perform for Miss Hampton upstairs. We're going to go around the circle and simply speak about anything and everything that comes to mind. How does that sound?"

All four of them continued to look at me blankly.

"All right, then; I'll start," I added.

This seemed to help a little, as they all now looked at me with apparent interest in what I might say, instead of fear pertaining to what I might expect to hear from them. To tell the truth, I had no idea what I would hear, but I was willing to listen, whatever they might decide to share.

"My name is Meredyth Summercourt, and I am twenty-four years old."

They silently waited for more.

"I have…I have three older brothers, the youngest of whom lives here in town. His name is Garrett. My two oldest brothers are Alex and Clyde. They live in New York City."

"I have a brother who lives in New York City, too," said a girl with blonde hair.

I didn't know her name, so I simply said, "Why don't you go next?"

"My brother—he's my twin—is named John. We're fourteen. He is an apprentice to a shipbuilder in New York City. Someday, when we are older, we are going to be together again and live in the same house. Oh, and my name is Jane Smithford." As she spoke, Jane fidgeted with her hands in her lap, and her hazel brown eyes bored into the floor. "I am very thankful that I have been sponsored to attend this school. I don't think I would be very good at making ships."

"I'm certain you'll be good at something, Jane." It was rather challenging to skim through the possible responses streaming through my mind and to pick out the ones that were appropriate to say, while filtering those that were not—such as any comment having to do with parents or what, exactly, the girls' station in life would be when they left the orphanage.

Were they aware of my specific station in society? What would they think if they knew that I had never wanted for anything in my entire life?

"I'll go next," said a girl with light brown hair and large blue eyes. "My name is Cornelia Bonneville. I'm almost sixteen and will graduate this summer. My father is an English gentleman from London who now sponsors my time here at this school. My mother was a maid at his manor, but she's dead now."

What a harsh reality. I really didn't want this to become a time of dwelling upon everything that was wrong with the girls' lives. Although, Cornelia didn't seem very depressed about the details she'd shared; rather, she came across as detached.

I looked to the next girl, who, like me, had auburn hair and freckles. I hoped, for her benefit, that hers would fade in time, as mine had.

"My name's Bridgie Nightingale."

"Do you have anything you want to share with us?" I coaxed her. "It can be anything at all."

"I want to tell you all about how, every night, I look out the window at the moon, shining above the city." Bridgie's eyes scanned the room, as if she were scared to find us laughing at her. "And every night, I think the same things. I suppose they're prayers, but sometimes it just seems like gratitude overflowing from my heart."

Her words took me aback. This girl, who looked to be no more than eleven or twelve, and who was quite alone in the world, had a heart overflowing with gratitude?

"The moon reminds me that God made it just for us," she continued. "And that back when Jesus lived on the earth, He went to sleep every night, just like me, and He, too, likely looked up at it—at the same exact moon I see every night—from wherever He laid his head. And where did He lay His head, compared to where we lay ours every night? On the dirt and grass of the earth. He took nothing for Himself, and now He provides me with a bed, and a roof, and all these friends, and meals...and this music class."

"Thank you, Bridgie." It was all I could get out. My chest suddenly felt utterly hollow...or unlocked...or, somehow, strangely filled. All I wanted was more of Him. More of God filling my life with gratitude such as this little girl named Bridgie possessed in abundance.

"I never thought of that before," Jane reflected. "At least we have beds and meals, and Miss Summercourt and Miss Hampton...even if we don't have families."

That both Jane and Bridgie had mentioned this silly music class among the things they were most grateful was a shock to me.

I thought of my plush, overstuffed bed at home. The wallpapered wall, the expensive furniture...all the many things I possessed. And Jesus hadn't had a bed to sleep in during the final three, most important, years of His life. Why would He provide me with all that I had? For what reason? What was I supposed to do with it all?

"And my name is Sicily Munroe, like the island off Italy...as I've been told," the last girl said. "I just turned fifteen, so, fortunately, I won't have to leave here for a whole year. I, too, am grateful for this orphanage." She sat with her shoulders straight, her head held high. "My whole family was killed in a carriage accident four years ago, and I am very happy to have a place to live and a school to attend. It's much better than the last school I attended. I'm glad that we're taught about God and Jesus and that we study the Bible."

"Do they teach Bible classes at this school?" I asked, intrigued.

"Dr. Wellesley teaches the class," Cornelia answered, though her tone was far from excited. "How wonderful—"

My response was drowned out by the sound of a multitude of tiny feet hurrying down the nearest staircase. Seconds later, the six youngest girls came scurrying in, Ainsley trailing them like a little shepherdess.

"It's simply amazing to me that I am able to teach these girls anything in such a brief span of time!" She had a happy flush upon her face, as if teaching piano lessons truly brought her joy.

Was that how Amaryllis had felt about teaching, too? She'd always seemed happy whenever I'd come to visit her class the year before, although she hadn't been nearly as spirited as Ainsley in her interactions with the girls.

There was no denying that they both had the talent for teaching, whereas I did not. Granted, I sometimes brought my violin to class, but I didn't teach. I suppose I was more trying to set an example of what hard work and diligent practice of any instrument could accomplish. Not that I was really that talented. But it did satisfy society into thinking me one step closer to being the accomplished young lady everyone expected me to be.

⌒

As Ainsley and I traveled with Agnes to Filene's—instead of attending the prayer meeting—I couldn't help thinking more upon Dr. Wellesley's Bible class. Specifically, I wondered whether I could find some way to attend.

I needed to figure out what I was supposed to accomplish with my life. What did God want me to do with this sudden, overwhelming feeling that I wasn't doing enough? Or was it, perhaps, that I wasn't living enough?

I certainly wasn't living with the same sense of purpose as Lawry and his sister. It was the strangest realization that I even wanted to—and quite desperately.

But then I remembered. How could I forget?

I lifted my gaze from the carriage floor to the window, hoping that Ainsley wouldn't realize I was on the verge of tears. How could I have so easily forgotten, even from that morning?

I already knew God's will for my life. And it had nothing to do with Lawry, or the way he lived, and everything to do with making things right between Vance and me.

SIX

The Snowstorm

"Few delights can equal the presence of one whom we trust utterly."
—George MacDonald

Astonished, I flipped the curtains back into place over the second-story parlor window.

I'd simply wanted to look upon the drifts of snow, which had reached five feet in places over the last few days. The last thing I'd expected to see was Lawry leading his heavily bundled younger sister up the walk of Commonwealth Avenue, shoveling the snow out of her way as they came.

The snow had started just as Ainsley and I were leaving Filene's on Tuesday, and it hadn't stopped for days. Needless to say, Lawry's plan to take me shopping for Wynn on Wednesday morning had been postponed. Everyone in Boston, and perhaps even everyone along the entire coast of New England, had been trapped inside by the snowstorm.

Figuring that Lawry and Ainsley were on their way to Summerton, I set to readying the parlor for visitors. With such dreadful weather barraging the city, I hadn't seen anyone but my family for days on end. Mother, feeling unwell, was resting in her room; Father had gone to the office, now that the snow had stopped; and Garrett was reading in the study. I hadn't seen much of anyone all day.

I collected my books and hid them in a pile behind a Christmas cactus propped on a tall plant stand beside the front window. As I did so, I heard the front door open.

Yes, Lawry and Ainsley had come to see me. And was I ever thankful! I'd been just about driven to distraction by the images of flowers and plants in my mother's botany books. I'd also tried reading *The Scarlet Letter*, practiced a few hymns on my violin, and dug out an old needlework pillow I'd started years ago and had never had a great desire to finish. After days on end of such mind-numbing activities, I was quite ready to see just about anyone.

Even Lawry Hampton.

Just the thought of seeing him sent an unexpected rush of elation racing through my veins. Which was no good. But since he was bringing Ainsley, I'd focus that elation on her and Garrett, manipulating the visit to somehow benefit my brother's obvious infatuation with her. If only Ainsley would just relax and let Garrett make her love him.

Smiling, I rushed down the hall to tell him about our visitors. I would find a way to have him entertain Ainsley alone in the parlor—I was certain that was all it would take. Garrett was known for being proficient at enticing ladies into falling in love with him.

I trusted him to behave himself, of course. And it was because he always behaved himself with the strictest of formalities that his skills were amazingly effective. He could, in only looking at and speaking with a young lady, have her hoping for a proposal within days of being introduced to him. It was simply part of Garrett's personality to please and to charm with no apparent effort. Unfortunately, he'd learned to use his skill more as a tool for his own amusement over the years.

I knocked lightly on the giant pocket door to the library, then immediately opened it. Garrett was slumped over the desk and staring straight at me, raking his hands through his short, wiry red hair. The fact that I'd entered the room did nothing to change the look of boredom in his eyes.

"Whatever's the matter with you?" I sauntered into the room as if I hadn't come in for any specific reason. "Sorry you decided to stay home rather than join Father at the office?"

"Meredyth, I think I'm losing my touch—and just when I need it most."

Shocked by this admission, I walked farther into the room. Everything about the way he'd acted around Ainsley for the last few months had made it obvious, at least to me, that he was falling for her. How fortunate, then, that Lawry had decided to shovel Ainsley's way to our doorstep this very morning.

"Well, you're in luck. Ainsley's come to call. Lawry, as well."

"With all the snow?" Garrett shot to his feet, sending his chair toppling with a loud clatter. "Why?"

"They've likely been as bored being snowed in at Hilldreth as we've been here. Come, they're waiting."

Garrett followed me into to the hall to the top of the staircase. To my surprise, Lawry and Ainsley hadn't waited in the parlor downstairs but were climbing the stairs to the second level, with our butler, Fenley, leading the way.

I immediately discovered that physical exertion looked extremely good on Lawry Hampton. He was smiling happily, although the task he'd completed—shoveling snow for all those blocks—must have been strenuous, especially considering the well-tailored suit he wore. What had he been thinking to do such a thing? His cheeks were still flushed as he bounded up the last few steps, looking straight at me.

"Meredyth, you're a sight for sore eyes!" Taking my hands in his ice-cold grip, he looked as if he'd genuinely missed me.

"I spotted you out the window as you walked up the street. I saw you shoveling, Lawry." I tried to sound disappointed in him, though that was hardly how I felt.

"I shoveled your front stoop while I was at it."

"You do realize we pay a servant to do such things, don't you?" I whispered as we made our way into the parlor. "And what of the servants at Hilldreth? Were none of them available to shovel your way here today?"

"I was doing the gentlemanly thing for the benefit of a much-loved sister. And I did it with pleasure." Lawry finally took his eyes off of me and looked to Garrett, who'd not said a word yet. "You'd do the same, wouldn't you, if Meredyth ever wanted to come and see me after a snowstorm?" Lawry seemed so spirited. Was it the result of the physical labor he'd just performed?

"Indeed." Garrett was doing his best not to stare at Ainsley but was failing rather miserably. He was obviously distracted, for he most certainly wouldn't have answered that question in the affirmative, had his head been clear. I was quite sure he would not degrade himself by shoveling any amount of snow for anything in the world.

Lawry and his sister lowered themselves onto the sofa, while I took a seat in one of the two chairs—the one in whose cushions the copy of *Leçons de Grammaire* was hidden. Ainsley was being rather quiet, and I wondered if she'd even wanted to come along. She didn't act like it. She hadn't said anything so far and looked stiff and uncomfortable.

"I have an idea." I stood, retrieved the pile of botany books I'd stashed behind the Christmas cactus, and set them on a small table. "Lawry, I want your opinion on what kinds of flowers I should try to cultivate in my garden this year."

"You want my help—and not Ainsley's?" He tilted his head skeptically.

"Ainsley cares nothing whatsoever about plants." I looked at her. "Isn't that right, Ainsley?"

Garrett moved to the sofa, taking the space on the other side of Ainsley, and she suddenly looked as white as death.

"Not really. However, I could—"

"See? I wouldn't want to bore her." I cut her off quite purposefully. "And you, Lawry—you've had your practice, listening to me harangue you plenty about flowers and plants in the past. Don't you remember my taking you through your mother's garden at Truesdale summer after summer? I think that was where I first truly learned to love… them."

"I do remember. Quite distinctly, actually." Lawry was already standing.

How had I completely forgotten those long walks through the gardens of Truesdale with Lawry as a youthful, starry-eyed adolescent? Now that I had remembered them, and had mentioned them with such fondness, I knew that recalling them in such a way was not beneficial to where I needed to direct my thoughts.

Away from *him* and his evident fondness for me.

There had been a strange balance of the old familiarity and something I wasn't quite used to in my dealings with Lawry since he'd come home from Bar Harbor. It was probably to blame for that blasted kiss, as well as the strange tension that now existed between us.

And yet, there I was, trying to get him to go with me up to the conservatory, alone.

Was it really worth the risk to allow Garrett a few unsupervised minutes with Ainsley? I was beginning to doubt it.

"Perhaps we can read," Garrett suggested. "Ainsley, are you familiar with the poetry of Victor Hugo? He's Meredyth's favorite." He sounded about as confident as a lion tamer trying to coax a giant cat out of a cage for the first time.

"No, I'm not," she answered dryly.

For a moment, I was exceedingly thankful for Ainsley's shyness and how she'd ended the matter succinctly; there was no use in trying further to persuade her.

But then she added, "I do enjoy poetry, however."

"I'll be right back, Ainsley. I left the book in the library." Garrett winked at me as he left the room. He seemed to have collected his bearings a little, while I felt as if I were losing mine altogether.

"I suppose that means we're going up without them." Lawry strolled to the door, seemingly eager to leave his little sister entirely alone in my parlor. Before Garrett returned with the book, Lawry was already leading me silently up the three flights of stairs to the very top floor.

My conservatory wasn't anything extraordinary. It was nothing like those that were built on to grand estates in the country, or like the one at our summer cottage in Bar Harbor. It had been constructed on the roof of our town house, quite simply because that was the only place for it, and the space was only adequate for planting only flowers and small shrubs. I'd tried cultivating a few different varieties of roses the year before, but I'd never become too interested in them. Perhaps, this year, I would try something more exotic.

And perhaps this would be the year when I finally carried a bouquet of my new creations down the aisle in my wedding to Vance Everstone.

Once we entered the humid glass room, Lawry shrugged out of his jacket and draped it over the middle of a set of two mahogany chairs with green velvet cushions joined together at the opposite arms in the shape of a twisted snake. Then he strolled about aimlessly, while I planted myself at the edge of the basin of the fountain at the center of the room.

"Thank you for bringing Ainsley to see Garrett."

Lawry turned at my comment. His face displayed a rather curious look, as if he thought I was wasting my time trying to conjure up an attachment between our siblings.

Even so, I continued, "You must have some desire to see a match, or you wouldn't have come."

"Precisely. Oh, and Ainsley...yes, I do suppose Garrett might be in need of some help, considering he's wooed only half a dozen or so young ladies in the last year alone, the poor chap. He apparently has no idea what he's doing." Lawry's cheeks scrunched up in a wide grin.

"He told me as much before you arrived—"

"Meredyth, as I've already said before, I have no interest in meddling with the affairs of our friends...or even our relatives." His smile was gone, his seriousness back.

How had I managed to take him from one extreme of emotion to its complete opposite in a matter of seconds?

"If they married, we would then be somewhat related," I pointed out. "You would be my...my brother's brother-in-law. Surely, that would make us something—"

"We're something already." He wasn't facing me when he said the words, and I had a feeling it was on purpose.

"But what? We're not truly related, though it feels like we are."

"I don't believe 'related' is quite the correct term...for us. No matter if Garrett somehow wins Ainsley's heart." After a few moments of consideration, he walked up to my bed of roses. They didn't look especially healthy, but that was my own fault. I'd lost interest in them soon after I'd learned that Vance had decided to remain in Europe instead of returning home with his father last summer.

"How is your father, Meredyth?"

"What do you mean? Father's fine, as always."

"It's just that I haven't seen him since getting back."

"Do you need to see him for some reason?" I refused to join him as he investigated the elevated flower bed.

"Your father's a good source of godly wisdom. He has a way of making the truth plain."

"Wisdom regarding a possible move back to Washington, perhaps?"

"Wisdom in general, Mere. It seems there isn't a whole lot of it to be found anymore." Lawry continued to walk about the perimeter of the room, giving his attention to the different plants my mother and I had cultivated over the years. "One sometimes encounters a situation that is difficult to figure out on one's own. Don't you ever wonder what you're supposed to do?"

Could he truly read my mind? If so, was I ever in trouble.

"I'm not going to ask my father anything. He hardly knows me anymore, Lawry." In fact, I scarcely spoke to my father, except for at dinner. And that wasn't exactly speaking. That was answering the same questions with the same answers, every day, no matter what the afternoon had entailed.

I stood and circled around the fountain until Lawry was blocked from my view. I hated that I couldn't be around him anymore without feeling deeply agitated.

Moments later, Lawry made his way to my side. "I thought you and your father were close."

"Not anymore."

We had been close before my life had been ruined in the matter of a single day's events. Since that day over five years ago, I'd pretty much ignored the fact that I used to have any sort of relationship with my father. I was certain that if he were to look into my eyes, he would know the truth.

Just as if I looked too deeply into Lawry's, I was sure he would know the truth. And that knowledge was the last thing I wanted to see coming from Lawry's gaze. Or my father's.

I fluttered the fingers of my left hand in the flowing water of the fountain. Lawry reached over, grabbed my hand, and grasped my wet fingers in his.

"What do you have against us?" Using both hands now, Lawry touched the sensitive skin between my fingers with the pads of his fingertips.

"I'm not holding anything against you...or Father." I pulled my hand free and crossed the room to sit on the closest piece of furniture that didn't resemble a sofa—the tête-à-tête where Lawry had laid his jacket.

"I meant, what do you have against men in general? It's widely known that you've turned down your fair share of proposals during the two years I spent out West and haven't allowed anyone to court you in the last year."

While his back was turned to me, I pressed my hand flat over the fine, smooth material of Lawry's jacket.

"I know what I want," I replied, "and, as it so happens, what I want wasn't what any of those particular men had to offer." I slipped my hand into the front pocket of his jacket and grasped a folded handkerchief, one of the dozens he likely had, although he'd insisted that Ainsley and I waste our time ordering him more at Filene's earlier that week.

"Is there a particular man who does have what you want?" Lawry turned to me, his gaze locking with mine, catching me just as I slipped the handkerchief up the sleeve of my dress. A smile lit his face, though I was certain he had no idea what I'd just done.

"I know for a fact that a gentleman does not ask such a question of a young lady unless he is seeking some sort of grand compliment to boast about to his friends. Remember, Lawry, I'm well aware of all the tricks men play. God didn't give me four brothers for nothing."

Lawry finally came and sat beside me, only he faced the door of the conservatory, his jacket still draped over the barrier between us.

He leaned over his jacket, and I realized that the piece of furniture I'd chosen to sit upon had been designed with one quite provocative goal.

To promote kissing.

I leaned back against the far rail on my side of the chair.

"It's a wonder all those men got to the point of proposing." Lawry placed his left arm over his jacket and leaned in.

"Believe me, Lawry, I gave them all plenty of reasons to take their suits elsewhere before they insisted upon making fools of themselves."

He laughed and sat back, his blue eyes sparking with some strange new look. "I wish I could have been there to see every single one of those proposals. How dare they presume to have captured the attention, and perhaps even the heart, of society's darling tomboy, Meredyth Summercourt?"

The fact that he insisted on holding me in such high esteem grated my nerves, no matter how I delighted in his words. How I dreaded the thought of him truly knowing me, of discovering that his good opinion of me was based upon pretense.

"Exactly." I was quite finished speaking on the subject. Even with all the chasing that had taken place over the last few years, not one gentleman had ventured to kiss me in the course of his pursuit.

Only two men had ever dared to do that, and both times had been quite accidental. The first was done in the throes of youthful passion, the second in a state of confusion.

Trying to seem unaffected by him, I kept my eyes downcast. "Do you think that perhaps Garrett and Ainsley are finished—"

"Oh, yes. Surely, they must be in love by now."

"They've known of each other their entire lives…it's the difference in ages which has prevented them from ever really knowing each other well. They truly are perfect for each other, Lawry." I lifted my face to his and was stunned to find his blue eyes focused not on my person as a whole but solely upon my lips. And he wasn't smiling.

In the next second, he seized his jacket and stood. Hearing the glass door of the conservatory open behind me, I turned to see Mother glide into the room. She didn't look to Lawry or me but gazed up at the ceiling for a moment, as if seeing it for the first time.

Finally, she focused her attention on us. "Poor Garrett. What were you thinking, Meredyth, leaving him to entertain Ainsley Hampton all on his own? Not that Ainsley isn't a lovely girl, Lawry…but you must understand. Garrett will think you're trying to entice him into thinking something more for her, and you know Garrett can't abide such things."

"But Mother, wouldn't you like to see at least one of your sons settle down and start a family? Heaven knows Alex and Clyde have no such plans in mind, running around New York City as they are."

"Yes, it would be nice, Meredyth—but I've always expected you to beat them to that station in life. They're men, after all. They have all the time in the world…whereas you do not."

"Mother, really." To say such things in front of Lawry was completely uncalled for—unless she was trying to plant a seed in his mind, which would be completely unappreciated.

"Well, Ainsley and I had better be off before it begins to snow again, or I'll have to shovel her way home, as well." Lawry took my arm, graciously ending the conversation.

There was no telling how things had gone between Garrett and Ainsley, for when the three of us returned to the second floor, they were standing silently in the hall. It seemed they'd already said everything they wanted to say. Ainsley held the poetry book in her hand, as if she were planning to take it home.

I stood before them all as Lawry and Ainsley readied to leave.

"I'll be here Wednesday morning to pick you up, Meredyth— remember our plans from last week that never came to be?" Lawry turned from Mother and took my hand in his. "I'm hoping the roads will be manageable by then." He gave me a peculiar look, and for a moment, I wondered if he was about to bring my hand to his lips. But then he quickly let go and accepted his shovel from Fenley.

When Lawry and Ainsley had gone, Garrett returned to the library, obviously having no desire to share with me about his time with Ainsley. Mother went back upstairs to her room, and I reentered the parlor, where I realized that Lawry and I hadn't even taken the botany books up to the conservatory.

I thought of Lawry's handkerchief tucked into the sleeve of my dress. I hated myself for sneaking it from his jacket. He would eventually realize that it was missing. Would he suspect that I had taken it? Would he wonder why I might do such a thing?

And why had I?

I pulled *Leçons de Grammaire* out from the plush cushions of the chair and sat. I had yet to open it to the significant page. It was too difficult. It was too close to my heart—or too close to what I wished my heart could have.

Lawry…and not Vance.

Finally, giving in just a little, I pulled Lawry's handkerchief out of my sleeve and pressed it to my face. It smelled like him. The familiar, woodsy smell of his shave lotion filled my senses until I forced myself to bury it within the pages of the book. I looked down at them, paired together, feeling disappointed in myself. Why was I amassing a collection of mementos in place of everything I'd given up and could never have, no matter how much I realized I wanted it?

But I did have Lawry, I reminded myself. He was still my best friend, even if the recollection of his kiss and of the strange profession of love to me all those years ago kept me awake late into the night.

Every night.

SEVEN

Secrets

"But love is blind and lovers cannot see the
pretty follies that themselves commit."
—William Shakespeare, *The Merchant of Venice*

After I had been sequestered inside Summerton for almost a week because of the snowstorm, Lawry finally picked me up, as promised, and we set out to purchase a few outfits and pairs of shoes for Wynn, as well as some toys.

The poor girl. I had no idea how she had been keeping herself occupied at The Waterhouse Inn. But the thought of her being inside instead of out in the cold was a comfort to me. There was no telling what would have happened to her if we hadn't chanced upon her the day before the blizzard. Lawry and I decided to take our purchases straight to The Waterhouse Inn and present them to Wynn.

"I've been thinking, Mere."

I looked across the carriage cab at Lawry, seated with a mountain of boxes piled next to him. "Since The Trinity School for Girls is filled to capacity, I'm going to ask Benta if she would try to teach Wynn her numbers and letters, and perhaps teach her to read, until—"

"Why Benta?" I wasn't asking because I didn't believe she was qualified. I didn't like being left out.

"Because she's handy."

"Do you even know if Benta can read?" I wanted to take the words back as soon as they were out. I knew the answer but was desperate to make him consider another option. "What about me?" I asked quietly, for lack of another idea.

"What about you?" Lawry asked.

"I'm not completely unsuitable—"

"Meredyth, Benta is perfectly suited for this—far more than you are. She lives in the same house as Wynn, and she probably needs the money I'm willing to pay. You certainly don't." Lawry sat back, his arms crossed at his chest.

"But I want to help." I felt I was fighting a losing battle.

"You would make the time in your busy schedule to come with me to see Wynn three or four times a week?" Lawry cocked his head to the side and waited for my answer.

"Yes."

His eyebrows came down. "Why?"

"You're not the only one who cares about orphans."

His eyes narrowed skeptically. "Do you care about orphans in general, or just one in particular?"

Why did he always seem to be testing me? I knew the best answer for any test was the truth. But was I prepared to tell him the truth?

"Tell me, Meredyth, just how interested are you?" Lawry broke in again, somewhat angrily.

And that was when I realized he already knew that Ainsley and I were teaching music at the school, and that his anger stemmed from my refusal to confide in him.

"Dr. Wellesley told you, didn't he?"

"No, Ainsley did. I didn't give her much of a choice. I already suspected as much when I realized you already knew Dr. Wellesley," he revealed evenly.

"Why was it important to you to force my secret out?"

He hesitated, as if considering the possible implications of his answer. "I wanted to know exactly why you, Meredyth Summercourt, felt the need to volunteer at a school for orphans—and why you wouldn't wish to tell me. Did Amaryllis ask you to do it when Nathan took her to Washington?"

Amaryllis probably never would have expected it of me, even though I'd come to visit and brought my violin on several occasions.

"Amaryllis has no idea. And, if you must know, I asked Ainsley to join me—not the other way around."

"But for Ainsley's sake?"

"No, for my sake, Lawry." I was revealing to him more of my wretched heart than I'd ever revealed to anyone. Almost more than I'd even acknowledged to myself.

"Why didn't you tell me?" Lawry raked both hands through his hair, obviously irritated with me. "I would have...it would have—"

I reached out and rested my hand on his knee for just a brief moment. "Lawry, I haven't told anyone. And, really, how would I have ever known you'd be one to care? You never spoke to me about helping orphans once until the day you got back from Bar Harbor, and you—" I felt my cheeks flame. What was I thinking bringing up that dreadful day?

"But, had I known.... Meredyth, I had no idea. I wouldn't have—" His face suddenly flushed. What was he saying? That he wouldn't have kissed me that day? Or that he wouldn't have stopped?

"Whether or not you knew about it then shouldn't matter. Everything would still be exactly the same as it is now." I hurried to close the subject. Whatever he'd been trying to say, I still believed that his finding out earlier wouldn't have changed anything.

"Have you told Garrett about your volunteer activities?" Lawry seemed perturbed with me for switching topics, but the fact that he'd let it go was just another confirmation that I probably didn't want to know what it was that he'd been trying to say.

"Why should I?"

"What's going to happen if we convince Garrett to stay strong in his regard for my sister?" Lawry's voice sounded strained, as if he were rather disappointed with me. "If he succeeds, she'll likely tell him she's been volunteering, and she'll also likely tell him how you've been there alongside her the whole time. And won't that be a shock."

"Fine, I'll tell him. Do we know of a date Wynn might be able to start at the school?"

"It won't be for a long while."

Perhaps, when she was finally enrolled, she would be one of the students Ainsley and I taught.

"Lawry, I think I'll bring my violin the next time we visit Wynn."

"That sounds like a wonderful idea. And I'll bring my guitar." Finally, Lawry smiled again; but the cool look in his eyes told me it was forced, more for my benefit than out of genuine delight in me or the topic of conversation.

"You have a guitar?" I smiled back awkwardly, enduring his gaze. I tried to picture Lawry holding such an instrument. "Can you play it?"

"Of course. And I know for a fact that Dr. Wellesley has a trumpet. Not that a violin, a guitar, and a trumpet even belong in the same room together."

"Certainly not." I was still amused at the thought of Lawry playing a guitar. Did he know many songs? What would he end up playing for Wynn? "Are you going to take Wynn back with you to Washington when you go?" I knew it was best for me to think and speak of his eventual return West with a casual tone. "You could actually take a few of the older girls back with you, to work at the orphanage—but they'd need a proper chaperone."

"Would you consider such a position?" There was a new light behind his bright eyes.

"Of course not. What would my parents think?" I replied with remarkable composure.

Lawry's gaze pinned me to the leather seat cushions behind me. "Perhaps they'd think you had found your life's purpose."

"Don't be silly." Keeping my eyes on his, I wrapped my arms around my torso, anxious to calm my erratically beating heart. "Orphans have no real part in my overall mission in life, Lawry, especially not after—"

Vance would return, and if I was to accomplish everything I needed to, there would be no room in my life for teaching orphans music lessons…or for Lawry Hampton.

"After what?"

I couldn't tell him. I'd never told anyone. If I did, I knew that the questions would not stop until I was made to explain why. Why would I want to marry Vance? Why indeed, when I hadn't seen or heard of him in four years? And why couldn't I change my mind?

Or let Lawry change my mind.

"After what, Mere?" He drilled me again.

I glanced at the floor, a black emptiness filling my soul at the thought of Lawry leaving Boston, and my never seeing him again.

"Lawry, a young lady never gives away all her secrets. You'll find out someday what I'm referring to. But now is simply not the time." For a brief moment, I wondered why it mattered to him what I did with my life. Did he seriously want me to—? No, he couldn't. There was no way I could chaperone a group of young girls on a cross-country train trip without being married. And married to whom? Him?

"Fine, Meredyth. Keep your secrets." Lawry sighed in resignation.

"Don't worry, I will."

Lawry didn't seem quite as angry after I said this, but neither did he continue the conversation. In fact, neither of us said another word for the remainder of the ride.

I forced my thoughts away from Lawry and back to Vance. Suddenly, I wanted Lawry to know there was a very real reason I was holding myself back from him—from whatever it was he was after.

Perhaps it was best he knew for certain I would be married to Vance someday.

I was sure I would. Vance would eventually see that we belonged together and why. And he would come home and marry me. He simply needed a little more time to himself. He would be back soon, and everything would work out as I'd planned for the last five, almost six, years. God would answer my prayers, and I would be able to fix all that was wrong in my life.

I hardly recognized Wynn when she greeted us as we entered the inn. She wore an outdated dress with light blue and white stripes with a brown ribbon tied around her tiny waist.

And a big smile on her face.

As we climbed the steps, Wynn caught my hand and pulled me inside. Then she turned excitedly to Lawry. "You brung her back!"

Once in the door, I knelt before her and gave her the hug she was begging for with her skinny arms outstretched. "Of course, I came back, Wynn. You're my friend."

While still in my arms, she looked up at Lawry and said, "Is she yourn?"

"Is she what?"

"She yourn?"

When I stood again, I noticed that Lawry's face was a study of unmistakable confusion. Apparently, he had not yet picked up on Wynn's funny way of speaking. I knew exactly what she was saying, but I wasn't about to clarify it for him.

"Mere'dy's yourn, ain't she?" The more Wynn repeated it, the more it sounded like a childhood rhyme. "'Course she's yourn, ain't she? Miziz Larry?"

I smiled at her nickname for Lawry. He never would've asked her to call him that. He hated that name.

"Wynn, his name is pronounced Law-ree," I said gently.

"What is she saying, Mere?" Lawry looked at me with pleading in his eyes. He wanted so badly to understand her. However, no matter how many times she asked the question, I was perfectly content to let him try to figure the puzzle out on his own.

Turning to Wynn, I strived to explain without giving away what she meant. "Wynn, my proper name is Miss Meredyth Summercourt, and this"—I reluctantly took Lawry's hand—"is Mr. Lawrence Hampton. Of course, you don't have to use our formal names, but, as you can tell…." *Our last names were not the same.*

Wynn grabbed our entwined hands and lifted them, as if they were evidence for what she believed. "But Benta was sure of it."

I stood and freed my hand from their grasps. "Well, Benta was mistaken. That's all."

"Wynn, I have a surprise for you." Lawry kept hold of her hand and led her into the parlor, where he sat on the sofa and positioned her before him. "On top of having gone shopping for you this morning, we've also decided that until we're able to enroll you at The Trinity School for Girls, Meredyth will come to work with you on your lessons. How would you like it if she came here a few times a week to teach you?"

"Oh, please!" Wynn jumped up and down, then climbed on the sofa and gave Lawry a sideways hug around his neck. He smiled up at me, his eyes sparkling.

I about melted inside at the charming picture they created.

Wynn let go of Lawry and continued to jump excitedly on the sofa. "Oh, Mere'dy!" she sighed loudly. "Mere'dy, I—I do love you!"

I grabbed her under the arms mid-bounce, unable to endure just standing there, looking at Lawry, while Wynn said such things aloud. As I hugged her to me, I turned away from him, trying to forget the last time I'd thought I was going to hear those very words from Lawry, in the midst of a passionate kiss...but it was impossible. The memory was etched permanently in my mind.

EIGHT

Pretending

"What greater thing is there for two human souls than to feel that they are joined...to strengthen each other...to be one with each other in silent, unspeakable memories...?"
— George Eliot

We visited The Waterhouse Inn almost every day that week, always with Dr. Wellesley as our chaperone. And if he wasn't available, Benta Allister was always willing to sit and listen to us.

Lawry had yet to bring his guitar, and I'd not remembered to bring my violin, so Lawry decided that once I was done teaching Wynn her lessons, we would read to her from the Bible. We started with Christ's Sermon on the Mount and then the Twenty-third Psalm, and I was interested in seeing what Lawry would choose next. It seemed that I hadn't seen many Bible passages in ages—not since my days in boarding school.

Yes, I went to church every Sunday with my family, but for some reason, I hadn't considered listening closely to the sermons every week as all that important. However, now that Lawry had effectively pulled me back into studying the Scriptures, I couldn't shake the feeling that in recent years, I'd been merely surviving... more lost than found.

Friday afternoon, Lawry sat on the sofa with Wynn beside him, while I took a seat in a chair facing them.

"Today, we'll begin with Jeremiah chapter twenty-nine, verse eleven." Lawry flipped deftly to the section of the Bible he sought. I didn't recall ever reading, or even hearing, anything from the prophet Jeremiah before. Lawry placed the Bible on Wynn's lap and pointed to the verse as he began to read aloud. *"For I know the thoughts that I think toward you, saith the* LORD...."

For the first time that week, I questioned Lawry's choice of Scripture. What would Wynn think of the Bible saying such things concerning her life? That it was God's plan for her to be born in the slums of Boston and then deserted to the streets in the middle of winter because of the untimely death of her poor mother?

"...thoughts of peace, and not of evil, to give you an expected end."

My thoughts were jarred from Wynn to myself.

"An expected end." Had God known my "expected end" all along?

"'Then shall ye call upon me, and ye shall go and pray unto me,'" Lawry continued, *"and I will hearken unto you."*

Wynn gripped Lawry's arm with her tiny fingers and looked up at him with a grin. "Did God send you to find me?"

I let out a breath and stood to my feet. Hearing Wynn express such simple confidence in God surprised me. How could Wynn, of all people, put her trust in God so easily?

I walked over to the fireplace, though I was far from cold. I was actually burning with the awareness that I didn't seem to trust God at all.

"That He has, Wynn. And I think He's finally hearkening unto my prayers, as well." Lawry added quietly, almost as if he didn't want me to hear, "After all these years."

They both said something more, but I couldn't discern their words; I was too preoccupied to pay them mind, entirely focused upon the raging fire burning in the hearth—and the revelations that had caught me off guard.

I'd thought I was ever so trusting—that I knew precisely what it was that God required of me. Had I not utterly failed Him? Was I not determined to do everything in my power to make what I'd done right? Suddenly, I had an overwhelming realization that all of my trust was in me, in my own actions and my own plans created out of a desperate search for peace.

Behind me, Lawry resumed reading. *"And ye shall seek me, and find me, when ye shall search for me with all your heart. And I will be found of you, saith the* Lord.*"*

Found. Like Lawry had found Wynn that day.

"I'm glad you found me when you did," Wynn said, and again I was struck by the frequency with which her words echoed the longings of my own heart.

Except, unlike Wynn, I wasn't found—I was still completely lost.

"Meredyth, are you feeling all right?" Lawry asked.

I turned to discover that Wynn had found her way onto his lap. His arms were circled around her, holding the Bible before them.

"I'm…fine." I stared at them as a new realization took hold. They were what I wanted. Not Vance Everstone.

It was becoming dangerous for me to be there with him…and her. This pretending to be a family for a few hours every day had to stop. No matter how I craved it. No matter how I loved *them.*

I couldn't have them.

I couldn't. I was tied, chained, bound, to Vance.

Wynn took hold of the small Bible and brought it closer to her face. "Now it's my turn to try."

"How about we play a game and come back to this later?" I stood before the fireplace, as if making a formal case against reading the Bible.

Lawry looked at me intently as he scooted Wynn from his lap. He always seemed to know when *he* was bothering me. But instead of retreating, as I kept wishing he would, he continued to advance, becoming more and more persistent in his mysterious quest every day.

What exactly did he want from me?

He stood. "How about hide-and-seek?"

"That sounds perfect." It really did. I wanted nothing more at that moment than to hide from his ever-searching gaze. "You count, and Wynn and I will hide."

Before the sentence had passed my lips, Wynn had raced out of the room and was scrambling up the stairs, squealing with child-ish delight. I followed in the same direction but turned back at the foot of the stairs. Lawry had moved an armless walnut rococo chair from one corner of the room and now sat straddling it, his face buried in the crook of his arm. I could hear him slowly count-ing down from one hundred.

I couldn't take a step. How often did I have the chance to just take in the sight of him?

And since when did I care to? Countless times over the course of my life, I'd seen him and thought nothing of him, beyond the fact that he was one of my dearest friends. Since when did I care to such a degree about the style of his hair, or the way the material of his jacket stretched around the muscles of his upper arms, or the way his legs, now superbly displayed, were scaled perfectly to his height?

I'd always had more gentleman friends than female friends, which likely had much to do with my having only brothers and no sisters. I had learned quite early that most women wanted to befriend me solely as a scheme to get closer to Alex, Clyde, and Garrett. Only Nathan Everstone and Lawry Hampton had been my true friends throughout the years, seeming to care nothing at all that I was a young lady.

At least, it seemed, until recently.

"...forty-five, forty-four, forty-three...." Lawry lifted his head and ceased counting. His piercing blue eyes seemed to implore *something* of me. He smiled as if he knew he'd held my attention the entire time he'd been sitting there. Had I truly been standing at the foot of the stairs, transfixed by him, for almost a minute?

"You can't be found if you're not hiding in the first place, Meredyth."

I swallowed hard. "Yes—of course. I was only giving Wynn a head start." I turned and ran up the stairs, glad that no one else besides him, Wynn, Mrs. Allister, and Benta was in the house to see me engaged in such childish antics.

After reaching the second floor, I started down the hall, peeking inside the few vacant bedchambers which weren't permanently occupied by Dr. Wellesley, Wynn or the other few boarders. The Waterhouse Inn was rather large, with eight moderately sized bedchambers and four newly added bathrooms. I looked in the half-empty built-in linen cupboard at the far end of the hall, but there was no sight of Wynn. That was where we'd concealed ourselves the first time we'd played hide-and-seek with Lawry, scrunched in the back of the deep closet, half hidden by some old musty-smelling coats hanging before us.

I came to the back stairs, which led down to the kitchen, and realized that the staircase there also led up to the attic. There I would find a dozen hiding places, no doubt.

I took the wooden stairs slowly, lest they creak and give Lawry a clue as to where I was headed. He had to be almost finished counting, unless he'd decided to give me more time. I hoped Wynn was up in the attic. We wouldn't have been able to hear her footsteps, as light as she was, even if she'd clambered up there as fast as her little legs could take her.

In the large, crowded one-room attic were four rather deep dormer windows that let in a fair amount of light—enough for me to see where I was going and to avoid tripping over anything that might be in my path. I was headed straight for the far dormer, thinking it would be the last place Lawry would ever think to check. It was perfect, especially with the tall stack of old trunks in front of it.

The hiding place also offered the benefit of a wide built-in window seat, and although it had no cushion, it was better than sitting on the dusty floor. Twisting around as best I could in my corset, I faced the window. The view was at the same level as the vista from my bedchamber at Summerton, but for some reason, as I looked upon Court Street through the cold, unadorned window, it seemed that I was much further removed from the world below. Not a minute after selecting my hiding spot, I heard someone else moving clumsily through the attic. I didn't think Lawry was light-footed enough to have scaled the stairs without my overhearing, so I assumed it was Wynn. But I wasn't sure I wanted her to find me. The overwhelming sense of envy I had felt at seeing her and Lawry situated so cozily upon the sofa earlier was still fresh in my heart, and I wanted to be alone. I needed to be alone in order to make my way through those unwanted emotions, to get back to my previous stance of steadfastness and determination—one that had nothing to do with her or with Lawry Hampton.

"Mere'dy?"

One timidly spoken word from that tiny girl, and my resolve turned to mush.

"I'm in the far right dormer window," I whispered. I couldn't help but answer; I didn't know how I would stand hearing her say my name with such pleading in her voice again.

She peeked around the pile of trunks. "I found you!"

"You did."

"I heard you come up—knew t'was you cause o' your skirts." Wynn climbed up on the wooden seat and huddled close beside me, only she sat upon her knees facing the window. "I wish my bed was up here. Then I could see everything all the time."

"Surely, it's too cold up here, Wynn. You'd freeze at night, even with a dozen blankets covering you."

"I've been colder than cold before. I slept in a barn after Mumma died." She shuffled around on her knees to face me. "I come here a lot."

"Do you? What do you do up here?"

"Look around…usually while Benta is in the kitchen. Nobody comes here but me—and now you!" Excitement had raised the volume of her voice by several notches.

"Shh." I held my index finger to my lips. "We're hiding from Lawry, remember?"

"But di'n't ya want him t'come find us? Then we can be together. This is my favorite place, here in this window." She turned and pressed her nose to the cold glass. "Did you know that you and Law'ry are my favorite people in the world?"

"You and Lawry are my favorites, too, Wynn," I admitted, thinking it harmless to tell her. She needed all the love she could get.

"Lawry! Lawry! Come find us, Lawry," Wynn shouted in the direction of the door. "We're hidin' in the attic!"

"Wynn, that's not quite how hide-and-seek is supposed to be played, you know." I continued to whisper, hoping Lawry hadn't heard her. What was the use of hiding in the first place if all we were going to do was call out to Lawry to find us?

We listened in silence for a few seconds until we heard Lawry's footsteps on the narrow wooden stairs. My heart leapt at the sound, challenging my mind, fighting for the right to love him.

"Lawry." I heard my own voice calling out to him, evidence of my inconstant will. "Lawry, we're in the far right dormer…waiting for you." And not really hiding at all.

"Ah, my two favorite people." Lawry popped his head around the pile of trunks, smiling.

He couldn't have heard our conversation, but I was glad he'd said it. It somehow reminded me that I was again pretending. That being with them, my two favorite people, wasn't something I could actually afford to do.

"We were having a lovely time, enjoying this view of…Court Street." I forced myself to smile, to forget what I suspected he was trying to create between us. To forget everything that had happened before I'd raced up the stairs.

"I should have started my search in the attic." He squeezed onto the seat with us, watching me closely over the top of Wynn's head. She pressed her face to the window once more, grinning happily. "I should have known you'd run to the farthest corner of the house to hide from me."

"What is that supposed to mean?"

"It means that I know you better than you think I do, Mere."

At the sound of a bell ringing—a ringing that didn't stop—Wynn jumped from the window seat and ran past the trunks. "That's lunch!"

Lawry remained seated beside me, seemingly uninterested in immediately following Wynn down to the kitchen. "Did you not like the verses I chose to read today?"

"No, they were very appropriate. I'd never heard them before." It felt very normal to just sit there with him, discussing Scripture. It reminded me of when we were young…when life was less complicated.

"You seemed bothered by something about that particular verse."

"The idea of God's expected end for me—" *Terrified me.* After saying as much, I thought better about sharing such concerns with him. He would only try to convince me that God loved me and wanted to bless me. Lawry had always been telling me things like that, for as long as I could remember.

I moved to stand, but Lawry reached out and blocked me, trapping me between his arm and the window. His face was mere inches from mine, and for the first time I realized that he could tell I was falling for him.

"You're still holding out for Vance, aren't you?"

"I don't know what you mean. Vance and I are friends, just as much as you and I." My voice wavered. "But I suppose something might eventually happen between us...." I should have specified "between Vance and me," but the words caught in my throat.

"Vance isn't a friend to anyone. How long has it been since you last saw him?"

"Since before you left for Washington. You know that. He left Boston years before you."

"Yes, he left before me, Meredyth. And before he left, he told me and Nathan that there was absolutely nothing holding him here. That he was bored with life on this side of the Atlantic, and that he needed to go back to Europe...where life was exciting and he could live without the burden of social proprieties—"

"How do you know he still—"

"Because he's a scoundrel, Mere. And everyone seems to know it but you."

"Be assured, Lawry: I know better than anyone what a scoundrel Vance Everstone is capable of being." It felt good to say those words aloud, to proclaim the truth candidly. But it didn't change a thing. I still had to marry Vance, no matter that I was beginning to realize it was merely my own convoluted plan of redemption—one that had absolutely nothing to do with God.

But God didn't really want me, no matter what Lawry thought or believed. I'd already failed Him, and now I had to pay the price.

Lawry's arm still blocked my way. His eyes searched mine, and for a second, I wondered if I'd said too much. But then, if I'd said anything, I hadn't said nearly enough.

An aroma akin to that of shepherd's pie wafted through the corridors of the inn as we made our way to the kitchen. Benta met us on the second-story landing. "We were just sitting down to eat…rather late, I'm sorry to say," she told us. "You're welcome to join us, if you'd like."

"That would be wonderful, Benta." Lawry was polite to everyone, but did he realize he was likely making the innkeeper's niece fall in love with him?

"Just this way, then." She led us down the servant stairs toward the back of the house.

Soon we found ourselves in the kitchen, a room I'd never previously visited. I was surprised to find that it was also where we would be sitting to eat the meal. Wynn was situated in a tiny high chair. Was that how she took all her meals?

Wynn's eyes lit up once she saw us, and she started to say something.

"Wynn, please don't speak with your mouth full," Benta gently reprimanded her. "They'll still be here once you've swallowed."

Even as wrong as it seemed to have her seated in a "baby" chair, Wynn's delicate frame seemed to fit it comfortably, and she appeared to be enjoying herself. Perhaps she needed a good dose of babying now and then. Who knew how much of that she had experienced in her short, hard life?

Mrs. Allister stood and offered us the two chairs at the opposite side of the worktable. "Would you like somethin' to eat?"

"That's all right, but thank you," Lawry said as he took a seat. "We've eaten already." He'd come to Summerton early and joined Mother, Father and me for brunch. Father undoubtedly thought Lawry was trying to court me, and I let him believe it because it was easier than telling him the truth.

As I lowered myself into the seat next to his, Benta asked Lawry, "Would you do the honor of saying the grace? You're so very good at it."

"Of course." Lawry shot me a look, for I'd said almost the same thing to him when we'd sat down to brunch. He really was much better at praying than anyone else I knew.

I watched Wynn as she clasped her hands tightly and closed her eyes. Benta and Mrs. Allister simply bowed their heads. I closed my eyes, bowed my head, and clutched my hands together at my knees under the table. I loved hearing Lawry pray, and I was yet again looking forward to what he might say. It seemed as if the words of the Bible somehow came alive when he spoke them aloud in prayer.

"Lord Jesus, I thank You for these dear women surrounding me, who've taken to heart Your command to love the least of these. Bless them as they strive to obey all of Your commands in every aspect of their lives, through want and hardships, as well as in times of abundance. Thank You for this inn and for this food You've generously provided. We thank You for the hope You give us as we attempt to achieve Your purposes for our lives. And, Lord, I thank You for Meredyth. In Jesus' name, amen."

Somewhere in the midst of the prayer, Lawry had slipped his right hand between mine and interlaced our fingers. For all the practice I'd had at keeping my feelings for him at bay, I couldn't help but sense that, by grasping my hand during prayer, he was taking possession of me before God. That he was trying to tear me from Vance's hold, and, in so doing, revealing to me what perfection would be like—what being *found* felt like.

If I ever, indeed, endeavored to deserve it.

NINE

Everwood

"Oh, beware, my lord, of jealousy!
It is the green-eyed monster which doth mock the meat it feeds on."
—William Shakespeare, *Othello*

T he Diamond Room." I couldn't help uttering the words under my breath as I entered the Everstones' large, immaculate drawing room. The dazzling crystal chandeliers that hung from the ornate ceiling always had a way of mesmerizing me. I remembered coming to this grand house years ago, when it had first been built, making a point to sneak in to see the sparkling crystals in the otherwise darkly decorated space. Years later, it was still my favorite room at Everwood.

It had been ages since I'd been in the room, as Everwood had been shut up while Bram Everstone and his children had been scattered about the world for the last few years. His daughter Natalia and her doctor husband, George Livingston, lived year round at the family's summer cottage on the outskirts of Bar Harbor, just up the coast from Lawry's parents. And, of course, his son Nathan had been in Washington State for the last few years with Lawry. William was studying at Harvard, and his youngest daughter, Estella, had been playing companion to her blue-blooded great-aunt Miriam Bancroft.

All while Vance gallivanted throughout Europe.

"You'll never believe what Will told me yesterday." Nicholette Fairbanks clutched on to my arm and led me to the far end of the room. Whatever her fiancé had said, she evidently felt it was important to keep it confidential. "It's about Vance," she added in a whisper.

Did she know what the mere mention of his name did to my nerves? Surely, by the inquisitive look in her hazel eyes, William had told her *something*. He must have.

"Oh, what's that?" asked twenty-year-old Estella as she followed us. The poor girl didn't know what to do with herself, now that Nathan, her favorite brother, had again moved cross-country, this time as a newlywed. It had surprised me that he and Amaryllis hadn't taken her with them when they had left for their honeymoon last summer. "Do you not yet know, Estella?" Nicholette asked dryly as the rest of the company filed into the room.

I straightened my back, returned Nicholette's steady gaze, and took another moment to collect myself before speaking. "Is Vance coming home soon?" I made sure to look at Estella as I asked the question.

"No." Nicholette snagged my attention once more as she turned the three of us to sit upon a chaise longue in a shadowy corner of the room. "He still refuses to leave Paris."

I had hoped that whatever she had to share was no graver than that. Vance's insistence on staying abroad was rather old news.

"Father has tried everything to get him to return to the States." Estella picked up a glass figurine from the side table next to her and cradled it gently. "But even Father's threats are no good in getting Vance to obey."

One would think, with his making so many threats of cutting off money supplies and canceling inheritances, that Bram Everstone could better control his three sons. The fact that Nicholette was engaged to William instead of Nathan attested to the fact that the Everstones would do as they pleased, no matter the cost.

By the lively look on Nicholette's face, I knew there had to be something more to the news than all that. And I didn't have to wait long for her to explain.

"Not when Vance is in love with a beautiful Parisian girl named Giselle Gerard he's already admitted he's been supporting. Now he insists he's going to marry her."

Oh Lord, help me.

Estella lowered her gaze, but I could tell she was still looking in my direction. How did she feel about learning such information regarding her own brother from someone outside her family? Or had she already known?

"He won't leave Paris without permission to marry her, and he already considers himself engaged, no matter what his father says," Nicholette went on. "He refuses to leave her side for anything."

Anything. Including me, of course.

I closed my eyes, and my heart thumped loudly in my ears. I couldn't breathe.

"Does his— Did your father know about this when he returned last summer?" I asked Estella. I didn't know why I even bothered. Vance didn't care what Bram Everstone thought. He never cared what anyone thought.

Least of all, me.

"We've known for some time...since Christmas." Estella still didn't meet my gaze. "Father was furious, of course."

"Isn't it scandalous, Mere?" Nicholette was too focused upon being the bearer of such provocative news that she hardly noticed my lack of response. "But you know Vance...."

Yes, I knew Vance—better than anyone could ever guess.

I'd had years of practice appearing calm whenever his name was casually thrown about between my friends and acquaintances. But this was a new breed of test. How would I ever make my way across the drawing room and through the gathering of the

Everstones' dinner guests before my tears began to fall, obliging me to concoct an explanation as to why?

I stood and walked to one of the front windows. The shades were still up, the curtains pulled back, likely so that anyone driving past would be able to see the extravagance of the party being held inside. I simply stared out at the blackness, not caring who might see me. Even from the street, I was certain all that anyone might be able to discern would be a green silk evening gown and a tall coiffure of bright ginger hair.

I was certain no one would really see *me*. Ever.

Not turning from the window, I asked, "Have you heard anything lately from Nathan and Amaryllis?" I was doing a fantastic job of conducting myself with remarkable civility, when all I really wanted to do was scream.

"Oh, probably the same old news you already know…about breeding horses and living on some strange island in the middle of Washington State," Nicholette replied. "Tell me, how is there an island in the middle of a state?"

"I don't know," I said to the window. "I suppose we'll have to go visit Whidbey Island in order to really understand."

"As I've explained before, Nicholette, the island is in Puget Sound," Estella tried to clarify.

"And what exactly does that mean?" Nicholette could be impossible at times.

"Do they plan to attend your wedding, Nicholette?" I asked.

"I believe so."

"Oh, good."

There was a long, awkward pause, but I wasn't about to turn around and face them again. "Where will you and William set up house after you're married?" I finally asked Nicholette.

"Will's purchased a large brownstone just down from my parents on Dartmouth Avenue. Of course, he's also having a summer cottage built for me in Newport, near my parents' and my grand-parents' cottages."

I'd been completely mistaken in thinking that this subject was preferable to speaking about Vance's disgraceful Parisian love affair. All I'd ever wished for was everything Nicholette was establishing with William, only with Vance.

Just then, William approached our secluded corner, looking as sharp as always—and much like Vance with his short, dark wavy hair and black eyes. "Sharing secrets over here, I presume? I hope they're not too horrifying, and that you're all still able to call this a 'wonderful' evening."

I refused to answer him. The evening was actually turning out to be one of the worst evenings of my entire life, and I had a feeling William knew exactly why. Had he been the one to put Nicholette up to telling me the news of Vance like this? And why just now, after they'd known for months?

Could William tell I was still *consumed* by the idea of marrying his brother? He'd really grown up while he was away at Harvard, and I was shocked that he seemed quite ready to settle down and marry at the age of twenty-four. Such a situation was almost unheard of for a young man with the last name of Everstone.

"We were just telling Meredyth about Vance," Estella said quietly. Was she embarrassed by her brothers? It was no wonder she favored Nathan, the most levelheaded of the three.

"Were you surprised, Meredyth?" Will studied me unscrupulously as I stood by the window. I stared back as he took a seat in a chair next to his sister's end of the chaise longue. If he thought he would discover anything concerning my thoughts about his brother, he was wrong.

"I, for one, wasn't," he divulged further. "Falling in love with someone inappropriate sounds just like something Vance would do—take delight in, even. He probably went to Paris with that singular goal. He does love to shock everyone."

"Yes, he certainly does." I came back to sit on the chaise longue with Nicholette and Estella. "What are you going to do after the double wedding this summer, Estella? Stay at Rockwood with Natalia?"

"Possibly." Estella took a moment before saying anything further, and in a matter of mere seconds, she seemed to muster up more determination than I'd ever seen on her face. "I've been thinking a lot lately...about going to live in Washington with Nathan and Amaryllis. They've mentioned the idea in their last few letters—"

"Estella, you do realize Crawford isn't in Washington, don't you?" Will asked her.

Her eyes nearly doubled in size at her brother's boldness. I couldn't believe his audacity—and to ask such a question right there in front of Nicholette and me!

"*He* has nothing to do with my wanting to live with Nathan and Amaryllis."

I determined, in that instant, never to think badly of my brothers. Even their worst treatment of me was nothing compared with the condescension that poor Estella had to endure from William—and probably from Vance, too, when he was around.

William stood and silently offered his hand to Nicholette. It was as if the two of them—two people who seemed to have everything they'd ever wanted in each other—needed to point it out to those of us who were not in a similar relationship. They seemed to delight in causing others to feel as if their dreams were unattainable, their heart's desires hopeless wishes—all under the guise of friendship and family relations, of course.

I was suddenly very happy that Ainsley and Lawry had been unable to attend the dinner party. I had a frightful notion that if Lawry were to see me in that instant, he would have been able to see my broken heart.

An irresistible urge to run into his arms possessed me. I imagined melting into the comfort of him again, and how very safe I'd feel with my cheek pressed to his heart....

I turned when I heard a tiny sniffle. I'd forgotten all about Estella sitting next to me. She was quiet. Always so quiet.

I forced myself to ignore my own desire to cry. "Moving to Washington does sound like a grand idea, Est—" Suddenly I couldn't speak. It was as if a door to my heart's greatest yearnings and desires had been flung open without so much as a warning, and I suddenly saw *myself* living in Washington with Amaryllis and Nathan.

And with Lawry.

"I do look forward to it, whenever it may come to be," she replied, evidently finding nothing strange about my abrupt silence. "However, I'm not at all certain it will. I'm not sure what I'm going to do when Father marries Madame Boutilier. And Aunt Miriam isn't well, and requires a nurse now. She doesn't need me anymore. She doesn't want me."

"You should go to Washington," I insisted, almost more to myself than to Estella.

She turned sharply, as though astounded at hearing such a charge from me. "Do you think I should give up on Jay, after so many years? He's still not gone West. He's working as a resident physician at one of my father's hotels—Everston, near Moosehead Lake. It's the only thing that has kept me from going to Nathan and Amaryllis." I looked into her eyes and saw that the tears I'd heard in her voice were long gone, replaced with a decided hardness. That she hadn't given up on him the summer before was surprising. Everyone knew she'd wanted him for years.

"I'm hardly the one to ask, Estella. I don't even know what I'm supposed to do with my own life, let alone...."

My mind returned to a more pertinent subject—everything Nicholette had just disclosed about her rogue brother.

Vance had obviously made his decision. He didn't want me—and now I didn't know what I was going to do.

Marrying anyone else was simply out of the question.

TEN

The Hancock Ball

*"For one human being to love another: that is perhaps
the most difficult of all our tasks...."*
—Rainer Maria Rilke

I stood beside Garrett against the railing of a long balcony overlooking the ballroom of the Hancock mansion. What would Wynn think of such extravagance? Would she ever get a chance to see such things—such wealth? My mind drifted to Mrs. Allister and Benta and the simple life they lived. What were they doing as I stood there in my gown of burgundy and gold, with jewels adorning my ears, neck, and wrists, all of which probably cost more than everything those two women would ever own?

In the month since we'd taken Wynn her new clothes and toys, Lawry and I had gone to visit with her and teach her nearly every other day. I still hadn't told Garrett that Ainsley and I had been teaching music classes for the girl's school, and I was pretty certain she hadn't told him herself. I'd hardly witnessed them speaking to each other lately.

As soon as I noticed Ainsley coming up the stairs with Lawry, Garrett disappeared, but not to attend to her, as I would have expected only weeks ago. Ainsley left Lawry's side, and I turned away. I didn't need anyone detecting how often my gaze stayed glued to him. I was sure that half of Boston probably thought he was courting me, given how frequently we were seen out and about together.

Sooner than I thought possible, he was at my side. I continued to inspect the bustling crowd below, but I could stand there only so long without looking at him. Like always, once my eyes were fixed upon him, I could hardly drag them away from the fine, even features of his face...and that slight bump at the bridge of his nose.

He smiled widely, showing me his straight teeth.

I pushed away from the balcony and stood with my back to the nearby wall, one hand still holding on to the railing. Lawry placed his warm hand on mine. I was sure it was an effort to comfort me, but consolation was far from the emotions his touch stirred. What I really needed was to see less of him. Much less.

And I wanted to lash out at him for making me feel things I didn't want to feel.

"Why did your sister come to town, Lawry?" I decided to ask. "She hardly seems willing to fraternize...even with Garrett. And she's known him her whole life."

"It was Claudine's idea...and Mother's, too," he replied gently. "And she's eighteen. It was time."

"You should have realized she wasn't ready. Pretty soon, she'll have the reputation of being a heartbreaker for the way she keeps treating her would-be suitors." I stared at the crowd below, avoiding his gaze.

"She must be taking pointers from you." They seemed like such harsh words, but when I cut a glance to him, I found he was smiling.

"I am not a heartbreaker. I'm just incredibly choosy."

"Meredyth...I don't think she's ready to deal with someone as experienced as Garrett. There's no point in foisting your brother upon her right now. Perhaps she's just as choosy as you are...and simply doesn't want him."

I stepped away from the wall, almost ready to hunt Ainsley down at that very instant. However, Lawry still held my hand captive on the railing, and I didn't want to break the contact.

"I'm going to find out what she does want. And why she came to Boston, if not to find a husband." Except I didn't move away.

He stepped closer, his hand still upon mine—only now he was caressing the skin at my wrist with his thumb. "And would you be willing to share with me the same information concerning yourself? I'd love to know just what you want...if not a husband who adores you."

My eyes flitted from his face to my hand and back again, my chest filling with the breaths I couldn't manage to release. Without giving an audible answer, I tugged myself free from his grasp and began walking through the throngs of people along the balcony and down the stairs.

Fortunately, he didn't follow. I had no idea what I was going to say the next time I faced him.

He was becoming much too...persistent.

Did he truly want me?

I paused at the foot of the stairs. What had been going on since that day he kissed me? Did he truly think he was courting me?

I glanced up at him, still standing where I'd left him. When he saw me looking at him, he disappeared from the railing, and I resumed my search for Ainsley.

After searching the crowds that filled the entire first floor of the Hancock mansion, I went back upstairs, having heard that Lawry was in the downstairs card room. It seemed he was avoiding me as much as I was avoiding him.

I didn't find Ainsley anywhere around the balcony, so I stood near the top of the staircase in hopes of spotting her from above. Finally, I saw her, dancing with Phillip Craven. I watched as her eyes trailed to something—or someone—close behind me. I turned to see who it was.

Garrett.

And what a look Ainsley was giving him!

How fascinating. Every little detail of how she'd been acting, and her revelation that she feared her mother didn't want her to marry young, all made sense...and I was immediately sorry for practically attacking Lawry about something I apparently knew nothing about. Though I was even sorrier for how our conversation had ended.

Ainsley was falling for Garrett, despite everything she'd said to me. Was that the source of her frustrations? That she wanted to encourage him but didn't think her mother would approve?

I let Garrett catch up to me, and together we descended the stairs. He didn't say much and practically acted as if he saw no one. Not even Ainsley. Had he already given up on her? Oh, if only he would be persistent! If only he knew how close he was to winning her heart.

Leaving Garrett's side, I went in search of Ainsley as soon as the dance was through and found her taking refreshment with Phillip.

"Ainsley, have you danced with Garrett tonight?"

"He never asked." She looped her arm through mine and led me out of earshot of Phillip.

"Why don't you ask *him*?"

"I wouldn't want your brother to think I have any designs on him. You know how Garrett is...."

"Why not? We're all old friends. And it's not like he hasn't acted as if he has the same designs on you. All winter, in fact—"

"Please, Meredyth. Garrett?"

It was time to put a stop to these silly games, once and for all. "What do you think of him, truly? Are you in love with him?"

She was visibly startled by the barrage of blunt questions, and by her failure to answer, I knew she was simply collecting herself in order to somehow turn the conversation around. Which only compelled me to prod further before she could do so.

"Well, if you don't, I've noticed that Hazel likes him enough. Very much, actually. I wouldn't be surprised if she's set on marrying him, herself...stealing him right out from under your nose."

Ainsley whitened. "Garrett's not the kind of man who marries."

"I think he's changed, starting sometime last summer." I placed a finger to my lips. "Around the time of the Everstone Ball last June, in fact. He seemed rather agitated to find that you'd grown into such a beaut—"

"No." Ainsley suddenly displayed absolutely no emotion whatsoever, which was very odd for her. "And I have no idea why you think he might have changed. He seems the same as ever to me. Really, Meredyth, I think you need to stop worrying about other people's affairs and focus on your own, instead. Like what you mean by spending so much time with *my* brother." And with that, she turned and walked away.

⌒

Ainsley wasn't acting like a heartbreaker; she just didn't know what to do.

Well, Lawry and I would fix that for her. I was sure he'd be thrilled to hear me admit how wrong I'd been. Though, I wasn't quite certain how he would react to the news that his little sister was already in love with my brother. I really didn't relish facing him again, but there was no one else I could tell.

However, when I found Lawry, most of my excitement about what I wanted to share had disappeared, replaced with a fear that he would disapprove of my actions. Especially if he knew how disturbed Ainsley had become because of my interference.

I made my way back through the crowded halls of the immaculate mansion until I found him in the card room. All four gentlemen around the table stood when they noticed me, allowing me to interrupt their game. Lawry took his time in studying me.

"Lawry, may I have a word with you?" I asked in my most pleasant voice.

Having this discussion while waltzing was out of the question, unless we wanted everyone to be gossiping about us even more. Then I realized what I was preparing to do—gossip about Garrett and Ainsley. But we were their family, and we cared about them. Surely, any words we might speak in the interest of helping them would not count as gossip.

The ballroom of the Hancock mansion was arranged to facilitate about as much privacy as anyone could ask for. On each side of the room were five alcoves concealed by massive aqua-blue velvet curtains. Every other alcove also had French doors leading out to the veranda that surrounded the ballroom's three outer-facing walls. It was the alcoves without French doors that were perfect for tête-à-têtes and secret rendezvous.

Not that I had frequented them. I'd been in one just once, with Vance, right before he left for Europe.

With our arms linked together, Lawry and I walked silently down the hall and into the ballroom. He followed my lead out a set of French doors to the veranda, which, unfortunately, was rather crowded. We moved at a slow pace all the way around the veranda, so as not to bring attention to ourselves, then reentered the ballroom through another set of French doors on the opposite side.

I looked up at Lawry and saw that he was smiling, obviously enjoying the game he thought I was playing.

The orchestra finished their waltz, and all the dancers stopped to clap their hands, the sound muffled by their gloves. We paused in our quest for privacy and applauded along with them.

"Would you not like to dance, Meredyth?" Lawry asked.

"No," I answered softly, "I don't…I don't think we should. We've already stood up twice. People would talk."

"I think people already are talking."

I ignored his comment, hoping it was not entirely true. "I just need you to follow me."

He smiled. "With pleasure."

When the orchestra started up again, I led him through the crowd of bystanders to the next alcove. As we neared the spot, I let go of his arm. When I looked into his eyes, I could tell he knew what I meant to do—and that he was perfectly willing to go through with it. Slowly, inconspicuously, I wove my way through the many people standing around and snuck behind one of the velvety blue curtains.

Fortunately, the alcove was unoccupied—a rare situation indeed.

Soon enough, Lawry was standing before me in the blue-tinted semidarkness. He was so close, I could smell the peppermint on his breath, and my stomach dropped a little at the thought of repeating the kiss from back in January.

"This is much better than dancing with you," he teased.

"Lawry, do be serious. I have something important I need to tell you," I whispered, coaxing the words out.

"What is it, Merit?"

Why was he using my childhood nickname now? His sudden mention of it nearly erased my every thought.

Still whispering, I began, "I wanted to tell you something that I—"

He stepped closer, presumably to better hear me over the strains of the orchestra. "You have no idea what you're doing, do you?"

I really didn't. What had I been thinking to bring him to such a secluded place?

But then I remembered. "Lawry, I think—I, um…do you…?" How did one say what I wanted to say without sounding like a silly, frivolous fool of a girl?

"You what?" he asked, stepping even closer. He sounded almost shocked at what I'd already said—which was absolutely nothing. "You do? You finally admit it?"

"I do what?" I asked impatiently.

"You admit it? You love me?"

"What? No!" I replied, still whispering. "I love—? No, I meant— I think Ainsley's already in love with Garrett!"

His beautiful blue eyes turned to slits. "You believe Ainsley loves Garrett? That's what you brought me back here to tell me?"

I put my hands behind my back and pressed against the cold wall. "Are you upset with me?"

"Yes, Meredyth," he answered curtly.

I hated the sinking feeling his response had created in my chest. He still stood incredibly close, and I wondered how I would ever escape—and if I even wanted to.

The blue-tinged light coming through the curtains wrapped around us provocatively in the long silence. I desperately wished we could simply go back and finish the last conversation we'd had upstairs. Yes, I wanted a husband who adored me. And, yes, I wanted to adore him back.

And I wanted it to be him.

Just as Lawry moved aside to allow me to pass, someone on the ballroom side of the thick curtains fell against them, pushing Lawry back toward me.

He caught himself with his palms against the wall, his hands on either side of me. And he stayed there, his face mere inches from mine, the smell of peppermint all around me. I heard his ragged breaths; I watched as his eyes searched my face. I knew the worst thing for me to do was to continue looking at him, but that was exactly what I did. Bravely, recklessly, I stared back, knowing what was coming—welcoming it, even. Lawry was going to kiss me again. I could see it in his eyes as his bristling gaze darted to my lips.

My hands were still behind my back, and I summoned every ounce of determination I could muster to keep them there. I wanted to reach out to him, but it was my turn to stand still, unmoving. If he wanted me, he could have me, but I would not throw myself at a man again in a moment of weakness.

I waited for what seemed like minutes, listening to his deep, unsteady breaths, wondering when the inevitable would happen. He would kiss me. Wouldn't he?

He would make me forget. He would change my mind. He would let me love him.

Oh, God—he would, wouldn't he?

"I won't make that mistake again." His words stunned me, and the breath I'd been unaware I was holding rushed out. "Not if you don't—" He shoved himself from the wall, away from me.

"Yes—yes, we'd best not," I uttered, trying my very best to seem as if I agreed wholeheartedly; that I didn't care in the least if he wanted to kiss away my memories of Vance or let them fester forever.

As Lawry stalked out of the alcove into the ballroom, I felt as if he'd hit me in the stomach. But he hadn't even touched me.

I stood there and listened as the orchestra, their music muffled by the thick curtains, ended one piece of music and began another. Could I stay there in the alcove for the rest of the night? Would anyone even notice? Would Lawry?

Perhaps it was best he didn't. Perhaps, what I really needed to do was better remember the one and only other time I'd been in one of those alcoves, with Vance standing in almost the same position in which Lawry had accidentally found himself.

When Vance had led me back there, I'd been certain he was going to propose. I was expecting it, wishing for it. Instead, what I'd heard as he stood pressed against me, whispering into my ear, was: "Meredyth…just look at you. You drive me mad. That's why I must leave, you know. You can't imagine what the sight of you does to me…."

It was a common theme of our private conversations, and I was quite aware that his words had everything to do with that day in the cave…and nothing whatsoever to do with a future together. I also knew, when he touched the delicate ruffles edging the low neckline of my gown, that his eyes were most likely leveled there, as well.

"Vance…you don't need to travel to Europe alone," I had whispered. "Marry me. I can go with you. It can be our honeymoon."

"I will, Meredyth, when I come back. I promise," he'd said before kissing my cheek. He hadn't kissed my lips after what had happened in the cave. Perhaps it was too much for him. Perhaps it was too personal.

Vance had left me in the alcove in much the same manner as Lawry just had, only not so much because of anger. Vance had departed in frustration. The same kind of frustration I always seemed to cause for him.

My thoughts drifted forward to what had just happened between Lawry and me—and how very odd it was that he would be able to induce the very same feelings that had led me into such a shameful situation with Vance. Only, I knew Lawry Hampton, and he never would have allowed himself to participate in what had taken place in the cave all those years ago. He valued me more than that. And I valued him enough to stop whatever was on the verge of happening between us.

It was useless, pointless, to pretend it could ever happen. It most definitely could not. Would not.

As I slowly collapsed to the floor of the lonely, gloomy alcove, I so wished I'd been able to resist Vance as much as I'd just resisted Lawry. That way, the fact that he seemed to be falling in love with me as much as I was falling in love with him wouldn't have seemed like such a disaster.

ELEVEN

The Guitar Song

"Angry people are not always wise."
—Jane Austen, *Pride and Prejudice*

Lawry did not come to call at Summerton the day after the Hancock Ball...or the day after that. Much to my relief.

I was actually thankful to not have to travel across town with him in his carriage...even though I missed seeing Wynn. However, when two full weeks had passed since my last visit at the inn, I found myself afraid that Wynn likely thought I'd deserted her. That Lawry didn't seem to care what she thought of my abandoning her bothered me considerably.

I had to find a way to get to The Waterhouse Inn on my own. But how?

That afternoon, Garrett came home from Father's office looking rather haggard. He practically collapsed into a chair. Unlike Alex and Clyde, he never had been all that interested in Father's business ventures. Or was this about Ainsley?

I was certain Garrett would be willing to take me across town, and then I'd be able to tell him about our volunteer activities at The Trinity School for Girls, if Ainsley hadn't done so already. Perhaps I'd even manage to find out more of what *wasn't* happening in regard to her.

I'd already convinced myself that it was a good idea, regardless of how worn he looked.

"Garrett, will you take me out in your coach? I simply must escape this house. I've been shut in all day."

He looked very much like he wanted to say no.

Instead, he said, "Where would you like to go? Hilldreth?"

"How interesting, but no." I smiled, knowing his thoughts must be quite wrapped up in Ainsley Hampton for him to suggest such a destination. "I'd like to take you to meet someone very special to me. There's a little girl Lawry and I have befriended—really, Garrett, don't seem shocked. You know there's more to the world than the towering stone mansions of Back Bay."

"I thought you'd been spending a lot of time with Lawry, at least before the Hancock Ball." He gave me the crooked smile he used when he thought he was on to something.

"Garrett, I must confess something to you...something we've been hiding. Lawry and I thought we might as well tell you..." I said, deliberately feeding his belief that he had figured things out on his own.

"I knew this would be coming—for years, in fact."

"For years?" I was stunned that he'd ever given any extra thought to me, let alone Lawry and me, for years. "Well, that's impossible, because the school was brought into existence only last year."

He sat up. "School? What school?"

"The Trinity School for Girls. Ainsley and I have been teaching a music class there every Tuesday afternoon."

Garrett shot to his feet. "What? Why?" His smile was gone, replaced with a scowl that scrunched his reddish-blond brows over his steel-blue eyes. I hadn't expected my news to cause such alarm.

"Because we want to...help?" If Garrett had such a reaction, what would my mother do if she ever found out? "Do you think it's really so bad to help those who are less fortunate?"

"Does Mother know?" he asked, lowering his voice. "Does Claudine? Was this Ainsley's idea?" He joined me on the settee.

"You pain me with such uncharitable words, Garrett! And it was actually I who dragged Ainsley into our volunteer work."

"Does Ainsley care that much about…?"

"I suppose she does, but aren't you at all interested in the little girl I said I wanted you to meet?"

"A little girl. Of what interest is she to Lawry—and why?" I could already tell he was conjuring up the worst possible scenario in his mind.

"She's an orphan we rescued from the streets, and she's the dearest little thing I've ever seen." Though, truth be told, I seriously wondered how Wynn might have changed in the weeks since Benta Allister had presumably taken over her schooling.

"What's her name? And does Ainsley know about her?" Garrett leaned forward, his elbows on his knees, his brows drawn together. Why he suddenly cared so much, I could hardly guess.

"Her name is Wynn Rosselet, and no, Ainsley doesn't know a thing about her."

"Rosselet?" He looked at me sharply.

"Yes, why? Do you know someone by that name?"

"Not anymore."

"Who did you know?"

"You knew her, too, Mere. Don't you recall Olivia Rosselet? She was about your age, came out a year before you, I believe. She was stunning."

Olivia Rosselet, who'd gone away one summer a few years back and never returned. Yes, I remembered, now that Garrett had mentioned her.

Was it possible that Olivia Rosselet was Wynn's mother? Had Olivia been disowned by her parents and then forced to spend the last few years hiding in the slums of Boston in order to look after her child? Did Wynn's father even know about his daughter? Had it been Olivia's secret hope that he would eventually marry her?

Well, it was too late for that. He'd probably supported them until he learned Olivia was gone, figuring her death absolved him from responsibility.

The cad.

"Do you remember what Olivia Rosselet was like, Garrett? Besides stunning? I don't remember her at all."

"Caused quite a stir among the men. Seemed everyone wanted her." He looked more comfortable now as he reclined against the deep-cushioned side of the settee.

"I meant, what did she look like?"

"Gorgeous, of course. Blonde hair. Green eyes."

She didn't sound like she could have been Wynn's mother. Everything about Wynn was so very dark.

Garrett stood. "Well, are you ready?"

Distracted by my thoughts, I'd completely forgotten all about my plans to visit Wynn…and my very real dread that Lawry would be at the inn, as well.

"Oh, yes. Let's go."

After helping me into his coach, Garrett asked, "Where to?"

"The Waterhouse Inn on Court Street."

"An inn? Lawry must be smitten, indeed." Garrett disappeared for a moment, in order to tell his coachman his orders. When he'd taken his seat, facing the back of the carriage, he continued. "Meredyth, you never did address the topic of what's going on between you and Lawry. Or what *was* going on, until a couple of weeks ago. What exactly happened between you two?" Garrett was being much nosier than usual.

Heat rushed to my face. "Don't old friends like to see much of each other simply because they're old friends?"

"Yes, but then, why suddenly stop?"

"We haven't stopped anything." I focused my gaze out the window on the cold, icy sludge in the street, regretting ever having told Garrett anything.

"I noticed you two roaming the halls at the Hancock Ball...."

I looked up and found his head cocked to one side as he waited for me to admit to something.

"There is absolutely nothing wrong with linking arms with an old friend as one strolls the halls of an extremely crowded social event." The conversation was not going in the direction I had hoped at all.

"If you say so, Meredyth, I'll believe you. Though, I will not believe Lawry has been the same since the ball. He hasn't, and that's a fact."

He was right, of course. But I was not going to discuss the topic with Garrett. Or with anyone else, for that matter.

Garrett's mouth twisted into a sneering smile. "You don't suppose Lawry's the father of this Wynn Rosselet, do you?"

"No, I definitely don't!"

His grin only grew wider. I could tell I'd responded just as he'd hoped I would. "Will you promise me, Meredyth, that you won't tell Ainsley about Wynn? If she learns of Lawry's interest in orphans here in Boston, she will more than likely find out about the orphanage in Seattle, and—"

"You know about Lawry's orphanage?" It felt like a slap in the face. Lawry had confided in me, said I was the one he'd wanted to tell more than anyone else.

"Yes, and I don't want her to know about it. Not yet." Garrett wasn't smiling anymore. I couldn't imagine the reason for his concern over Ainsley's knowing this detail about her own brother.

"What do you think she would do if she found out?"

"One of two things. She could take the information straight to her parents—you know how overprotective they've always been."

"And the other thing?"

"What if she wants to follow Lawry to Washington? None of us would ever see or hear from her again. Unless, of course...."

"Unless she marries someone who is set on staying in Boston?" I finished for him. "You don't really think Ainsley would follow Lawry to Washington, do you?"

Garrett's auburn brows were again bunched together, as if he had no way of making heads or tails of Ainsley. "There's no telling what that girl would do. She's so...curious."

"Curious" was a strange way to describe her, but I supposed Garrett didn't really know what to think about any pretty young lady who wasn't hounding him for his attention.

Just as I was about to prod him more regarding what he thought of Ainsley, I noticed we were turning onto Court Street...and that Lawry's carriage was already parked in front of the inn. "How fortunate," I muttered. "Lawry's visiting Wynn today, as well."

⌒

Once Mrs. Allister had admitted us into the front hall, Wynn came running from the parlor, shouting, "It's Mere'dy! It's Mere'dy!" She stopped when she saw Garrett behind me. "Who's this? Aren't you Lawry's, Mere'dy? Or is you his?"

Oh, bother. Was she still convinced that Lawry and I belonged to each other?

"Wynn, dear, this is Mr. Garrett Summercourt, my brother," I gently explained.

Her question answered, Wynn was beside me in an instant, taking my hand, as well as Garrett's.

"You must be the Miss Wynn I've heard so much about. It's a pleasure to make your acquaintance." Garrett bowed, and I couldn't help but smile at the sight of his large hand enveloping Wynn's tiny one. I could not recall one instance when I'd seen my brother in the presence of a young child. But that didn't mean he wasn't able to charm the little nymph from the first instant she laid eyes on him.

"You're a nice brother, huh?"

"The very best kind of brother, in fact."

He was better than both Alex and Clyde put together, but he was nothing like the kind of brother Lawry was to Ainsley and Daphne.

Garrett drew Wynn down the hall to the wide entrance to the parlor, and I followed. I quickly spotted Lawry leaning against the wood frame of the curtained doorway, his arms crossed over his chest. A large brown guitar rested on the floor at his feet. He'd finally brought it along.

Also in the parlor was Benta Allister. Had she so fully assumed my place in becoming Wynn's teacher in the last few weeks that the three of them now enjoyed the family setting I missed so much?

Not daring to look Lawry in the eye, I willfully stepped right past him without a word. He was, after all, the one who had excluded me. What kind of stories had he made up to explain my absence to Wynn, or to Benta and Mrs. Allister? Did they think I'd so easily forgotten my duty? And did Benta take delight in spending time with Lawry?

"Good morning, Benta," I greeted her. "I'm so happy you've been able to fill in for me while I've been away. I've missed coming… so very much."

Benta smiled uneasily. "It was no trouble, Miss Summercourt. It was actually my pleasure."

Of course, she would take pleasure in spending time with Lawry. He was exceedingly likable, on top of being exceedingly handsome. Actually, he was probably quite appealing to any woman, especially when he smiled. Not to mention the fact that he had such a remarkably generous, loving heart.

I sat next to Benta on the settee. Garrett and Wynn remained standing in the doorway as Lawry picked up his guitar, took the nearest seat on the sofa and cradled the instrument in his arms. "I was just about to play Wynn's favorite song. Victor Hugo and I made it up while I was living in Washington." He smiled dashingly. Wynn finally let go of Garrett's hand and sat close to Lawry. She tapped her fingers against the wood at the base of the guitar, making a deep, hollow thumping rhythm.

"You know very well that Victor Hugo has been dead for over five years, Lawry." I smoothed my skirts around me, trying very hard to keep my eyes on Wynn and not traveling to Lawry's face. I didn't want to see the look he might be giving me. "And I highly doubt he ever made it to Washington State…even while he was alive."

"Ah, but that hasn't stopped us from getting together to create a quite brilliant song. I thought you might even recognize it, Meredyth. It's called 'The Guitar Song.'"

Benta stood. "I should get back to…my real work." She raced out of the room.

Wynn immediately jumped up and ran after her. My heart lurched with envy before I could stop it.

Garrett peered skeptically about the stuffy room, which was a far cry from the parlors he was used to being entertained in.

I glanced at Lawry quickly enough to tell that he hadn't especially minded Benta's hurried exit. Wynn came back into the room moments later with half a cookie in her hand, the other half in her mouth.

"Would you like to hear it, Meredyth?" Lawry asked evenly. "I know Wynn does. She's been begging me for the last hour to play it."

"Oh, yes, Lawry, do the guitar song, like you said you would." Wynn smiled adoringly at him and shoved the rest of the cookie in her mouth.

Lawry strummed the chords of the guitar in a lively tune.

I'd never seen Lawry play a guitar before. To the best of my knowledge, he hadn't known how before he'd headed off to Washington. I wondered how he'd come to learn. And then I wondered how long I'd been staring at him.

Lawry stopped his fingers over the strings, silencing them. His eyes met mine, and I swallowed the dry lump in my throat. No, he definitely didn't hate me.

"Do the guitar song again, Lawry!" Wynn bounced on the sofa cushions, causing both Lawry's arm and his instrument to shake.

I searched Garrett's face. Seated across the room from me, he'd said nothing so far about our involvement in the life of a six-year-old orphan. I hoped I hadn't made a giant mistake in telling him about her and bringing him to meet her. Would he end up telling Mother?

"I know, I know, Wynn—it's coming, I promise." Lawry charmed her into submission by lifting one corner of his mouth in a smirk that was hardly visible, though the smile lines around his lips and eyes were still quite evident. "Mere, I'm going to need your help to sing the song properly, which Wynn hasn't had the delight of hearing yet. The song is somewhat of a duet, you see, and Benta was too shy to sing it with me." He'd caught me staring again, and suddenly all the charm was gone, replaced by an almost angry glare.

"But I don't know your song."

"All you need to know are a few words. First, I'll sing a verse, and you'll end it by singing the word 'how' three times. After the second verse, you'll sing the word 'dream' the same way. It's that simple." He was being so cut-and-dry, and so unlike the Lawry Hampton I'd always known.

"Fine." I gave in to him entirely too easily. "'How' and 'dream' three times each. I suppose I can handle that."

Lawry immediately began strumming the guitar again, filling the room with the song's sweet melody. "How shall we flee sorrow—flee sorrow? How, how? How shall we flee sorrow—flee sorrow?"

I was so transfixed by the timbre of his voice, I almost forgot I had a part to sing. It had been years since I'd heard his smooth baritone voice. The faultless way he hit each note made my chest swell with emotion, and suddenly I wanted to cry.

Lawry nodded to me, indicating that it was my turn.

"How—how—how?" I did my best to match the notes he'd sung, trying very hard to ignore the way his clarion voice was able to prod at something hidden, something I'd purposefully buried long ago.

"How shall we see pleasure—see pleasure? How, how? How shall we see pleasure—see pleasure?" He nodded again, and this time my response was considerably more composed.

I was even able to smile, somehow. "Dream—dream—dream!"

"How shall we be happy—be happy? How, how? How shall we be happy—be happy?"

I stared at Lawry, bewildered. He hadn't mentioned a third verse.

"How shall we?" I whispered.

"Love." He spoke the word plainly as he continued playing the song—no melody in his tone, no smile on his face. He stared at me evenly, his blue eyes cool and calculating.

Trying to keep with the tempo of the song, I faltered, "Love…?"

"Just sing it for Wynn," he whispered. "If it's too difficult to—"

"Love—love—love!" I answered in song…and a cold chill crept up my back as I recalled Lawry's biting words. *If it's too difficult to*"—what? Sing the words to him?

Garrett interrupted my last "love" by spitting out a menacing laugh. "How you shall be happy, indeed!" Then he stood, and before any of us even realized what he was doing, he was out the door, slamming it shut behind him. By the time I reached the front door, with Lawry at my side, and opened it wide, Garrett's carriage was moving away from the curb.

"I suppose he was under the misguided impression that I wanted to escort you home," Lawry said, turning away from me as I watched my brother's coach disappear down the street.

TWELVE

A Poetic Reading

"Life is one fool thing after another, whereas love is two fool things after each other."
—Oscar Wilde, *The Happy Prince and Other Tales*

After being forced to sing Lawry's ridiculous song, followed by a long, awful, silent ride home with him, I decided not to try to see Wynn on my own again.

I missed seeing her; she was such a funny little girl. I tried not to dwell on the fact that the reason I liked spending time with her was because she seemed to adore me. That had been true especially when Lawry and I had first gone visiting. It had felt like we were playing make-believe…pretending to be a perfect little family who all adored one another.

I really missed that.

And I missed him, too. More than I'd thought possible.

I tried hard to be all right with all this, with hardly ever seeing Lawry and Wynn. I knew it was for the best, and that was the only reason I was able to endure it.

In the weeks since my last trip to the inn, I'd seen Lawry only once, at a benefit for The Children's Aid Society of Boston hosted by Nicholette Fairbanks's parents. I'd been rather confused all that night about what, exactly, The Children's Aid Society did and whom they helped. No one I'd asked seemed to know the answers.

And I never did have a chance to ask Lawry. He'd spent the evening ignoring that I was alive, let alone in the same room with him.

Prior to receiving the invitation, I'd never heard of The Children's Aid Society—at least with my heart. I'd probably heard the name before with my ears but hadn't allowed the thought to travel any farther. Exactly how had Mr. and Mrs. Fairbanks helped the poor and needy children of Boston by putting on such a show of lavish spending to entertain their wealthy friends?

A few days after the benefit, I was forced to attend a very small poetic reading hosted by Dr. and Mrs. Craven, though I was in absolutely no mood to listen to love poems. Weeks ago, when we'd received the invitation, I had thought it bearable—but not now.

My parents and I sat near the back of the room, saving seats for Claudine, Lawry, Ainsley, and Garrett, who was coming only because I'd long ago commissioned Lawry to convince him. That had been before everything became so complicated between us. When the group walked in, a few minutes late, I discreetly motioned to the two vacant seats next to me and to the pair along the aisle a few rows in front of us.

I knew the only way I was going to get Garrett and Ainsley to take the seats a few rows up would be by waving directly at Lawry and indicating that I wanted *him* to sit next to me. Much to my surprise, he accepted my invitation, a beaming Claudine lowering herself into the seat next to his. I was pretty sure she had the same sort of ideas regarding Garrett and Ainsley that I did.

When Ainsley realized she was being forced to sit with Garrett, she briefly cut me a scathing glare. But I was certain she'd alter her facial expression once she resumed conversing with Garrett about poetry. I knew she was scheduled to read a short poem by Victor Hugo, probably from my book Garrett had lent her.

For the first half of the evening, Ainsley stayed motionless, sitting rigidly next to my brother. Just about as rigidly as Lawry sat next to me.

I missed being near him, talking to him, looking at him. My heart grieved the loss of his laughter and his almost lover-like friendship. Was this what life would be like after he moved permanently to Washington?

"I still don't think Ainsley likes him," Lawry whispered in my ear.

"Nonsense. She's in love with him," I replied, doing my best to hide my hurting heart. "What woman in her right mind would be able to resist attention from Garrett?"

"What, exactly, do you mean by 'attention'? He's hardly spoken to her since before the Hancock Ball."

"Your mother—" I spoke softly so that Lawry alone would hear me, no matter that I had to lean in close to make sure. Let everyone else in the room suspect that Lawry and I were courting; what did I care? "Ainsley thinks your mother was sorry to see Daphne marry so young."

"She was, indeed." It was a rather detached, logic-based conversation we were having—with absolutely none of the passion behind his words that I'd become accustomed to hearing.

"But that's only because Daphne moved to Germany immediately following her wedding and didn't see your mother for almost a decade. If Ainsley married Garrett, your mother would still see her—because I highly doubt Garrett would steal her off anywhere." I looked at my program. The poem Ainsley had selected to read was called "Morning." I didn't know the poem, but it sounded like something she would choose. Something safe.

"What's to say Garrett still wants Ainsley?" Lawry asked with a shrug. "Seems to me he's changed his mind."

"It's that look he gives her, and the fact that he hardly talks to her anymore. When has Garrett ever been at a loss for words with a young lady? I believe it's simply this: He detests the fact that he cannot stop his unruly feelings for her, so much so in fact, that he feels he loves her against reason, even against his will...no matter her response to him."

Lawry's expression turned to stone. "That's a rather complex hypothesis."

"Shhh." From the other side of Lawry, Claudine pointed a long wrinkly finger in our direction. Oh yes, people were reading poetry at the other end of the room. I'd forgotten. I focused my attention on the reader, who was droning on and on about grass and trees.

"Will you help me?" I lowered my voice to the faintest of whispers. "We need to get him back to wooing her...and we need to change her mind."

Lawry cocked his head ever so slightly. "Just how does one do that—get a young lady to change her mind?" He was suddenly more interested, the stone wall strangely gone.

"That's the problem." I was mesmerized by the closeness of Lawry's jaw in relation to my nose when I leaned in to speak. "I haven't the slightest idea."

"I'll see what I can do." Lawry smiled down at me, his face near mine. I breathed in, and the soothing scent of peppermint surrounded me. Did he ever think back to that almost-kiss at the Hancock Ball?

I exhaled my pent-up breath and opened my eyes once I became aware that they were closed.

Before I knew it, the people around us began to rise from their chairs for refreshments. When I looked over Lawry's shoulder, I saw that Claudine was already gone, but that Garrett and Ainsley were still seated next to each other.

"Hurry, let's leave them." I stood and pulled Lawry by the arm. Thoughts of the last time I'd led him about a public event flooded my mind...and, of course, the result of that leading.

I unlatched myself from his arm.

"As you can tell, I did end up accomplishing the task you once asked of me," Lawry said as we found our way to the line for the refreshment tables. "Garrett came to this reading solely to appease me…in order to appease you."

I definitely did not want to get into the subject of Lawry's desire to appease me. I knew that if he'd done such a thing at the Hancock Ball…. Heavens, why was it that kissing Lawry was the only thing I could focus on?

"I had a question about the benefit at the Fairbanks's." I forced my thoughts off Lawry and back to how frustrated I'd been that night. All the tables of extravagantly prepared foods, meticulously set up at the benefit; all those bottles of expensive wine and champagne that had been consumed; everyone devouring an overabundance of food and drink—were we really helping anyone?

Lawry frowned. "What's the matter? Are you still trying to determine how the benefit helped any of the unfortunate children of Boston?"

"Do you know?"

"I haven't a clue. I heard you were asking around, though." He seemed genuinely pleased with me for half a moment, and I felt overcome with something like merit—until my thoughts went to Wynn, starving on the street with no one to give her food or shelter or protection from bullies. Where would she be if Lawry and I hadn't driven by when we had?

I wasn't hungry anymore and decided to forgo the refreshment table altogether. Lawry followed me out to the hall. Not that I knew where I was going. I really just wanted to be alone. But being with Lawry felt almost the same.

If Lawry hadn't taken the initiative to run to Wynn's rescue, what then? What about the other children in the same dreadful predicament she'd been in? Why had no one ever explained it more fully to us?

The only other person I knew who really seemed to care was Lawry.

Was it possible that this was the reason Jayson Crawford Castleman wanted nothing to do with our society, and how he was able to stay away for so long? And if Jay understood, did Estella understand, also?

"Estella. Have you seen Estella? I need to ask her a question." Because it was becoming clearer and clearer that I desperately needed someone else to whom I could voice such disconcerting thoughts...someone besides Lawry Hampton.

He took me by the arm and led me through the rooms filled with people, but Estella was nowhere to be found. We eventually reached the back of the house. I knew that heading down the empty halls of the Cravens' brownstone mansion with Lawry on my arm wasn't the best idea; not since the last time had ended with him—

Just as Lawry turned around to lead me back to the front of the sprawling house, we heard a high-pitched, giggly squeal.

And I knew just whose squeal that was. Nicholette Fairbanks.

Lawry tried to stop me by pulling at my hand, but I shook myself free and continued on until I came upon Nicholette and William. With one hand, he kept a firm hold on her tightly corseted waist; the other was embedded in her waves of golden hair as he pressed her against the wall and kissed her quite zealously. My standing there did nothing to deter him.

My feet were glued to the floor. I couldn't stop watching.

Behind me, Lawry cleared his throat, and Nicholette flew out from between William and the wall faster than I'd ever seen her do anything in her life. Her face was flushed, yet she still smiled, as if she couldn't help it. And I was sure she couldn't.

Next to me, Lawry bowed slightly as he took my hand in his. He interlaced his fingers with mine and tugged me back in the direction from whence we'd come. "Excuse us," he murmured.

"Of course." Nicholette's hand lingered possessively on William's arm.

William looked as if our disruption was hardly worthy of his notice. Obviously, he wanted to get back to what he'd been doing before being so rudely interrupted.

"Shall we continue our search for Estella?" Lawry asked as he pulled me down the hall. "What did you need to see her about?"

"Oh, nothing." Only everything I never wanted to speak of to him ever again.

As we walked back to the main hall in silence, visions of that passionate kiss raced through my mind, only it wasn't Nicholette and Will I pictured.

Lawry practically pulled me back to the drawing room, and I could tell he had one thing on his mind: getting me as far away from those lovebirds as quickly as he could. Were his thoughts running along the same avenues as mine? Was he thinking of the time we'd found ourselves nearly doing the same thing at the Hancock Ball?

Up ahead, Garrett and Ainsley still sat next to each other. I could tell that Ainsley seemed more relaxed than before. And from what the program said, she would be reading her poem directly after the refreshments.

Lawry and I sat alone in our seats a few rows behind them, awkwardly ignoring what we'd just witnessed, as we waited for the audience to reassemble.

Once the room again filled with people, shy little Ainsley walked to the front. For some reason, it didn't surprise me when Garrett followed her, red-faced. Not that I knew what they were doing—but I had a notion.

Ainsley gripped my book of Victor Hugo's poetry in her hand and slowly cracked it open to one of the very last pages. "I know the program of events says I will be reading a poem by Victor Hugo called 'Morning,' but I'm afraid it was a misprint. Instead, Garrett Summercourt and I will be reading another poem, 'First Love,' also by Victor Hugo."

The name stunned me and wiped from my face the smile provoked by their walking to the front of the room together.

I knew that poem. It really wasn't a poem at all but a dialogue between two lovers. The thought of hearing those particularly ardent words once again sent shivers through me.

Those never-forgotten words and their potency—those very words I'd memorized long ago in the form of a prayer for my future husband—it astonished me that they so accurately described what I felt for Lawry, and that, as I was beginning to realize, I had never come close to feeling for Vance.

I stared at Ainsley and Garrett—who were standing silently before one another at the front of the room—preparing myself to think only upon them and what the words could possibly mean to them...for each other.

Never in my life had I thought I'd be jealous of one of my brothers, especially when it came to love, and especially since I'd chiefly been the one trying for so long to get Garrett and Ainsley to acknowledge their love. I just wasn't prepared for it to happen so quickly, without warning. Hadn't Lawry and I just been wondering how we might accomplish this very thing?

"And something else," Ainsley stated apologetically, yet sounding more resolute and authoritative than ever. "I will be reading the part of Didier, while Mr. Summercourt takes the part of Marion."

Garrett took his position and began: "You're strange, and yet I love you thus." He didn't speak to the audience; he spoke the words directly to Ainsley, and my heart about hit the floor. She hadn't even passed him the book.

"You love me!" Ainsley said to Garrett, feigning utter surprise. And then she looked to the book in her hand and read, "Beware, nor with light lips utter that word. You love me!—Know you what it is to love with love that is the life-blood in one's veins, the vital air we breathe, a love long smothered, smouldering in silence, kindling, burning, blazing, and purifying in its growth the soul."

She looked up, but again, not to the audience—her eyes were on Garrett. She put her free hand to her heart and went on. "A love, that from the heart eats every passion but its sole self;—love without hope, or limit, deep love that will outlast all happiness; speak, speak; is such the love you bear me?"

In the silence of the crowd, I could hear my heart thundering in my ears. Could Lawry hear it, as well? We were still sitting incredibly close to each other, since the chairs were crammed into the room so tightly. What did he think of these passionate words?

"Truly," Garrett finally replied, his voice booming with confidence.

It was no wonder Ainsley had taken the part of Didier. Garrett probably wouldn't have been able to handle more than his two tiny lines, especially with the way Ainsley was practically declaring her love for him in front of everyone.

"Ha! But you do not know how I love you! The day that first I saw you, the dark world grew shining, for your eyes lighted my gloom. Since then all things have changed; to me you are some brightest, unknown creature from the skies. This irksome life, 'gainst which my heart rebelled, seems almost fair and pleasant; for, alas!" Ainsley held the book before her for a moment and then gently closed it. "Till I knew you, wandering, alone, oppressed, I wept and struggled, I had never loved."

And…silence.

I was still in shock at what I'd just witnessed, and I believe the effect was universal. I looked down and saw Lawry's hand clutching the edge of his chair, his knuckles white from the strain. He must have been stupefied after hearing his baby sister profess her love for my older, somewhat wild, brother for the whole world to hear, and with quite an unconventional display of poetic affection.

While the crowd gave them a polite round of applause, Lawry merely stared at Ainsley and Garrett, who held hands and bowed ever so slightly. "What just happened?" Lawry asked slowly.

"I believe Garrett somehow changed Ainsley's mind…without needing our help at all." I continued to study his hand as he pried his grip from the seat and then laced his fingers together, flipped his hands around, and cracked his knuckles. It was rude to do such things in public, but at least the applause mostly covered the noise. It seemed all the people I knew by the last name of Hampton had a strange penchant to embarrass themselves outrageously.

Suddenly, the next reader had begun her recitation—something about a lady floating down a river. I really wasn't paying attention. The only thing I could do was stare at Lawry's hands, now clenched into fists and propped upon his knees. It seemed a safe enough place to focus until I realized what I was imagining him doing with those hands. I wanted to feel his fingers entangled in my hair, the way I'd seen William's in Nicholette's not twenty minutes earlier.

"Seems we've been witness to all kinds of displays of affection tonight," I whispered. For some odd reason, I wanted to make Lawry sorry that he hadn't kissed me in that alcove at the Hancock Ball.

He should have.

He really should have.

Lawry turned his blue eyes to me, and for a moment, I saw something like sorrow shift across his handsome features. It brought to my mind how jealous and, yes, even grief-stricken I'd become at Garrett's first—and practically his only—line in his performance with Ainsley.

"*You're strange, and yet I love you thus.*"

"Are you happy with the way that just played out?" Lawry asked quietly.

"I'm happy for Garrett and Ainsley…and also for Nicholette and William." The subject begged to be addressed. "Those two seem to have fostered some affection for each other since becoming engaged, considering they did so without so much as a courtship."

"Passionately kissing in a back hall at a poetic reading doesn't necessarily signal true affection, Meredyth." His sharp answer had a tone of finality about it, as if there was nothing more important he could ever say to me than that one rather poignant sentence.

Little could Lawry have known he was wasting his time offering me such knowledge. I likely knew more about it than he ever would. I'd already tasted an excess of so-called affection and its ramifications, including excess guilt.

But Lawry knew nothing of that, so what was he referring to?

Was he hinting at his kissing me? That *his* unplanned kiss, and whatever had been going on in the alcove of the Hancock Ball, did not signal any amount of affection?

I steeled my back against my chair, stared straight ahead, and focused on keeping my attention fully set on the young lady reading Edgar Allan Poe's tragic poem "Annabel Lee." Up until that moment, it had been a favorite of mine. But now I didn't know how I would ever be able to think of the poem without also recalling such an awful sentiment from Lawry, no matter how badly I needed to hear it.

THIRTEEN

Warm

"The remedy for wrongs is to forget them."
—Publilius Syrus

Before church, Lawry wouldn't look at me.
No smiles. No winks. Nothing.
What had happened to us?

I tried not to care. I really did. He'd been absent from my life for two years, and I'd been fine. And then he'd disappeared again for another four months after that, and I'd hardly missed him. So what did it matter that he was in Boston yet again, only now farther away from me than ever before?

I forced myself to think of Vance Everstone instead.

After learning all that I had about Vance's plans to marry some Parisian girl named Giselle, I wasn't delusional enough to think my plan to marry him could still become a reality. No, I was now forced to face the other prospect. The one I hadn't considered thinking much upon before because it was so disheartening.

I would become a spinster. Just like Claudine Abernathy.

I felt my nose wrinkle at the thought and quickly corrected it before anyone noticed. Either I would marry Vance, or I would never marry. That had been my scheme all along—my only other option.

I looked over at the Everstones' pew, where Estella and William were seated with their father; where Vance had sat every

Sunday before leaving for Europe. He would always stare at me throughout the service, searing me with his black eyes, willfully prompting me to remember my greatest sin.

Did he really think I could forget?

Had he known what he was doing that day?

I would never know now, not if he married this French girl. Not that we'd ever really spoken of it much before he'd left. That day had simply created an invisible bond between us, and it was a subject that was usually treaded upon only with our eyes.

I looked back to Lawry, sitting between Ainsley and his aunt Claudine. I couldn't help it.

He was the better man. I knew it with every fiber of my being.

He'd stopped himself from kissing me in that alcove at the Hancock Ball, even though it had been clear he wanted to. He'd been so close, mere inches from me. Inches from all of me—and yet his self-control had prevailed. Probably because of his utter lack of affection for me.

Oh, why did I insist upon seeing that as such a terrible thing? It was for the best…for everyone. I would marry no one, and Lawry would marry someone…eventually. Probably the beautiful Amelia Grendahl.

When the pastor concluded his sermon, I realized I hadn't heard a single word. Everyone stood for the closing hymn. Garrett held the hymnal between us, but I only stared at it blankly. I wasn't planning to sing. My heart couldn't take it.

"Be still, my soul: the Lord is on thy side."

That first line burned in my heart. I wasn't able to concentrate on the remaining lines of the first verse as they filled the sanctuary. Those first words simply repeated over and over in my soul until the very last line of the stanza caught my attention.

"Through thorny ways leads to a joyful end."

I wished it was possible. But how could it be, with so many pieces of my life—and, yes, even my heart—scattered about, not fitting together properly?

After church, Estella came over and walked alongside me as I sifted through the crowded aisle toward the door. She'd completely broken away from her father, her brother, and her soon-to-be stepmother.

Her face and her brunette hair were half hidden under the brim of her hat, but I could tell by the tiny glimpse I got of her brown eyes that she had something she desperately wanted to say. And whenever Estella Everstone had something to say, it was likely important.

Once freed from the bustling crowd, we stood together in a deserted corner of the vestibule attached to the sanctuary. Estella grabbed my hand. "Meredyth, please say you'll accompany me to Bar Harbor. Nicholette and William are insisting I travel up there by the end of May."

I wasn't used to hearing so many words come out of her at once. She seemed more than a little vexed that her brother and his fiancée were ordering her around. But then again, perhaps she was merely distressed at the whole prospect of soon acquiring both Madame Boutilier and Nicholette Fairbanks into the tight confines of her family.

"Can they not handle the wedding plans on their own? I thought that your sister was helping, too."

"It seems Nicholette has convinced Daphne to make a huge to-do about the entire week before their double ceremony. Father and Eva—forgive me, Madame Boutilier—insist upon going up early next week. And Natalia is already too fatigued...did you know she's finally in the family way after all these years?"

"No, I hadn't heard."

"Will you come with me? We received the telegram concerning Nicholette's new plans just yesterday." Estella looked pleadingly into my eyes. "I've already asked Father, and he says you may stay at Rockwood until your own family comes up to open Summerhouse."

The idea of escaping Lawry's presence until the wedding in June did sound awfully tempting, as I was getting more and more troubled by his treatment of me—as well as my own responses to him.

"Yes, I'll come. I'm sure my parents won't mind my absence. What day will you leave?"

"Monday, the twenty-fifth." Estella smiled.

I'd never been particularly close to her, though we'd known each other our entire lives. Neither of us was really particularly close to many people, actually. Estella always seemed to live in the shadow of her brother Nathan, and I'd always had Lawry. But even the fact that Nathan and Lawry were the closest of friends growing up had not helped a friendship to form between Estella and me. Perhaps it was about time, since she no longer had the steady comfort of Nathan's presence, and I had only the immense discomfort of Lawry's.

I could handle another week and a half of Lawry Hampton. I was sure of it. Especially with the way he'd been acting. After that, it would be easy to leave—easy to travel hundreds of miles from him.

It would be good practice for when those miles numbered in the thousands.

⌒

"Does anyone know where Sicily Munroe is today?" I asked the nine exceptionally quiet girls standing before me. Not one of them would look me in the eye. And no one offered an answer to my question.

Ainsley had not felt well the day before, and I'd insisted that I could handle teaching the last class of the spring semester on my own. During the summer months, the girls would observe a completely different school schedule that wouldn't include the music class.

Today, I had finally brought my violin with me. If anything, I knew I could entertain the girls with some music, and then perhaps let them each have a chance to play a few notes. That was how I'd first become interested in the violin, myself—I'd witnessed an older cousin of mine play, and I'd immediately fallen in love when she'd let me hold the instrument and push the bow back and forth over the thick strings. Yet it frustrated me to no end that no matter how much I practiced, no matter how much time I spent with that polished wood pressed under to my chin, I would ever be called only a "fairly good" violinist.

But that didn't stop my heart from almost bursting with joy every time I brought the instrument out of its case. I truly loved my violin, although it wasn't anything exceptional. When it was clear I would never become truly proficient at creating moving moments of musical delight for my friends and family, Mother had seen no sense in purchasing a better-quality violin, insisting that the one I had would do. That was fine with me; I never had looked forward to giving it up for a "better" one.

I'd hidden my brown leather violin case in a closet before the girls had arrived, and now, as I lifted the instrument out, I heard their squeals of delight behind me. The melancholy mood regarding Sicily's absence was somewhat forgotten as they huddled around me.

"They rather flock to her, don't they?"

I was shocked to hear Lawry's voice echo through the large, practically empty classroom. Turning, I found he'd walked in with Dr. Wellesley...and Wynn.

I almost dropped my beloved violin.

"What are you doing here?" I didn't know to whom I was directing the question, exactly, only that it wasn't to Dr. Wellesley. He came by for a few minutes almost every Tuesday.

The girls remained bunched around me and now stared at Wynn, while I gawked at Lawry and the amused look on his face. That was certainly not the kind of expression I would have expected, though I suppose seeing me surrounded by a group of young orphans would be entertaining to him. He was probably still trying to understand how I'd found myself in such unusual circumstances. I still didn't understand it, myself.

"Girls, I'd like you to meet Wynn Rosselet." Dr. Wellesley's hand was on Wynn's shoulder, and I think he was trying to get her to walk toward me and the girls. "She's making a special visit to the class today."

Wynn's beautiful, blackish-brown eyes were wide with terror—she looked even more frightened than she had when Lawry had carried her to his carriage the day he'd saved her. I remembered her comment to me that day about never having had any friends. What were Lawry's plans for her during the summer? Would he take her to Bar Harbor when he went up for the wedding? And would they leave soon after that?

I awkwardly held out my violin, knowing Wynn had always looked forward to the day when I would bring it to The Waterhouse Inn—which I had never done before Lawry stopped taking me with him.

"I brought my violin today," I said to her. "I know you've been— I mean, I know you'll probably enjoy—" I stumbled over my words as I realized it was probably best not to let the other girls know of my prior relationship with Wynn.

I turned to Dr. Wellesley. "Where is Sicily Munroe?"

"Sicily has had the good fortune of being adopted, Miss Summercourt," he responded with a lopsided smile.

"Oh, isn't that wonderful?" But then I realized why the other girls had been so down when I'd asked about her. They knew she'd been adopted—no longer living at the orphanage, no longer needing to attend the charity school. She wasn't considered an orphan anymore. Sweet-tempered, optimistic Sicily was now part of a family.

No one made a reply to my inane comment; not Wynn, not Dr. Wellesley, not Lawry, and not a single one of the nine girls from the orphanage. My gaze landed on Wynn—who, from what I'd gathered over the months, hardly even realized she was an orphan without a family. But she probably had Lawry to thank for that. And Benta.

Dr. Wellesley left the room without a word, as usual.

Lawry still stood silently near the door, leaning against the wall, his arms crossed over his chest. That stance seemed to be one of his favorite ways to torment me. Did he realize that standing like that made him appear more attractive than ever?

"Girls, if you'll please be seated…." I strived to take control of my thoughts…and of my classroom. "Wynn, you can sit here at the end of the row, right next to me, if you'd like. I was just about to play something on the violin."

Lawry pushed himself away from the wall and walked across the room. "If this is going to be a concert, do you mind if I stay and listen?" I could tell he was measuring his words carefully, as if he weren't quite willing to forgive me just yet.

"Girls, I'd like you all to meet Mr. Lawrence Hampton, one of the school's generous sponsors. He's a gentleman of great caliber—in fact, one of the very best gentlemen I've ever had the privilege to know and call my friend." I glanced over the row of faces, ending with a big smile for Wynn. "Who was just leaving."

"You won't play for me?" Lawry asked with a mock pout, stopping to stand behind the row of chairs that separated him from me. "I promise not to cringe…too much."

"I have a job to do, Mr. Hampton, and I really would prefer to do it without an audience." I tried my best to seem stern, for I really didn't need him there observing my friendly association with the girls. For some reason, it bothered me that we both had a fondness for helping orphans, each in our own way.

"All right." He agreed. "I'll be around, though. I'll be taking Miss Rosselet back to—"

"The one across town?" I asked quickly.

Lawry fortunately understood my intent and replied accordingly. "Yes, the one across town."

It would not help Wynn to announce that she lived at The Waterhouse Inn instead of at an orphanage; I was certain it would only cause jealousy and strife among the girls. For as much as most of them seemed thankful to live at the orphanage, living anywhere else, even if it was with a "pretend" family at an inn, would seem infinitely more desirable. For a moment, I wondered how we would explain to Wynn that we had essentially lied to the girls for their benefit. What were we supposed to do—foster resentment and dissension?

Lawry left the room, and I hoped I wouldn't have to see him again that day. Lately, encounters with him, no matter his demeanor, brought out the strange sense that I had no idea what I was doing—with him, with those orphaned girls, or with the rest of my life.

Instead of beginning the class by playing my violin, I decided to give each girl a chance to play a few notes, beginning with Cornelia, who was the oldest, and working my way down to Wynn. With each of them, I would first play a few notes, instruct her on where to place her fingers, and then together we would glide the bow back and forth over the strings, usually making rather appalling sounds that no one could ever call music. When it wasn't their turn, the other girls watched rapturously, laughing at the funny "notes" produced.

By the conclusion of class, I'd given all nine of the girls from the orphanage their lessons while Wynn watched quietly. She'd laughed with the rest of us, and I'd tried to catch her eye as often as possible to make sure she knew she wasn't there alone, that I was glad to have her there.

After class, I allowed Wynn to stay behind. I could tell by the longing in her eyes through all the lessons that she could barely wait for her turn.

My violin was too big for most of the girls, but they hadn't seemed to mind too much; however, it looked enormous in Wynn's little hands. We sat next to each other on two wooden chairs, the violin between us. As soon as she felt comfortable, Wynn tapped the hollow, polished wood with her dainty fingertips, just as she'd done with Lawry's guitar.

"Now, Wynn, you don't need to hold the violin to your chin to make a note," I explained. "We can hold it right here between us, like this."

"All right." Suddenly she seemed rather cheerless. Did she not like the idea of attending the school?

I handed her the bow and helped her position it over the violin, which was mostly resting upon my right leg. Knowing she had little chance of creating anything that would sound like a true note of music, I placed the fingers of my left hand upon the fingerboard, hoping that whatever came out would resemble C.

As soon as Wynn was making all manner of noises with the bow, literally scraping it back and forth across the strings, her smile returned. I didn't have the heart to stop her, she was so happy to "pretend" she was playing.

Then she unexpectedly stopped, lifted the bow, and silently handed it back to me.

Perhaps she, too, realized that pretending wasn't all that great. Not when compared with the real thing. I thought back to the times I'd caught myself pretending with Lawry and Wynn at The Waterhouse Inn all those weeks ago. How perfect life had seemed for those few days.

Wynn looked up at me from her chair, her legs dangling over the edge, her feet whipping through the air. "Mere'dy, why'd you stop comin' to see me?"

I really should have known that question was coming. I should have been more prepared. "Well, Wynn...." What was I going to say? I couldn't lie to her; it seemed I did entirely too much of that with everyone else. I needed there to be at least one person on earth with whom I was honest. "It's rather complicated, actually... but it has nothing to do with my not wanting to see you. If I could convince my brother to escort me to your inn, I'd come every day. But he's...become particularly busy, of late."

"Why not come with Lawry, then? He comes 'most every day. You could ride with him. You did before." She gazed at me with sorrow in her eyes.

"It's rather complicated, Wynn." I really didn't know how to explain the situation to myself, let alone to a solemn six-year-old.

"You said that."

"Do you remember how you felt when you came into this room for the first time, a little over an hour ago, and you saw all those girls you didn't know?" I looked down at my violin and fingered the strings, scared I would lose my nerve if I saw Wynn cry because of something I'd done.

"Yes."

"Do you remember the uncertainty you felt? Like you didn't know what they thought of you, and you were scared of truly finding out?"

Wynn touched my sleeve with her tiny hand. "I di'n't want to come in. But then I seen you, and I felt all better, mostly."

"Well, that's how I feel sometimes...with Lawry." I finally looked at her, certain she wasn't on the verge of tears—like I was.

"You feel safer with Lawry, too?" She smiled.

That wasn't at all what I was trying to say, but as the words registered in my heart, I knew they were the truth. There was no one on earth I felt safer with than Lawry Hampton.

And that frightened me more than anything.

Something kept me from telling Wynn that she'd missed my point. I supposed I could see why she had missed it—Lawry was perfection in her eyes. Why would she ever fear what he thought of her? She knew he loved her.

"He is a very honest and truthful person," I began, simply trying to get the conversation out of the awkward place where it had landed.

"And warm." Wynn smiled, and her face was instantly transformed. Yes, being loved by my honest, truthful friend did have a rather profound effect on a girl.

"Why exactly do you think he's warm, Wynn?"

"It's prob'ly because of Jesus," she answered without so much as a flutter of her full, black eyelashes. "Lawry's good at love. Just like God is."

I closed my eyes, hoping to quell the tears I felt rising up within them. "Yes, Wynn, you're right. Lawry is warm…and very good at love…because he loves Jesus so much."

"I want to be warm, too, and loving. And you know what? I think Lawry's teaching me how." She looked as if she were telling me a secret—as if it were a surprise he was planning for her. "You want to learn to be warm, Mere'dy? I'm sure he'll teach you how to love, too."

"Yes, perhaps he could." I stood, because I couldn't sit there and continue with such a conversation. Wynn was too straightforward, too insightful, though I had a feeling she had no idea of the magnitude of what she was saying. She was just a little girl speaking the truth, as only a child could.

I carried the violin and bow across the room to my case, open on the floor. I didn't want Wynn to see that my eyes had welled up with tears, and I most certainly didn't want Lawry to come back to collect her and find me crying all because he was *warm*…and I wasn't.

FOURTEEN

The Pocket Watch

"What is that you express in your eyes? It seems to me more than all the print I have read in my life."
—Walt Whitman, "Leaves of Grass"

Wynn and I found Lawry waiting for us in the hall, leaning against the wall. He insisted I send my carriage home and join him in returning Wynn to The Waterhouse Inn. I tried to gauge whether he'd overheard our conversation in the classroom, but it was impossible. I supposed it didn't matter if he had. Anyone acquainted with Lawry Hampton would agree with all I'd said.

Benta met us at the door of the inn and immediately led us past the parlor, where a small group of people I didn't recognize were gathered, and up the stairs to Wynn's tiny room.

Lawry had mentioned having helped Benta switch some of the beds around, giving Wynn the smallest bed since she was, indeed, the smallest boarder. It gave the room the appearance of being a bit larger, but not by much. The furniture was still limited to the cot and one dresser beside the tall window with ratty white curtains.

"Sorry about the full house downstairs," Benta said. "We take pride in boarding only those with good references and such, but sometimes we just have to learn to share with those who have more friends than we're used to." Benta grabbed Wynn by the hand before she could follow us into the bedchamber. "I've already begun your bathwater, dearie. I was sure a nice, hot bath would help after such a trying day—"

"Would you like some help?" I asked, hoping to avoid the impropriety of being stuck waiting in the room alone with Lawry, even if the bed was just a tiny cot.

"Oh no, Miss Summercourt. It's best you stay right where you are. Lawry has some news. We'll be back shortly." She turned and led Wynn down the hall toward the back stairs.

"Thank you, Benta," Lawry called over his shoulder. He was leaning against the doorjamb, blocking my escape, and seemed perfectly happy with the arrangement.

I crossed the room to stand near the window. I couldn't look at him, not when I sensed him staring at me across the tiny space. I hated how desperately I wanted to go back to the time before we'd lost our friendship. I wanted to start over. But where? Too much had happened since he'd come back from Bar Harbor. And I was so confused.

I pulled aside the worn linen drape and looked out the window, up at the sky.

"Something up there caught your attention?" he asked.

The sky was clear blue with a scattering of bright white clouds. There was nothing terribly interesting about it. I directed my gaze back into the room, to Lawry. I was ashamed to admit, but gazing at him was much more satisfying. The look in his eyes surprisingly mirrored my thoughts.

"No," I finally answered. "I was simply trying to avoid looking at you."

"I've given up such things, myself. I find it only makes matters worse."

"That it does."

Lawry didn't answer for a while. We both just stood there, silently waiting for…something.

"I need to apologize, Meredyth, for ignoring you and not taking you with me to see Wynn since the Hancock Ball." He straightened, as if he meant to enter the room. However, when I backed myself against the wall, he quickly returned his shoulder to the doorjamb. "I can tell you've missed her, and she you. I don't know what I was thinking, being so inconsiderate of you both."

I still didn't know what he was thinking, either, but I realized I didn't care any longer—as long as he was sorry.

"Has Benta been teaching her anything? What have they been doing?" I hated that I'd allowed so many weeks to pass without making my own way to see Wynn. What kind of person was I to do such a thing to a friendless little girl?

"Benta's been doing what she can, but it doesn't compare to how you are with her. For some reason, Wynn is quite enamored of you."

"Yes, 'for some reason.' Heaven knows what she sees to love in me."

I'd meant it to be a good-natured jab at myself, but at the severe look Lawry gave me, I decided against continuing with my self-degradation. "Are you finding it any easier to understand her speech?" I asked instead. "It does seem quite improved."

"Yes. But I still can't believe how easily you picked up on almost everything she said early on, without trying. All but that one line about your belonging to me."

A burst of nervous laughter escaped my lips. "You—you finally figured out what she was saying that day, did you?"

"After a while. I had to run it through my mind about a dozen times before I understood." He looked at me intently. "I suppose it would have seemed that we were together."

"As if there's no place in the world for a woman except tied to a man," I added quickly, wanting desperately to redirect the conversation.

"Is that...is that what's stopping you?" He was still a safe distance away, leaning against the door frame, but I could tell he was fighting the urge to enter the room.

"From doing what?" I turned around, grabbed the nearby curtain, and began absently wringing it with both hands.

"Falling in love, marrying." He filled those four treacherously combined words with so much passion, I wanted to turn around, to look in his eyes. Instead, I lowered my gaze to the scuffed floorboards, my fingers still busily twisting the curtains.

He was playing so unfairly all of a sudden. What had changed to make him abruptly act so kind toward me after weeks of such frustration? I almost preferred his being angry, for I knew very well that kindness and gentleness were the most effective weapons he could endeavor to use against the weary strongholds guarding my heart.

"I've never been very interested in marrying...anyone." I faced him with reluctance after such an abhorrent lie.

"That's not the answer you gave the last time the subject was brought up." He stayed as he was, only now his arms were folded over his chest once more.

"Oh? What did I say then?" I released the curtains.

"You said you knew what you wanted, and I gathered you were beginning to realize *who*, as well." Lawry moved away from the doorjamb, but instead of coming into the room, he reached up and inspected the wood trim.

"And now I'm saying what I want is to never marry. It's really not that difficult to understand," I answered sternly.

"But you didn't say as much before. You gave the impression you were merely being choosy, and that you'd already decided... just who you wanted." With his one arm still extended to the top corner of the door frame, his eyes darted from the trim to me, catching me off guard.

"Well, I haven't."

I didn't like seeing the sudden hardness in his eyes, even if it lasted only a moment. It was the same look from the ball, and I'd also seen it sometime during our conversation at the poetic reading. But I knew it was best I did see it, and that I kept on seeing it until the day came that Lawry would again be on his way to Washington.

Thankfully, he was still standing in the doorway, keeping his distance. Though he was no longer inspecting the trim but staring at me, waiting for me to allow him to enter.

"Mrs. Allister had something interesting to tell me the other day." Apparently he was finally giving up on trying for an answer from me that he approved of.

I let out a deep breath, relieved. "Oh, what is that? Has the rent on Wynn's room and board gone up already?"

"She told me you and Benta had learned quite a bit about Wynn's mother that day we found her. I've tried to get her to talk about it, but Wynn won't say a word. Why didn't you tell me she'd opened up to you that day?" Lawry took a bold step into the room.

"I...I guess I forgot." How was I so utterly concerned with only myself that I'd never thought to share the information with Lawry? I was a horrid friend, indeed—to both Lawry and Wynn.

"Well, as it turns out, old Mrs. Allister actually knew of Libby Rosselet. Her sister and brother-in-law own a boardinghouse called The Olde Ram. That's where Libby and Wynn had been boarding for a short time before—"

"Really, Lawry? Don't you think that seems a bit too convenient?" I turned toward the dresser, reflecting on the conversation we'd had with Wynn about her mother. It had seemed of the utmost importance at the time, and then I'd completely forgotten it. "Benta didn't seem to know the Mr. and Mrs. Dunk Wynn mentioned. Don't you think she'd know her own relatives?"

"Benta is Mrs. Allister's great-niece, and the owners of The Olde Ram are Benta's great-aunt and great-uncle, so it's highly probable she'd never heard of them. Moreover, Wynn wasn't calling them by their proper names. Rufus and Lena *Duncan*."

"Oh." I met Lawry's gaze in the mirror and gave a sheepish grin. "Do you know who I believe Libby Rosselet was, Lawry?"

In the glass, I saw him lift his eyebrows in mock surprise. "Olivia Rosselet, perhaps?"

I turned around, suddenly unconcerned that we were in the room together, standing only feet apart. "You figured it out on your own, didn't you? What do you think happened?"

His glance shifted to the cot. "You really want me to go into the details?"

"No." I felt a blush creep into my cheeks. I couldn't help my own gaze from traveling to the small bed. "It's only...do you remember anyone who might have courted Olivia Rosselet the year before she disappeared? Do you have any idea who Wynn's father might be? Garrett said she had scads of men after her—"

"You've spoken about Olivia Rosselet to Garrett but not to me?"

"I'm not the only one who took Garrett into my confidence. You told him about your orphanage."

"It's my secret to tell, Meredyth." Lawry looked genuinely angry with me, once again. "And ever since I told you—"

"Yes, we've been increasingly at odds with each other." We'd *never* been at odds before that day.

"Mrs. Allister told me all about her sister, Lena, and the unfortunate man she married." Lawry's anger had not abated, but I could tell it wasn't exactly directed at me, as I'd first thought. "He bought the run-down boardinghouse, thinking to get into the same business as his father-in-law, Mrs. Allister's father, hoping to prove himself worthy of inheriting the inn. However, Mr. Duncan's not a worthy sort of fellow, on any account. He used the income from The Olde Ram to support his obsession with gambling instead of sustaining the boardinghouse. Mrs. Allister had been widowed early on in her marriage, and her father ended up leaving the inn to her as a means of providing an income for her."

"Have you been to The Olde Ram?"

"It's a run-down pile of sticks."

"What did Wynn do when her mother died? All I ever learned was that she slept in a cold barn."

"From what Mrs. Allister says, at first, Mrs. Duncan tried to get Wynn to stay with them, even to adopt her, since their own children were raised and gone. But then, something changed her mind drastically, and she insisted that Wynn leave for her own good." Lawry took a step forward and stood beside me. He fingered the knob of one of the tiny trinket drawers that protruded from the top of the dresser.

"For her own good? How could starving on the streets—sleeping in a drafty barn—be better than having even a dilapidated roof over her head?"

"Mrs. Duncan had a suspicion that her husband wanted— It just wasn't safe, Mere. That's all I'm going to say." He caught my gaze in the looking glass and held it for a moment.

"How long had Wynn been on the streets?" I, too, began fiddling with the knobs of the dresser drawers. There really wasn't much else to do in such a small, sparse room to distract me from my ever-deepening awareness of Lawry Hampton.

"Just a few weeks, but I'm sure they were the longest weeks of her life."

"What happened to her mother's things? She must have had something for—"

"After Olivia died, Mr. Duncan immediately had her body taken away and then ransacked her room for clues as to who'd been supporting her. I suppose he thought Wynn's father might be some public figure or wealthy gentleman he could blackmail."

"Poor Wynn. She has nothing of her mother's?" It seemed safe enough to watch Lawry in the mirror, but I found myself moving away from him regardless, inching toward the window.

"He didn't find anything valuable because Mrs. Duncan already had most of Olivia and Wynn's most precious possessions hidden away. You see, before Olivia died, Mrs. Duncan had been nursing her quite faithfully...." Lawry stayed facing the dresser, seemingly unconcerned that I'd backed away. "I believe Mrs. Duncan is a good sort of woman who unfortunately made a very bad choice regarding one of the most important decisions of her life. She married good-for-nothing Rufus Duncan."

"Does Mrs. Duncan still have Olivia's things?" I found I was able to face him, as long as his gaze was concentrated on the dresser—and not me.

"No. They're here. I was going to give them to Wynn today."

"You've already been to see Mrs. Duncan? What did she have? Were there any clues as to the identity of Wynn's father?"

"Some quite discernible ones, actually." He opened one of the smallest drawers—the one whose knob he'd been fiddling with—and pulled out something wrapped in a handkerchief. "I doubt Wynn's father cares one way or the other about what happened to Olivia or his daughter. He's made absolutely no attempt to provide for Wynn since the death of her mother."

I looked closer. The handkerchief was Lawry's, embroidered with his initials in royal blue thread that matched his eyes. It looked new, and I realized it probably came from the package Ainsley and I had ordered for him at Filene's over a month ago.

Lawry walked the short distance from the dresser to the window—and me. He paused, and I studied his face. He looked almost fearful as he slowly opened his handkerchief.

What he'd had cosseted away were a pile of folded letters and an expensive-looking gold pocket watch.

"I think you'll be surprised to know who fathered Wynn, Meredyth—though I can't say I am. It's someone we know quite well." He held the items out to me, still half wrapped in his handkerchief.

I lifted the chain of the pocket watch from his hand and held it before me, swinging like a pendulum. Etched in the gold back was the monogram VEX. I sucked in my breath as the chain slipped from my fingers. The watch clattered on the floor. I knew only one person with those initials: Vance Xander Everstone.

Leaving the pocket watch on the floor, Lawry stared at me intently, watching for my reaction. He'd stopped short of freeing the letters from the ribbon that held them together. I shook my head frantically; I couldn't open my mouth. What if I said too much? Could Lawry already see my shock? My pain? My disgust? I turned around to face the wall.

"Are you really that surprised?" Lawry asked dryly.

Wynn's dark eyes came to mind...her curly black hair. How old was she? Six? That meant Vance had done the same thing to Olivia Rosselet as he had to me, one year before. What kinds of lies had he told her? Were they the same ones he'd told me?

I wanted to retch. Inescapable sorrow overwhelmed me until all I knew were the tears streaming down my face. So, this was the end. The answers I'd always wanted but was too afraid to seek. I could hardly catch my breath between sobs.

I hated that I was acting so outlandishly in front of Lawry. Why couldn't I stop this insufferable weeping? My self-control and resolve, so effective at keeping out the world, always seemed to crumble whenever Lawry was around.

I turned to dash for the door, but he caught me in his arms, his hands splayed across my back. I didn't move. I couldn't—not once I was assaulted with the realization that safe in Lawry's arms was truly the only place I wanted to be.

Almost immediately, I calmed. How did he do that? How did he make me forget about Vance so entirely? His hands traveled slowly from my back to my waist to my elbows, then up to my shoulders and my neck to my face, as if he were examining me, trying to figure out what was wrong with me so he could fix me. His brows were drawn, and I'd never seen him look so grave.

When I realized he was looking into my eyes, my gaze darted about the room, finally settling on the floor. The folded letters were scattered all over the marred floorboards.

Lawry held my jaw gently with both palms. Almost involuntarily, my hands came up to cover his. I could tell his fingers were drenched with my tears, but he didn't seem that interested in wiping them dry. The only thing he seemed concerned about was gazing into my eyes.

But I wouldn't let him. I couldn't face him in the state I was in. I couldn't. He'd see.

"Meredyth, if you don't look at me, I'm going to kiss you again."

I immediately looked up, knowing a kiss would tell him something more dangerous than my eyes ever could.

"Have you read them?" I didn't dare look at the letters all over the floor. Not if Lawry planned to make good on his threat.

"Yes."

"What do they say?" I forced myself to maintain the calm Lawry had achieved by his holding on to me. If only his hands would never leave.

"You can read them yourself, if you'd like." By the look in his eyes, it was almost a challenge. "Actually, you should. You ought to read every one of them."

"No, that's all right. I think I need to...I need to go home." I dragged the words out, quickly realizing I didn't really want to go to Summerton at all. I would have stayed there at The Waterhouse Inn forever if it meant I could remain safe with Lawry, cradled in his arms.

He loosened his grip on me, but my fingers still clung to his hands. "Take my carriage. I'll stay here awhile. I could use a long walk." He took advantage of having my gaze fixed upon him; I'd hardly stopped looking into his face. I couldn't seem to stop. "Take the letters with you."

"I don't— Don't you think Wynn will want them?"

"She doesn't need to know what they say. Not until she's much older." Lawry freed his hands from mine and reached down to collect the letters, as well as the pocket watch. "In the meantime, she has this."

"Vance's pocket watch." I forced myself to say the words aloud, evenly, and without tears.

"It's Wynn's now. I'm certain this watch is the most she'll ever receive from that good-for-nothing— If you'd read the letters, you'd agree completely." Lawry stood, wrapped his handkerchief around the watch, and pushed the letters into my hand.

I saw one line.

My dearest Olivia...

Yes, it was settled. Somewhere deep inside, it was settled. Vance was a cad who'd used Olivia Rosselet.

And, a year later, me.

And God only knew how many others. Even without the involvement of his *petite amie*, Vance never would have married me. He wouldn't even marry Olivia Rosselet, and she'd come from just as good a family as I—and had borne his child.

Wynn Rosselet...Everstone.

⌒

All the way home, alone in Lawry's carriage, I stared blindly out the window. I didn't care about the letters in my hands. I didn't even care that I'd been rude in leaving the inn without as much as a good-bye for Wynn.

I cared about one thing—and that was that Lawry had stood before me. Loving me.

I knew I needed to read the letters. And I needed to read them alone. There was no way I could have read them in front of Lawry.

Stopping in the second-story parlor only long enough to recover the copy of *Leçons de Grammaire* from its cache in the cushions of the overstuffed chair, I hurried up every flight of stairs until I reached my bedchamber. Then I lowered myself, breathless, into my reading chaise, the letters and the book in my grasp, my door locked. As I read the letters, I would keep Lawry's handkerchief and the French grammar book beside me. And perhaps, after I was through with reading, I would turn to the page I hadn't seen in ages.

How had I utterly forgotten that day for so long? And all of those long walks through the gardens of Truesdale...had Lawry truly been courting me that spring? And what had I been so focused upon that had kept me from seeing it until now?

I knew the answer, of course. It was Vance Everstone. The answer was always Vance Everstone.

While Lawry had practically been falling over himself, trying to declare his love, I'd been too infatuated with Vance to even notice. And after Vance had taken advantage of my fascination with him, I'd hardly been able to see anything else as I'd searched for a way to make right what had happened that day.

But what if I couldn't? What if there was nothing I could do to fix what had happened? I'd been over everything before, but never with such tangible evidence against Vance in my hands. I'd always believed that by marrying him, I would be doing us both a favor. He'd obviously wanted me—at least, he had back when I was eighteen—and I thought that by reserving myself for him, I was doing what was best.

However, finding out about Olivia Rosselet had changed everything. Vance didn't love me. He'd simply wanted me the same way he'd wanted Olivia Rosselet—with no strings attached.

And now he wanted to marry someone else.

Did this mean I was free? Vance apparently wanted his French mistress enough to sacrifice his rightful fortune, and I was beginning to realize I wanted Lawry Hampton enough to give up my plans of self-retribution.

I still wasn't sure if I could allow such a thing. I didn't deserve Lawry. And I was quite certain I never would.

I looked to the letters. I didn't really want to read all of them. I just wanted to see one.

Keeping them folded, I carefully sorted through the stack. The dates were clearly visible, given the way they'd been folded—as if they'd been catalogued long ago and read through often. However, they were all out of order, since Lawry had dropped them in his earnestness to hold me. There were about three dozen in all, and once they were back in order, I found that they ranged from before Wynn was born to earlier that very winter.

The only date I cared to see was one around the time of June 19, 1885. And I wasn't disappointed. Or rather, perhaps I was. Yes, I was disappointed that Vance had gone from seducing me in a cave to going home to write the mother of his illegitimate daughter a letter.

My dearest Olivia,

I must apologize for not writing sooner. My summer, so far, has been filled with family outings and old friends wanting so much of my time and attention. You understand, don't you, why I must keep this up? I have years upon years until I reach my majority. Until then, I'm afraid I have only a meager allowance on which to get by. I do hope you like the new rooms I've acquired for you. And I hope you both are well.

Vance X. Everstone

Wynn would have likely been born by then—and he'd hardly acknowledged her existence.

I tried to imagine what Wynn and Olivia's circumstances must have been like back then—living in a dirty boardinghouse while Vance spent the summer at Rockwood. It wasn't as if Olivia Rosselet didn't know how he passed the summer months. She and her family had likely done the same thing, up until he'd ruined her life.

I couldn't help but feel grateful that my "brush" with the incomparable Vance Everstone hadn't landed me in the same situation. I still had my family, my friends, and at least some of my dignity. I had a feeling Olivia Rosselet hadn't had any of that. And now she was dead, and her illegitimate daughter was all alone in the world—or had been until Lawry had saved her.

How strange that God would throw us all together in such a way—Olivia Rosselet, Vance Everstone, Wynn, Lawry Hampton...and me.

It was good for me to have such a reminder of that day. Just as it had been to my benefit to have the handkerchief I'd stolen out of Lawry's jacket the day he'd visited during the snowstorm. And the book, of course. They were all good reminders of what I would never have.

Had it really been four months since I'd taken the French book from Hilldreth after he'd kissed me? Lawry hadn't brought it up once. Did he even realize I had it? Had he intentionally selected it from the shelf that day, remembering the last time we'd both seen it? I flipped the book open for the first time since bringing it to Summerton, but then I closed it quickly, unsure if I was ready to see those words again.

I recalled how I'd almost cracked it open that day in January, just before Lawry had retrieved his hidden photographs from the secret cubby in the study. Yes, he must have remembered, for it was likely the reason he'd then kissed me, as if it were the only thing he'd thought of doing for years on end.

And, for some reason, I had let him, knowing full well that doing so was a very, very bad idea. It was the most idiotic thing I'd ever done—well, the second most idiotic thing. It had only made me wish for the impossible, for everything I would never deserve. All while breaking my heart even more.

Not that I'd ever really felt heartbroken until that day. It was more that I'd been numb, oppressed, and completely lost in everyone else's seemingly perfect world.

Life had been much easier when I was numb, when I knew I was helplessly lost. When I knew there was only one thing to do—to marry Vance Everstone.

However, ever since being enraptured in the warmth of Lawry's embrace for those long, dreamlike minutes, and in a thousand moments since, I'd realized that allowing myself to lean into the comfort of his strong chest was more like being *found* than anything I'd ever experienced before.

FIFTEEN

The Woods

"*Are we not like two volumes of the same book?*"
—Marceline Desbordes-Valmore

As discomposed as I was becoming on a daily basis, it really didn't surprise me when Mother awakened me one morning, reminding me that my family had, weeks ago, planned a picnic for that day at Boston Common with Claudine, Lawry, and Ainsley. It was clear to me at the outset that the entire purpose of the outing was to allow Garrett and Ainsley some time to strengthen their attachment to each other. Personally, I didn't think they were in need of any more help. I was quite certain they would become engaged before the double wedding at the beginning of June.

I stood alone on the front stoop of Summerton and watched Garrett, holding a basket of food and a blanket in one arm, escort Ainsley by the hand along the sidewalk. Mother, Father, and Claudine had already left in the carriage.

I wasn't interested in participating—not since it would mean spending an afternoon with Lawry. Everything I'd seen in his eyes at The Waterhouse Inn had been much too tempting.

When Garrett and Ainsley had disappeared from sight, I turned and found Lawry standing at the foot of the steps, a hamper of food in his hand, a bundled blue and white quilt tucked under his arm. I'd known he would be coming for me, but that didn't mean I'd been prepared.

I descended the steps to meet him and silently looped my arm through his. There wasn't much to say, except that I was quite possibly falling in love with him. And I wasn't about to divulge that.

Lawry led me along the sidewalk in the same direction in which Garrett and Ainsley had gone, toward Boston Common. I made no attempt at conversation, and it seemed Lawry didn't have much to say, either.

I desperately hoped that his silence had nothing to do with my own reasons for not wanting to speak. I didn't know what I would do if Lawry actually declared aloud all the things I'd seen in his steadfast blue eyes the last time I'd looked. Suddenly, it dawned on me that all I had thought about in the days since learning about the connection between Vance and Wynn was that Lawry obviously had feelings for me, stronger feelings than I'd ever dared to imagine. Oddly, I had not been consumed with thoughts of Vance and the implications of his being Wynn's father. Instead, learning the truth had been almost freeing.

Once Lawry and I reached the Common, he chose a nice grassy knoll to picnic upon, somewhat near Garrett and Ainsley. He set the basket down and whipped the blanket free from its folds, which only made a rumpled mess of the thing. He bent to gather up one end, while I fixed the two opposite corners.

I sat on the nearest corner, and Lawry grabbed the basket from the grass and positioned it at the center of the quilt. Then he reclined on his side, rested his weight upon one sturdy elbow, and faced me. The self-confidence of his pose had a queer effect on me. He was lying mere inches away, looking at me with a mixture of mirth and desire—and I couldn't move.

The dearest wish of my heart was that I could somehow attain the freedom to encourage his attention.

And by attention, I do not merely mean the attentiveness of a best friend. I'd enjoyed that my whole life. Even when I was a girl of only four or five, Lawry was my favorite person, my ever-faithful champion.

No, what I wanted now had more to do with the lightning that had run through my veins when the lengths of our bodies *hadn't* touched behind the thick blue curtains of the Hancock ballroom...and the peaceful sense of belonging I'd experienced in his arms just as I'd begun to kiss him back in the study at Hilldreth.

Oh God, could I have him?

The answer that seemed to break through from my deceitful heart was, Why not?

"It does seem, at times, that you can," Lawry began quietly, "have a strange knack for seeing the innermost desires of the hearts of your closest friends...and relatives. You did it with Amaryllis. I never would have thought she was falling for Nathan, given how little of a response she always gave him." He quickly averted his eyes, and fiddled with one of his fingernails. "I must concede, it seems Garrett was in love with Ainsley all along."

"I'm not sure how, but I could see all the pieces fitting together quite perfectly." I situated myself a little farther from him—it seemed rather too intimate to speak when we sat so close. We barely needed to raise our voices above a whisper in order to be heard. "Do you remember the day you visited during the snow-storm...when we left them alone in the parlor?"

"Of course I do."

"I saw it even months before then, while you were still in Bar Harbor. But that was the day I knew for sure."

He chuckled. "How remarkable."

"What?" I pulled the hamper nearer and peeked inside. Not that I was hungry. I couldn't have eaten anything if I'd tried.

"That you can so easily recognize the pieces of your brother's love affair with Ainsley fitting together, while you're completely blind to those of your own."

He seemed to think this was something to smile about, but I found the matter rather disheartening. For when I imagined myself having a love affair with anyone, the only person who came to mind was Lawry—no matter all the years I'd spent thinking about Vance. But I simply could not allow myself to have Lawry. He would end up knowing my shame. And then what would he think of me?

I pulled out a thick wedge of cheese wrapped in a yellow napkin, then searched for the cutting block and cheese knife I'd made sure to pack. While sorting through the hamper, I wished I'd brought the French book with me, so I could return it.

He would understand what that meant, wouldn't he? My relinquishing the book would make things clear—that I would not give in to him, no matter what he endeavored to say to me. That he was wrong—and that I was wrong. I wasn't free to have him.

Even so, I needed to at least keep our friendship intact. I couldn't lose that, even if he lived in Washington and I in New England for the rest of our lives.

"As you know, I'm leaving for Bar Harbor Monday with Estella and her father. I'm going to miss Wynn so much." *And you.* "I don't know when I'll see her next." I cut off a few slices of cheese, placed them on a small plate, and offered it to Lawry.

"Don't worry, I'll make sure you see her before you leave. And don't think you won't see her this summer. I plan to bring her to Truesdale when I come up." He took the plate, popped a morsel of cheese in his mouth, and chewed for a moment. "Why are you going so early? The wedding isn't for weeks."

"Nicholette asked Estella to come early, and Estella asked me to join her. Probably to keep her and Daphne from strangling each other."

"Do you think Bram might consider taking Ainsley and Claudine up, as well? I'll be in New York City by then, and I probably won't travel there until right before the wedding."

"We could always ask. There's plenty of room in the railcar." I smoothed my skirts over the quilt, trying to think of something to add to the conversation. I didn't want to dwell on the fact that it would soon be time to say good-bye to him forever, but it was a fact that was suddenly becoming all too real. "You haven't had your camera out much lately," I observed. "You used to have it with you at all times."

"I suppose I've been a little distracted since returning to Boston in January, between you and Wynn." He lowered his gaze and took another piece of cheese from the plate, but then he put it back and looked at me. "You're not hungry?"

I swallowed the lump in my throat and fought to control my breathing. "No."

"Then let's take a walk." Lawry stood and offered me his hand. After helping me to my feet, he guided me the short distance to the edge of the trees. I went willingly, thinking of our much-needed discussion concerning *his* future in Washington, where he would surely, eventually, marry Amelia Grendahl.

We strolled further toward the nearby woods, neither one of us speaking for some minutes. And then I brought up the one subject I knew would help me get through the afternoon: "So, are you going to marry Amelia Grendahl when you get back to Seattle? She looked pretty in the photograph." I ignored what my mention of the photograph brought to mind—how all of them had landed on the carpet when Lawry had taken me in his arms that first time.

Yes, I was ignoring all of that.

Lawry tightened his grip on my hand where it rested at the crook of his elbow. "She is rather pretty, isn't she? But her blonde hair is nothing compared to these stunning russet locks." He took hold of several loose strands of my hair and coiled them around his finger. "However, she does have one thing going for her that's hard to match—her remarkable eyes. But, again, they're nothing like yours. Let me see…." He released my hair and tried to turn my head toward him, to look into my eyes, but I resisted. He was suddenly being much too…personal.

"I suppose she'll be a wonderful wife, though. What is she like, besides having blonde hair and remarkable eyes?" I freed my hand from his arm and walked toward a large, straight oak.

"Amelia is a very sweet, good-natured young woman, and, of course, she's wonderful with the children. As you said, she would make any man a very good wife."

"She sounds grand. Why did you decide to come to Boston before marrying her?"

"I'm not going to marry Amelia Grendahl, Meredyth."

"Why ever not?" I scanned the park, still refusing to look at him. We'd walked rather far into a secluded, garden-like area where paths meandered through bushes and trees and well-manicured flower beds. When it was obvious he wasn't intent on answering, I continued, "I thought you hated secrets."

"I do. Complete frankness is always the best route." He paced before me for a moment, then leaned his hand against another oak a few feet away. "If only I would practice what I preach," he said quietly.

"Are you ready to tell your parents about the orphanage? Do you think they will understand how you want to exchange their place in your heart with a stark building full of scruffy children?" I looked off into the woods. I knew I needed to tread carefully, or he might turn the conversation to my own secrets, to my own depressing plans for the future. *Spinsterhood.* Yet I couldn't stop myself. "From the way Ainsley describes your mother these days, I really don't think she'll be prepared for such news."

From the corner of my eye, I saw him turn to me sharply. As much as I wanted my words to hurt him, to make him stop loving me, I dreaded actually seeing that hurt in his eyes. Was I really ready to never see Lawry's love for me radiating from his smiling blue eyes again?

I pushed away from the tree and headed further into the woods.

Lawry didn't follow me; he stayed cautiously at the edge of the forest, still leaning against that tree. When I glanced back from the shroud of dim, green darkness I'd entered, I could see his light hair and blue eyes still brightened by the intense early-afternoon sun.

"What do you have planned before we settle down to eat our lunch?" He watched me closely as I made a noisy path through a scattering of saplings. "Hide-and-seek in the trees?"

The idea did seem quite novel. We used to play the game in the woods between Summerhouse and Truesdale as children. But we were adults now—adults who had to, for the most part, act in accordance with the dictates of propriety.

"I wish Wynn were here," I said with a sigh. "Could we bring her sometime? She'd like this, and it wouldn't seem so improper for us to go traipsing through the woods together if she were with us."

"I rather like the idea of its never being improper for us to be alone *anywhere* together."

Yes, being alone *anywhere* with Lawry did sound rather diverting.

Behind me, I heard him venture into the trees, loudly snapping twigs and ruffling leaves as he came. Without a thought, I was irresistibly drawn back to him. I walked around a clump of pines and came to stand beside him, still facing the thicker part of the wood. Lawry glanced behind us for a moment, then wrapped his arm snugly around my shoulders.

"Lawry...." I turned my head, and my nose just grazed his jaw. I did fit there so perfectly, at his side. "Lawry, I'm so...I feel so trapped." It wasn't what I'd planned to say, but it was the only thing that would come out. I had no idea why I'd disclosed as much, vague though the comment was.

Lawry pulled me closer. "Have you read Vance's letters yet?"

The thought that Lawry had somehow drawn a line from my feelings of being trapped to Vance's letters terrified me. "You've read them. Isn't that enough?"

"I don't believe it is. I want you to read every one of them. I want you to know just what kind of man Vance Everstone truly is."

"I already—"

"Trust me, he isn't worth it." He stood rigidly beside me, as if the same awful thoughts dredged up in my mind were polluting his, as well. But that was impossible, or he wouldn't be standing so close to me, half shrouded in the outskirts of the shadowy woods.

"Did you know— Do you realize that no one means as much to me as you do, Mere? That there's no one else I'd rather be alone with than you…anywhere?"

And if he knew, he certainly wouldn't be saying things like that.

I couldn't open my mouth, for the answer was yes. I knew. And I felt the same.

I tried to escape his grasp, but instead of letting me go, he quickly twisted me around and pressed me back against the straight-standing oak.

"I never answered your question earlier…about why I won't be marrying Amelia." He had me trapped, hidden, facing the woods, with one hand propped against the tree trunk near my shoulder, his other hand reaching for my face. He lifted my chin, catching my gaze for a second.

"Oh? Why is that?" I forced myself to smile, to play off the tension building between us. I immediately regretted opening my mouth, for doing so only drew his attention from my eyes to my lips.

In trying to avoid his touch—and, in all likelihood, another kiss—I leaned to the left, causing my neck to come in contact with his arm. I stilled and found myself resting my cheek against his forearm, knowing full well I was participating in a losing battle—and that I wasn't nearly as prepared as I should have been for what was coming.

SIXTEEN

Claudine Abernathy

"Whatever our souls are made of, his and mine are the same."
—Emily Brontë, *Wuthering Heights*

B ecause I happen to be—" Lawry's lingering gaze suddenly shifted from me to something on the other side of the tree I stood against. He removed his hands from both my chin and the tree, took a step back, and called out, "Aunt Claudine, would you like to join Mere and me for our picnic lunch?"

After taking a moment to regain my composure, I circled around the tree and found Claudine standing a few feet away on the lawn. She was holding the folding chair Father had brought for her, as well as her cane. Obviously, she'd come searching for us when she'd found our blanket and hamper abandoned.

"Oh, yes, if you don't mind. It seems Arthur and Annabelle wanted to take a short walk through the park before going home. I'm not particularly feeling up to doing so, and I couldn't even find Garrett and Ainsley. Their quilt was deserted, as well. Finally, I saw you, Lawry.... You don't mind my interrupting you, do you?"

"Of course not," Lawry and I said together. He took my arm and walked me out of the clumping of trees and onto the grassy lawn.

"The more the merrier," I added as I wriggled free from him.

Lawry took the folding chair from Claudine in one hand and grasped her arm with the other. I followed behind as we wandered back to the deserted blanket.

Lawry positioned the chair and helped Claudine settle onto it, then sprawled out on his side, just as before. "Have you already eaten?"

"Yes, thank you. I've had all I want. Go ahead and enjoy your meal. I'll just sit here and bask in the presence of two of my most beloved young people."

Striving to concentrate upon anything but Lawry, reclined as he was, and what he had almost said to me in the woods, I opened the hamper and began pulling out the wrapped sandwiches.

"You don't have to do that, Meredyth." Claudine reached down and tugged the hamper in her direction. "I'll serve the two of you, since I'm the one intruding upon your romantic picnic lunch."

I couldn't very well rip the basket from her aged hands and tell her we were having no such thing, so I let her have the basket, hoping to God that Lawry wouldn't be encouraged by my failure to correct her terminology.

Claudine served me and then Lawry. I still wasn't very hungry and was hardly able to take even a bite of the cheese we'd left out. As I sat there, not eating, Lawry watched me attentively.

"Are you certain I didn't interrupt something?" Claudine asked.

I looked up to find her studying me, as well.

"No, not at all." There was absolutely nothing more Lawry and I needed to discuss...or do.

"You both seem so quiet. Usually, you are the ones having the most fun together. I've always admired your friendship, you know. It reminds me of a dear friendship I once had. Long-lasting friendship is the best beginning to a lifelong love."

I stared at her, not believing my ears. Surely, Lawry could hear the erratic beat of my thudding heart, even from where he lay at the other end of the quilt.

"Oh, Meredyth, you probably think I don't know a thing about love. Poor Claudine Abernathy, who never had the chance to marry and, for all Boston knows, never even had a serious beau."

"Who was he?" Lawry looked keenly interested. But then, I supposed the topic was of interest to him—if he indeed didn't already know anything of Claudine's secret beau.

"I was once engaged to someone in England."

Against my will, I was drawn by her words. "Would your family not let you marry him?"

"Oh, no; I'm sure my parents would have been thrilled. However, not even they ever knew."

I suddenly didn't want to ask what had happened to her fiancé. Since she'd obviously never married, the story was bound to have an unhappy ending.

"Who was he?" Fortunately, Lawry's attention seemed solely engrossed in Claudine's story, and I felt a little relieved. It was so difficult to have him stare at me and know why.

"He was a confirmed bachelor at one time and had quite the reputation about London, with all kinds of scandalous rumors surrounding him. And, of course, what young man with a rakish past doesn't have a strict determination to never marry?"

"You wanted to marry a rake?" I asked, somewhat shocked. But then I realized I'd long wanted to do the exact same thing. For that was just what Vance Everstone was—a rake.

"He'd changed over the years, and so, by the time he was nearing forty, he was so much more like Lawry, here, than a rake." Claudine smiled to herself and rubbed the smooth handle of her cane with her thumb. "You see, I'd been very good friends with his family for almost twenty years. His sister was one of my dearest friends; I met her while on my grand tour at sixteen. She was the reason I went back to England so often. And then, after meeting Eliot, the fact that he was often there didn't hurt."

"What made him finally see you after so long?" I asked.

"Now, don't think I set out from the beginning to win his heart, Meredyth." Claudine raised her gaze to the high branches above. "Over the years, Eliot and I had formed quite an unconventional friendship, much like you and Lawry have had for all these years." She looked from Lawry to me, then back again. "However, as time went by, and I chose to spend my summers and autumns in England, it somehow came to the point that Eliot and I...well, we both wanted more from each other than mere friendship."

After a few moments, Lawry broke the encumbering silence. "You loved him, despite his reputation? Despite his past behaviors?" Only he looked at me as he asked, instead of at Claudine.

"Yes, Lawry, I did forgive him for his rakish past. I couldn't help it—I loved him. I had for years, in fact, only I didn't realize it until he broached the subject."

"And you were engaged to him?" I asked quickly.

"Yes. After all those years of friendship, we were engaged and were going to marry."

I looked to Lawry, which was a mistake, for it only created a desire to throw myself at him and wrap my arms around him. Instead of acting upon this irrational desire pumping fervently through my veins, I simply put my hands to my cheeks, which, I was certain, were flaming red. Knowing quite well that Lawry would have welcomed such an outburst, and that his aunt probably would have been just as delighted by it, I forced myself to think of Claudine's broken heart. I forced myself not to dwell on the realization that my future was shaping up to be so much like Claudine's present.

Claudine Abernathy, the token lonely spinster, who hardly had anyone but her great-niece Amaryllis—living thousands of miles away—and Lawry's family, only distantly related to her. If Ainsley and Lawry weren't staying with her at Hilldreth, she would be utterly alone, save for her servants. It was no wonder she'd gone to England to see her closest friends for those two years Lawry had spent in Washington.

I stared down at the quilt spread beneath Lawry and me, realizing that no one had said a word for some time. Was Lawry just as afraid as I to hear what had happened to Eliot—why he had never married Claudine?

I had to be brave. I would need a courageous heart to do what I needed to do with my future—while knowing that Lawry Hampton was in love with me. And I needed to begin practicing posthaste.

I raised my eyes to Claudine. "What happened?"

Claudine looked sad, almost on the verge of tears. I was immediately sorry I'd asked.

"I came home. I wanted to tell my parents in person, and I needed to collect my things. I was going to move to England permanently, to marry my Eliot—" Her voice broke off suddenly, and I was struck by the strangeness of the subject we'd happened upon for a picnic lunch at the Common on such a beautiful spring day.

Had he married someone else? Had he broken Claudine's heart by ending the secret engagement after she'd left because he'd had second thoughts or had he changed his mind? I couldn't ask. I'd already inquired too closely. Lawry remained silent, looking as if he, too, had a string of equally sorrowful questions streaming through his mind.

"He died."

Again, my gaze was glued to the quilt. And again, my gaze followed the blue rings beneath where I sat all the way to the other end, where Lawry was still sprawled on his side, supporting his weight with his right elbow. He didn't seem to be as carefree as when he'd first taken the position—he must not have known this sad story, either. His eyes were downcast as he, too, studied the quilt, looking serious and morose.

"Eliot was killed in a carriage accident on his way back from London." Claudine held out her left hand, flashing the large square-cut diamond on her ring finger. "He'd been to town to purchase this engagement ring...for me."

I'd seen the diamond probably hundreds of times before, but never had I imagined that the gorgeous ring was tied to such heartache, such awful memories, for Claudine. Her fiancé had likely been holding that very ring, thinking of a younger Claudine Abernathy, when he'd died.

Claudine must have endured so much pain throughout the last twenty-some years of her life.

How sad that I would experience the same kind of misery—only it would be infinitely worse, because Claudine hadn't made the choice to lose her dearest friend and lover.

And I had.

"Speaking of unlikely engagements," Claudine piped up, as if trying to get us off the heartbreaking subject of lost love, "have you heard that Vance has married his Giselle Gerard?"

Lawry's eyes immediately met mine.

"No, I hadn't heard." I had to force the words out, my eyes darting from Lawry to Claudine's enormous engagement ring. I couldn't think of anything, save for one sentence that continued to stream through my mind: *Vance is married?*

Which meant I was free, right?

Vance was married. God had taken him out of my reach.

So why didn't I feel freed?

"Neither had I," I heard Lawry say. My eyes shifted to him, as if I were just awakening from a daze. He still stared at me.

"They'll arrive in time for the double wedding," Claudine added.

I wished again that I could ignore the hold Vance Everstone seemed to have upon my soul. I didn't want Vance—and even if I did, I couldn't have him, because now he was married. He'd chosen someone else.

So why did I still feel chained down? Why did it still feel so wrong that I was in love with Lawry? And why did it feel wrong that I wanted to disregard everything I'd been set upon doing for nearly six long years in order to have him?

"Claudine, would you like a ride home?" My father's voice crashed through my nightmarish thoughts. "Annabelle and I were just heading back to Summerton. Would you like us to take you along to Hilldreth? Or we could send a carriage back a little later."

Lawry and I stood as Father helped Claudine up from her chair. My family's carriage waited in the distance, across the sloping green yard, with Mother inside.

"Oh, leaving does sound like a splendid idea," Claudine said. "I do have other things to do today, after all...."

Father folded the chair, tucked it under his arm, and offered his other arm to Claudine. He turned a quick smile to Lawry. "I trust you'll take good care of my girl?" Father's kind, blue eyes slid to me, and I could tell he, too, thought there was more to our picnic than met the eye.

"Of course, Mr. Summercourt. It would be my pleasure, as always," Lawry answered, taking far too much delight in my father's request.

Father walked Claudine toward the carriage without another word. I turned back to Lawry, who seemed pleased at the prospect of having me all to himself again.

"You don't have to look so smug, Lawry. He didn't mean forever."

He took hold of my hand and pulled me toward the blanket, that rather dangerous look gleaming in his eyes again. "I would, you know. Quite willingly."

I wrenched my hand free and turned away. Father and Claudine hadn't yet made it to the coach. I still had a chance to escape before it was too late, and I was left there alone with Lawry once again.

"Father, do wait up," I called after them. And as rude as it was, I ran away from Lawry, leaving him with the entire picnic to pack up and take home on his own.

It just had to be done. I simply could not bear to hear another word from him. He was getting far too daring, much too intent on exposing his heart to me. Just imagining what he felt for me had already been difficult enough to deal with over the months; I didn't need to actually hear the excruciating words and then be forced to live with the memory of them. No, I didn't need them to be *real*.

SEVENTEEN

Relentless

"There is no remedy for love but to love more."
—Henry David Thoreau

Hours later, I still hadn't gained control of my reeling emotions.

Even with as little as Lawry had said, it had been too much. With the news of Vance's marriage to Giselle, and that he was bringing her home soon, the walls keeping me from giving in to Lawry were beginning to crumble, no matter how I tried to stop them.

After I'd arrived home from the picnic at the Common, Garrett and Ainsley had stopped by to see me and informed me that Lawry had walked home to Hilldreth with his basket and quilt. Once they'd established that I really had nothing worthwhile to do at home, they'd insisted I accompany them on a stroll through the galleries of the Athenaeum.

"What do you two beautiful ladies say we head back to Hilldreth for afternoon tea?" Garrett asked, seated across from Ainsley and me in his coach, as we traveled back toward Summerton. He had a peculiar expression on his face, as if he were hiding something. And I suspected it had to do with this proposed afternoon tea. I also suspected that Lawry would be in attendance.

"What a splendid idea, Garrett," Ainsley said, as casually as ever.

"Haven't we been out and about enough today, Garrett? I want to go home."

"Nonsense. Going to Hilldreth is just like going home."

Or, at least, it had been at one time.

I walked slowly up the steps of the portico at Hilldreth, dread filling me. I wasn't ready. I still wasn't prepared. I didn't know what I wanted. I didn't know what I needed to do.

The door opened, and Higgins greeted us, welcomed us into the foyer, and took our things. "Claudine is out at the moment, Miss Ainsley, but your brother is home."

Lawry emerged from the study at the back of the house, probably having heard voices echo through the hall. Upon seeing me, he tensed. "Meredyth. What a surprise. I gathered you'd already seen enough of me today." Had he not been party to our siblings' little trick of getting me to Hilldreth?

"Yes, well, Garrett and Ainsley insisted I join them at the Athenaeum...." That was when I turned and discovered that they'd gone back out the front door—right past Higgins—and were in the coach. Leaving me.

When I looked back at Lawry, I saw a sly grin spread slowly across his face. I must have appeared ridiculous, turning back and forth in circles as I was. I looked to Higgins despairingly.

"And what would you like me to do with Miss Summercourt, sir?" The butler asked carefully. It was clear that he, too, was at a loss.

"Show her to the drawing room, please, Higgins. I'll be with her directly." Lawry had already started down the hall. "And do bring her some tea."

"I'm not in need of any tea," I said, still standing in the middle of the foyer.

Lawry spun around with a sober glance that lasted some seconds. "You heard her, Higgins. She doesn't want any tea." And with those stark words still echoing through the dark, wood-paneled hall, he disappeared into his study.

Higgins escorted me to the drawing room, where I sat restlessly without the comfort of tea, even though I knew it was because I'd foolishly declined it.

What was I doing there? Was I supposed to simply sit in the drawing room all afternoon until Lawry decided to see me? There wasn't much to do as I waited. I stood and wandered the perimeter of the room, first looking at paintings, then at the many framed photographs displayed atop the box grand piano and the mantel over the fireplace.

There was a large studio shot of Amaryllis and Nathan, and another of Lawry, looking quite underdressed before a background of some steep mountains along the edge of a great body of water. Presumably, it had been taken while he was out West. There were many others that were considerably older, and I could only wonder if one of them featured Claudine's dead fiancé.

After a few minutes had passed, I mustered the confidence to walk down the hall to the study to find Lawry myself, completely disregarding what Higgins might think if he caught me. When I opened the pocket door and peeked inside, Lawry was reclined in the chair at his desk, his feet propped upon the large, ornately carved library table, his hands clasped behind his neck.

He smiled when he saw me.

He must have been watching the door, waiting for me, for after I slid it open enough to enter, he was, in essence, staring at me, as if he were an archer waiting vigilantly in the woods for his unsuspecting prey.

I entered the room, leaving the door open, and dared look him in the eye. "What are you doing in here?"

"Waiting for you."

"Then why ever did you have Higgins show me into the drawing room?"

"I wanted to see how long it would take you to decide to come and find me." He released his hands from behind his head and lowered his feet from the table. "Which, as it turns out, wasn't nearly as long as I expected."

I remained near the door, perplexed. "I didn't come to Hilldreth to see you at all. My brother brought me here for— We were going to have tea."

"Tea?" He frowned for a moment, but then all emotion disappeared from his face. "It seems everyone we know is suddenly intent on seeing something of a more amorous nature develop between us."

"Yes, they've been quite relentless, haven't they?"

He speared me with another stare, and I wondered just what he thought of my leaving him in the park earlier. Was he really that angry with me?

"Won't you have a seat?" As he stood, he motioned to the two leather chairs facing the table. His detached manner of speaking, devoid of any emotion, made me wonder if he'd given up—if my longstanding resistance had finally reached the point of turning him away.

Something in me decided to forgo the chairs he'd indicated, and I directed my feet to the deep leather sofa at the other end of the room—the one facing the fireplace I'd sat upon the last time I'd been in that room, months ago.

"I've changed my mind. I would like some tea, if you don't mind." I made myself comfortable on the old, familiar piece of furniture.

Lawry pulled a cord that caused a bell to ring in one of the rooms across the hall. Seconds later, Higgins appeared in the open doorway. "As it turns out, Higgins, Miss Summercourt now desires to have some tea, if you please." When Higgins left, Lawry made his way across the room to me and the sofa. "If I'm not mistaken,

Meredyth, you haven't been one for sitting on sofas lately. Not since the last time we were both seated on this one, in fact."

The look in his eyes was almost predatory, and it sent a chill down my back.

I stood to my feet, suddenly thinking better of the seating arrangement. Oh, what had I done? I was behaving as if I wanted him, as if I wanted him to think that I—

"No, sit. This unplanned and, dare I say, 'forced' visit of yours just became vastly more interesting."

I did as he commanded, a little scared for my heart, for I didn't know how much more it could take before giving in to his persistence.

"So, Vance is married now." Lawry stayed at his end of the sofa, his eyes glinting dangerously. It was definitely not the direction I'd expected him to take the conversation, but I was relieved. The subject of Vance and his new wife was much preferable to learning for certain that Lawry loved me.

"Yes, that was shocking to hear, was it not?"

Higgins came into the room with the serving tray and set it upon the nearby tea table. He served mine with ample sugar and a touch of cream, just the way I liked it. He always remembered. I brought the cup to my nose. Of course, it was peppermint tea.

Higgins served Lawry's tea black and then left us once more, closing the door most of the way, likely out of habit.

"Were you really all that shocked to learn of the marriage? Did you not know he was engaged?"

"I knew. It's just…I always thought Vance wasn't the type to marry anyone, even if he promised or proposed." I took a tiny sip of my tea. Oh, what a muddle I was making of things.

"Had he promised or proposed marriage to you?"

I struggled not to spit out my tea. And then I coughed, as the tea I had swallowed was still rather hot and had gone down quite improperly. "Of course not." I set my teacup on its saucer with a click.

"Of course not?" His brows were lifted a half inch higher than usual. Was he mocking me? "You know, that actually surprises me."

"Well, not in so many words," I amended.

"What words did he use, if not 'Will you marry me?'" He spoke slowly, and for a moment, his gaze gave the impression that he meant those last four words with all his heart. "Why, if Vance had said such a thing to you, would he then act as if there was no such understanding between you? Why would he have left the country and, years later, married someone else altogether?"

"I don't know." I brought my teacup to my lips once more, pretending to take a long sip, as my eyes scanned the books at the second level of the study, then the vaulted ceiling of stained glass.

Lawry sighed, then stood and gently placed his untouched tea back on the tray. "You do realize, Meredyth, that choosing whom you'll marry is one of the most important, one of the most serious, decisions you'll make in your entire life, don't you?"

"Yes," I answered, even though the decision would never be one I'd make. I couldn't marry—not until I felt freed from the insufferable ties binding me to…I didn't even know what anymore. I wanted to move further down to the far end of the sofa, but I didn't, lest I spill the tea from the cup in my hands. I took another small sip, for it was too hot to down in one gulp; otherwise, I would have done so. "You know, I meant to bring back that book I borrowed from you in January."

He sat back down, closer to the middle of the sofa this time. "*Leçons de Grammaire?*"

"Yes, that's the one."

"What have you been doing with it all this time?"

"Nothing." It came out sounding so like the lie that it was. I took another sip.

"Do you like the tea so much?" Lawry inched closer with each word.

"It's very hot...even with the cream."

"You're drinking it quickly enough. Do you want more? I know just how you like it."

"No, I think this will suffice." It was almost half gone, and I was just about to scoot down the sofa when he slid another foot nearer.

Strengthened with the resolve at my success in resisting him thus far, I said, "I know what you were trying to do that day, bringing out that book."

"That's odd, because I don't recall knowing what I was doing... until I was kissing you."

Oh, that had come up much too quickly. I took a long swallow of tea. "You can say anything you want, Lawry, about what happened that day—"

"Not a day goes by that I don't regret standing up from this sofa so quickly," he whispered into my ear. He was right beside me, his sturdy arm resting upon the back of the sofa behind me.

I still faced forward, staring at the magnificent mantel of marble and mahogany, as if I'd never noticed it there before. "Lawry, really, I won't be made to think that—" I gulped the final mouthful of tea and turned to him, finding him much closer than I'd expected. However, I couldn't pull away. In fact, I found myself leaning in further. "I won't be made to think that you...."

He remained silent for a moment, then quietly asked, "What?" He searched my face with those resolute blue eyes that saw everything. "That I love you?"

His words wrecked through me, forever damaging any barricade I had managed to erect. It was completely crushed under the knowledge of what he felt for me. What he'd long felt for me. He loved me. It was more than just a kiss, more than all those looks. He'd said the words, made them real. Lawry Hampton was in love with me.

I didn't realize my empty teacup and saucer were shaking in my hands until Lawry took them from me and they ceased their rattling. He placed them on the high table behind the sofa, his eyes never leaving my face. I could tell I wasn't fooling him, even with my silence. He knew me too well.

What did I care that he knew I was in love with him? I wasn't free yet. I didn't know if I ever would be. Then a crazy thought came crashing through my mind that would not leave. Perhaps, if I said the words aloud—if I let him know for certain what I felt for him—maybe it would break the chains binding my heart, and I could somehow be free from Vance and my guilt.

"Yes," I sighed.

Reaching his arms around my waist, he leaned in and pressed his lips to my ear. The contact sent chills down to my toes. "You don't believe me?"

"No. Yes. I do believe you, and I...." Straightening my back, I looked him in the eye and finished my sentence, rather more straightforwardly than planned: "And I love you, as well."

He stilled.

I stayed just as I was, my eyes riveted upon his face, as I watched my unforeseen words take effect.

He cleared his throat. "Is that merely as my friend, or...?"

I wondered that he had to ask, with how close I was letting him get. He was practically on top of me.

"More than that." I didn't feel that I had broken free yet. It was more like I was losing control. But I would go on. I had to. I wanted Lawry too much not to try wholeheartedly. "I don't know why, but you're the only one—" I took a deep breath, placed my arms around his broad shoulders, and draped my legs over his lap, cuddling close. "I just want you."

His arms tightened around my waist, drawing me even nearer, and he simply held me for the longest time. I could feel his heart racing. "Truly, Merit?" he finally asked, his voice cracking with uncertainty.

All I could focus on was his perfect mouth smiling in front of me. I lifted my chin and pressed my lips to his, grasping him closer—if that was even possible.

Deliberately and carefully, he kissed me back, as if he were leading me down a steep and winding road. Oh, and I knew what a slippery road it was—how well I knew—which was why I reveled in the caution of it all. Lawry wasn't kissing me accidentally this time. No, this time, it was much more intentional.

Lawry broke away from me for a moment, but only to take in a ragged breath, as if he'd been caught unawares, as if he could hardly fathom that I truly wanted him.

Of course, he was still uncertain. Who would blame him? I'd willfully fought against him for all those months, for nothing. And now, out of the blue, there I was, confessing my love and letting him kiss me in the exact same spot where I'd so shockingly allowed him to kiss me the first time.

The thought of his standing and breaking the contact, as he had that first time, strengthened my resolve. He would know I meant this. That I loved him, and I wanted him to be mine.

He was my only safety.

"Oh please, God, I just want Lawry," I whispered, pleading, almost praying, as my lips were again pressed to his. My heart wanted to burst inside my chest. This was what I was made for— loving Lawry Hampton.

"Good afternoon, Higgins!" I heard Claudine exclaim from the front hall.

Lawry bolted upright, looked me in the eyes, and swallowed.

I still gripped the lapels of his jacket, reluctant to let go. I'd completely forgotten that the door to the study was still ajar. How had we gone from having tea to this?

As Claudine's footsteps echoed through the house, Lawry stood, mumbled something under his breath, and hurried to take his seat at the desk on the other side of the room. He assumed the same position I'd found him in when I'd entered the room, only he didn't appear nearly as composed as before.

My nerves were a mess. I simply had to calm myself, or Claudine would know how guilty we were merely by looking at me! I shook out my hands in front of me, as if that might help. Then I stood and hastened right past Lawry to the door. I had to intercept Claudine in the hall before she had the occasion to come barreling into the study, looking for us.

As I opened the pocket door, I met her face-to-face.

"Meredyth! How delightful to find you here. Higgins said you were having tea with Lawry. It's difficult to get enough of him, isn't it? Having dear friends like Ainsley and Lawry...they are such a blessing, are they not?"

"Oh, yes. It is difficult—I mean, yes, he is a tremendous blessing to me. I could never do without a friend like Lawry." I could barely think, just recalling what had just transpired. Oh, for shame. Would I ever be able to have another intelligent conversation?

"May I join you for more tea in the—?"

"I should actually be going...but it was good seeing you again." I walked toward the front of the house to collect my things.

Claudine followed me. "You're leaving so suddenly?"

Lawry still hadn't exited the study, and I wasn't composed enough to return to the room for any reason, whether to have tea or to make my proper adieu. How did one even do such a thing after the tea we'd had?

"Mere." Lawry emerged from the room and walked slowly, nonchalantly, down the paneled hall, appearing ever so composed. How did he do that? Was his body not still screaming for mine? "Would you like a ride home? I was going to drive downtown to take care of a few errands."

"Oh, no. I can walk home; it's only a few blocks." I made my way closer to the door, desperate for escape. Both Lawry and Claudine followed, as well as Higgins.

"Let Lawry walk you home, Meredyth," Claudine said. "It's the least he can do."

"All right." I gave in too quickly. But, surely, nothing shocking could happen between us as we walked together down Commonwealth Avenue.

As we walked out the door together, my hand resting on his strong arm, the only thing I could think of were my last words to him in the study. I'd practically begged God aloud for Lawry, in the midst of that last kiss.

In spite of the awkwardness, there was a sweet, silent camaraderie between us as we strolled up Commonwealth toward Summerton. It was just as I remembered from years before in the gardens of Truesdale, walking down to The Cleft Stone to while away the hours, talking and watching the tide come in or go out. How had I gone so far off course over the years that I'd been blind to the fact that Lawry and I were obviously meant for each other?

I hardly knew what to say to him. All the words we'd exchanged that afternoon seemed to have forever changed the world around me. What did one say to someone to whom she'd just reluctantly, yet wholeheartedly, admitted to being in love with?

Anyone who happened to see us walking along would have a hard time detecting any trace of the passion that had flared between us a mere ten minutes before. But that might have been because I didn't dare look at Lawry.

"Je t'aime, Meredyth." Lawry breathed the words into my ear as he rubbed his thumb across the fingers of my hand that was resting on his arm. A rush of happiness unlike any I'd ever known spiked through me. Was this really happening?

That strange, foreign sensation brought tears to my eyes—happy tears. I was so unaccustomed to crying for any reason other than sorrow that I still couldn't say a word. Or look up.

"Hey." Lawry stopped our trek down the sidewalk and nudged my chin up with his bent forefinger. He gently held it there until I met his gaze. "Don't cry. This is the beginning of our happily ever after."

I nodded. It was all so difficult to take in, all this happiness... this sudden freedom.

"You did mean it, didn't you?" His eyes turned stormy for a moment, until I nodded again.

"Yes, I meant it. I do love you...so much. It's only...I didn't realize I was going to say so until it was out."

"Well, it did take some prying, I'll give you that." He turned me back toward Summerton and resumed leading me home. His smile was back, and his hand no longer seemed content to simply hold mine as it rested on his forearm. His fingers strayed to my wrist. "All that matters now is that you finally admitted it."

The delicious sensations scorching through me made me sigh. "If it makes you feel any better, Lawry, I wish I could kiss you all the way to my door."

His lips slanted into a cocky grin. "You know, that does make me feel better. Perhaps we should even give it a try...give the neighbors a little something to talk about. You know they're already talking...and wondering...."

There was a familiar gleam in his eyes that suddenly made me want to change the subject. I knew it wouldn't take much for Lawry to convince me to duck behind a brick wall, concealed from the street, to steal a much-coveted kiss, even if we would be in plain sight of numerous second-story parlor windows.

"Wednesday is your thirtieth birthday, is it not? You're getting rather old, aren't you?" I teased.

"You don't have to tell me. I've spent many of those long years praying for what happened today."

I knew his words weren't meant to make me feel guilty, but they did nonetheless. If only I'd recognized Lawry's love all those years before, I never would have gone into that cave with Vance. Never.

When I didn't answer, he went on. "Benta's making a cake for me tomorrow. When she and Wynn found out, there was no stop to the party planning."

"Why are they not having the party on your actual birthday?"

"I have to be in New York early tomorrow afternoon, remember? Right up to the wedding."

The same void that I'd felt when Lawry had wrenched himself from my grasp and stood after kissing me for the first time came rushing back. I'd found everything I wanted—what would I do without him for the next few weeks? How would I survive seeing Vance again without Lawry beside me?

"Did you want to come for the party tomorrow?" he asked.

"That's a silly question if I ever heard one." I tried my best to cover my cheerlessness. "Of course, I want to come."

"Are you free around ten thirty?"

"That sounds grand."

"I'll try to finish all the business in New York as quickly as possible, Mere, to join you in Bar Harbor as soon as I can. The only thing I want for the rest of my life is to be wherever you are."

"Me, too." I was so fearful of saying anything more. What did all this mean? I'd told him I loved him and then kissed him as if he was all I wanted. Oh, and I'd said as much, too. More than once. Was I really ready to allow myself to blissfully entertain thoughts of being with him, loving him, for the rest of my life?

Lawry led me up the front steps of Summerton and kept hold of my hand, still resting at his elbow. "I should probably head home and finish getting everything in order for the trip. It's nearly dinnertime, and I have yet to start packing." We stood before the door, facing each other. Lawry tugged playfully at my chin. "New York will be terribly boring without you."

"Just as Boston will be without you, and Bar Harbor, for that matter." I glanced to my right, toward the boulevard, where dozens of other couples walked and talked. Did any of them feel as awkward as I? Were any of them having such a trying time conversing with the one person on earth who held her heart in his hands?

"Well, for now, we have the party tomorrow. I'll pick you up at ten thirty." The way he spoke the words, they were much more than a promise to retrieve me with his carriage. He reached for my hand and tugged at the fingertips of my glove until it slipped off. I watched as he caressed my palm and then intertwined his fingers with mine. The intimate contact sent thrills down my spine.

He suddenly encompassed everything, my whole world. There were no thoughts of anything—my going to Bar Harbor, of The Trinity School for Girls, of the orphanage, of Washington—not even of Vance Everstone—that his presence didn't settle. My eyes darted to his, and I sighed. "Lawry."

"Meredyth." He stood as close as propriety would allow and brought my hand to his lips, his fingers still entwined with mine. "I love you. Don't forget that. I will always love you, no matter what." His penetrating gaze held mine for a long moment before he clicked the knocker against the door with three short taps.

Fenley opened the door almost immediately, and I turned to enter.

Lawry gave a small bow as he released my hand. "Remember, Meredyth. No matter what."

EIGHTEEN

Found

> *"All brave men love;*
> *for he only is brave who has affections to fight for…."*
> —Nathaniel Hawthorne

After an awkward greeting in the foyer of Summerton in the presence of my father, Lawry didn't say a word as he helped me into his closed carriage the next morning. Before I sat down, I buried his birthday present—his French book wrapped in the monogrammed handkerchief I'd pilfered—inside the large pocket in the leather lining of the wall. When I did take my seat, he was already seated across from me, seeming somewhat anxious.

Perhaps he, too, had passed a sleepless night, thinking about us, wondering if everything would be the same when next we saw each other. My own doubts and fears were difficult enough to handle—what could I say to reassure him?

I didn't really know what to say, but anything seemed better than nothing. "So, who all will be at this party?"

"Besides you and me? Mrs. Allister, Benta, Dr. Wellesley, and Wynn." Lawry flexed his fingers, cracking them loudly.

"You tired of such things long ago, did you not? I remember you telling me once that you had forbidden your mother to throw you any more surprise birthday parties."

189

"Yes. As I recall, I was turning three and twenty at the time, and I believed—and still believe—I'd quite outgrown them. However, a birthday party for the sake of a six-year-old? That is reason to celebrate, if I ever knew one."

"Yes, that is a good reason to celebrate." With a sudden brazenness, I propelled myself from my seat and plopped down next to him, pulling down the nearest window shade in the same instance.

He lowered the shade of the opposite window and immediately turned to me, desire blazing in those steady blue eyes, a boyish smile transforming his face. "And so is—"

I silenced him with my lips, crushing myself against his chest, wrapping my arms about his neck. I think I surprised him, but it didn't take him long to join in the revelry. He reached his arms around my waist and held me close. His lips traveled over my face, from my mouth to my jaw to my ear. I could hear the heaviness of his breath, the wild beating of his heart pressed against my chest. I couldn't resist anymore; I found his lips once again, and he kissed me as if I were the water his thirsty soul had long thought only a mirage, as if he were parched for me and couldn't stop drinking.

Minutes later, he breathed against my cheek, "I can't believe you're mine."

"I do love you so, Lawry. You were all I could think about last night." I knew that such an admission was quite unladylike, but how on earth was one supposed to behave like a proper young lady while deliriously in love?

The carriage halted before I could kiss him again, and we both reached around to open the blinds.

"Turn your head, Lawry. I don't want you to see your present yet."

He rubbed his hand over his face and sighed but did as I asked.

Yes, it was rather frustrating that we couldn't simply kiss in his carriage all morning and afternoon until it was time for him to leave for New York. It was unfair that we had to be separated so soon after finally coming together.

I retrieved the book from the wall pocket, then pressed it against my stomach while he helped me out of the carriage. I glanced up at his face in the sunlight and hoped I didn't look nearly as disheveled as he did. His face was flushed, and I didn't think he could have stopped grinning if he tried with all his might.

Benta must have been watching from the window, for the door flew open before we could knock, and she greeted us, her excitement bubbling forth with more smiles and laughter than I'd ever seen the stoic young woman display. "It's good to see you again, Miss Summercourt. I'm glad you're feeling better. It was a shame you had to leave so quickly last Tuesday. Seeing you is all that Wynn's spoken of since."

"Where is Wynn?" Lawry asked, looking into the empty parlor. The little girl was usually at our feet the moment we were in the door.

"She's upstairs in the attic. It's her favorite place to spend her time." Benta closed the door and moved toward the stairs. "I can fetch her now, if you'd like."

"Oh, you don't have to do that." I made my way past her and climbed a few steps, "Lawry mentioned that you were making him a cake. I don't want you to have to go to any more trouble. I'll gladly retrieve her."

"That's mighty considerate of you, Miss Summercourt," Benta said softly. "Don't hurry down. I haven't even begun icing the cake yet."

"Benta, you know you have my permission to call me Meredyth," I said over the railing as Lawry followed her down the long, narrow hall to the kitchen.

It surprised me that he hadn't chosen to join me.

As I walked up the stairs and down the hall, I noticed all the bedchamber doors were open. I heard old Mrs. Allister humming and saw her changing the linens in one of the rooms as I passed.

I didn't usually see much of her when visiting. She was always buzzing busily about the inn, accomplishing task after task. I stopped in the doorway. "Good afternoon, Mrs. Allister."

"Hello, deary. What's that you've got there?" She crumpled the dirty sheet she'd just stripped from a double bed. "Somethin' special for our dear Lawry's birt'day?"

I hid the book behind my back. "Not exactly. It's not so much a present as it is a few belongings of his I've been meaning to return. But don't worry if you—"

"We got something for him, too." She gave me a rare, bashful smile. It didn't surprise me that whenever I did find her smiling, it had something to do with Lawry.

"That's very sweet of you."

"He's a sweet man, that one. Any normal society miss would be hard-pressed to deserve such a man, but I do believe he's found somethin' special in you, as well, Miss Meredy." She bent over and collected a large pile of soiled sheets and blankets.

I backed into the hall, out of her way. "Oh, I don't know about that." I was unaccustomed to hearing such praise, especially from people who were almost strangers.

"Why, he's been a courtin' ya over the months—Dr. We'sley says he seen it in his eyes the moment Lawry first brung ya to him." Her arms laden with sheets, Mrs. Allister walked past me down the hall, then tossed the load down the back stairs. "He's in love with ya, ain't he? O' course, you is with him. Any gal would be. Otherwise ya wouldn't'a come here so often with him. Not a proper miss like yourself. You must be fixed somethin' awful to come here on and off as ya have all these months."

With my handbag now hanging from my wrist, I clutched the handkerchief-wrapped book to my stomach and backed toward the attic stairs. "Yes, we are...in love."

Somehow, I hadn't pictured the craggily Mrs. Allister as the first person I would take into my confidence regarding Lawry. I didn't really know how to share the news with anyone.

"Well, that there is enough for me. I wish you joy together, Miss Meredy. I know, if ever two people could find it, it'd be the two of yous."

She headed down the back stairs to the kitchen, and I was left standing there, feeling rather warm and happy. I'd admitted my love to Lawry, and now to Mrs. Allister. It was becoming easier and easier to accept that my dreams were coming true. Of course, the kisses in the carriage had helped.

As I started up the attic steps, I removed the handkerchief from around *Leçons de Grammaire* and tried to cram the book into my handbag. It seemed as if it should fit, but it simply had too many corners. I didn't know what I'd been thinking to give Lawry the book back for his birthday. It was such a bad idea.

I stuffed the cloth up my sleeve, not sure I wanted to give it up yet, either. Lately, I'd been sleeping with it draped over my pillow, savoring Lawry's woodsy scent in my dreams. But soon, once we were married, I would have the real thing—Lawry next to me all night long.

And we would be married. There was no question about that.

A delightful spring breeze flowed through the house, and I felt a rush of coolness from the attic door, which had been left ajar. As I neared the top of the attic stairs, I felt as if I were getting closer and closer to being *refreshed*.

Refreshment was something my soul hadn't experienced in years.

I stepped through the door into the dimly lit attic. Every window was open. "Wynn? Are you up here?"

"Mere'dy?" came her tiny voice.

"Where are you?"

"Behind the trunks."

I thought it odd that she hadn't come out of her hiding spot to greet me. As I reached her, I saw why.

Wynn had opened one of the old trunks and was dressed in a massive, moth-eaten wedding dress.

I stifled a laugh behind my hand. "Is that what you're planning to wear to the party?"

"I think it's too big."

An understatement if I'd ever heard one. "Do you want me to help you out of it?"

"Yes."

I set the French book and my handbag on the window seat, then stepped around the wedding dress, reached over the flounces of white lace and ruffles, and tried to lift Wynn from out of the sea of material. "How did you get in there?"

"I crawled in from underneath."

"Perhaps that's how you need to come out, unless Lawry comes and helps."

As if I'd summoned him by saying his name, I heard heavy footsteps coming up the attic stairs. Even before we could see him, he was speaking, knowing just where to find us. "Wynn, Benta wants you to help ice the cake. Do you want—"

"Yes!" Wynn's dark curls disappeared under the white lace ruffles, and before I knew it, she had crawled out from the dress and made a run for the stairs.

I heard a few more quiet footsteps and then a whisper from the other side of the trunks. "Now, where could my dearest Merit be?"

I desperately wanted to answer him, but my words were stuck in my throat. He was the only one who'd ever called me that, and I loved hearing the name from his smiling lips. It reminded me of when we were children, and he would take a break from playing with my brothers to spend time with me. Had I begun to love him even back then?

"Meredyth, are you there?"

That was a much easier question to answer.

"I'm here." I attempted to lift the wedding dress off the floor. It was heavier than I'd expected, and I had no idea how I was going to get the enormous thing back into the trunk Wynn had pulled it from. I had it clutched to my chest when Lawry casually strolled around the stack of trunks.

"What an appealing vision you are."

I hurriedly dropped the dress into the trunk and stepped around it, further into the dormer. It was the only direction I could move without progressing toward Lawry. Based on our encounter in the carriage that morning, I knew it wasn't the best idea to be alone with him for long periods of time—not when he made me feel the way he did.

"Meredyth, there's something I've been meaning to tell you."

"You've told me a number of significant things lately, Lawry." I laughed almost breathlessly, as if everything he'd said to me in the past few days had been mere trifles rather than words that would change my life forever. "How could there possibly be anything more?"

Lawry stepped forward, leveling those heartbreaking blue eyes on me. "I overheard your discussion with Wynn after your class on Tuesday. I was in the hall when the two of you were speaking."

"Oh?" I turned toward the window seat, welcoming the sudden breeze on my face, and closed my eyes, trying to recall what I'd said in regard to him. I could think only of everything I'd been dwelling upon at the time—how I'd thought I could never, ever have him.

"Wynn was certain I would be willing to teach you how to love."

I swallowed.

"And you agreed that perhaps I could."

Hearing him move closer, I turned around. He was only a few feet away.

He closed the distance between us, blocking my escape entirely, completely disregarding that he was wading through the bottom hem of an ancient dress overflowing from a nearby trunk. "That was my first inkling that you might allow…that you perhaps finally desired my love. You realize, don't you, that I've been waiting, that I've been in love with you for much of your life?"

"Yes." I took a step back and stumbled, landing on the window seat.

"I tried to stay away. I tried to move on, but I couldn't."

He came closer still, and it was all I could do to resist reaching out and touching him. All night long, I'd tried to convince myself that what was happening between Lawry and me was real. And I still had a difficult time believing it.

"I tried to love Amelia…tried to forget you. But it was impossible. You were too much a part of me already."

If I'd thought his confession of love the day before had overturned my heart, hearing him explain just how he'd loved me throughout the years lit a flame in my soul. With a new, raging confidence, I grabbed the French book from the seat and stood.

"Do you remember the first night I saw you upon returning home from Washington last year? I was scared to see you again. I didn't sleep for days after. Poor Amaryllis—she probably thought I was a crazy loon when she found me fully dressed in the study in the middle of the night, racking my brain for what to do about you." Lawry took one final stride closer. "You're the reason I came home. The reason I've been East and not out West these last fourteen months." His eyes held mine, the true blue of them penetrating something in me, pinning me where I stood on the wood-planked floor. Not that I wanted to be anywhere else.

"Last summer, at your family's Cove Party, when I realized you still wanted Vance, I didn't know what to do with myself. That's why I stayed in Bar Harbor. I couldn't go back to Washington. Not without telling you how I felt. I had to at least try, one last time. I just didn't know how or when."

"The night you told me about the orphanage. The night you kissed me." I held the book before me, but he didn't notice. He was too focused on keeping my gaze, which I returned willingly.

"When I heard about Vance and the French girl he ended up marrying, I thought perhaps I had a chance. I'd wanted to tell you about the orphanage all last year, Mere. I wanted to know how you felt about my doing such a thing. But I was scared out of my mind. What if you thought I was a fool?" Lawry ran his hands down his face. "I honestly didn't mean to kiss you. I was just so relieved by your reaction to my telling you about the orphanage. I was afraid you'd think…." He was rambling, but I didn't care. It only proved to me how much he needed to get everything out, how he wanted me to know all that I'd been doing to him.

For the first time, I wondered if he'd already figured out why I'd been set on marrying Vance for all those years. Every time Lawry had brought up Vance in recent days, it was as if he were testing me, trying to get me to tell him the truth of the matter. And now—now that I could see the love pouring from his eyes—I knew I needed to tell him.

But would he still love me?

I bravely held the book up for him. "You stole my heart that day…from the clutch Vance had upon it."

Lawry immediately reached for the book with one hand and my waist with the other, pulling me to him. "Lesson four." With both arms around me, he leveled his forehead with mine, and we stood nose to nose. His eyes refused to leave mine. "I'm going to marry you."

"I don't deserve you."

"It doesn't matter what you think you deserve." He released my waist and reached up to touch my jaw, then my cheek. "None of that matters." To hear him tell me that I could have him even though I didn't deserve him soothed the constant self-doubt in my heart.

Yes, I could have him. I was good enough for Lawry Hampton. *Somehow.*

Cautiously, I slid my hands up his chest to smooth my fingers over his collar and then his neck, finally tunneling them through his hair. I lifted myself on my toes and kissed his lips.

He dropped the book to the floor with a thud, and I could feel his heart pounding against my chest. His tender kisses and his unfaltering love gave me courage to hope that what I'd foolishly allowed Vance to have of me didn't matter. I loved Lawry now, and he loved me. I would be forever faithful to him. I needed him. His love was strong and steadfast, having endured through the years, despite his best attempts to forget all about me.

He easily could have given up. When I thought of all the times I'd pushed him away—and not just from the months he'd been back from Bar Harbor, but all the years we'd lived mere houses apart from each other, either in Boston or in Bar Harbor—he'd loved me all along.

I turned my head, breaking the searing contact, needing air. He was so close, the scent of peppermint drifted over me with his every breath. I felt safe, guarded...and somehow liberated. As if I'd found my one safe place in the crazy world I'd been lost in for so many years.

"We were meant for each other, Mere. I've known it since...I think I've known it forever." Lawry held me tight, his face buried between my neck and the mess of my hair, which had fallen from its pins. "You can't imagine how long I've wanted this, dreamt of this—of you, my Meredyth, loving me back." I could hear tears in his voice.

I didn't know how he did it, but when I was with Lawry, he made it easy for me to feel that I belonged to God, that God indeed wanted me and loved me, as if God's very love radiated from him.

I pulled myself closer around his neck. "I'm sorry, Lawry. I'm so sorry I took so long to—"

"There's no need to apologize." He lifted his head and held my face gently in his hands, his eyes searching mine. "You simply lost your way for a while, Merit. But, suffice it to say, I think you found it again." He kissed a hot trail from my cheek to my ear. "And I love you, regardless. That's all that matters."

"The cake is done!" Wynn's excited voice echoed through the attic as she came up the stairwell.

I immediately broke free from Lawry's arms, putting a proper distance between us.

"Wynn," Lawry said to me. "I want to take her with us to Washington."

"It's all ready to eat!" Wynn appeared from around the trunks and stopped by the one containing the wedding dress. She had globs of chocolate glaze lingering around her lips and clinging to her fingers.

I stepped toward Wynn and guided her by the shoulders away from the white fabric. "Wynn, don't touch the wedding dress."

"I won't, I promise," she answered as she backed up. "What were you doin'?"

"We were just discussing your future—"

"But I di'n't hear any voices."

"Wynn Rosselet!" Mrs. Allister's voice boomed up the stairs. "You get yourself back down here and let them two have their time together!"

Wynn disappeared again behind the pile of trunks, and we heard her little feet patter back down the stairwell.

I'd kept my back to Lawry as I'd spoken to Wynn, and I maintained that stance for a moment after she was gone. I bent to retrieve *Leçons de Grammaire* from the floor, almost scared to face Lawry again once I stood. When I felt him pull at a ruffle on my dress, I leaned back against his chest, and his arms came around me, both hands splayed upon my waist.

"I do need more time with you," he whispered into my hair, his breath tickling my ear.

I turned in his arms and pressed close as he leaned against the wall. With my nose, I nuzzled his clean-shaven jaw as my hands slid daringly inside his open jacket and around his waistcoat. "Then don't go to New York."

"I don't want to, but I must." He lifted my chin, forcing me to look into his eyes. "Especially if we plan to travel to Washington soon."

"Is Seattle near Whidbey Island—and Nathan and Amaryllis?"

"It isn't far."

"And are we to live at the orphanage?" It felt invigorating to speak so candidly with him about our future. The orphanage was something I'd wondered about for months, often thinking back to the photograph I'd seen of the large house but never allowing myself to care enough to ask about it.

He chuckled, as if greatly amused. "Don't worry, there's plenty of room for you. When I bought the house, I was thinking only of you. I hoped you would be there with me someday." He stretched his fingers along the nape of my neck, as if he were going to kiss me again, and whispered into my ear, "Hmm...perhaps we can convince Daphne and Nicholette to make it a triple wedding."

"I'm surprised Nicholette even suggested having a double wedding. I don't think we would be welcomed." I leaned back and cocked my jaw to the side, urging his lips down my neck. "When do you think you'll make it up to Bar Harbor?"

"There's no telling. But I will come as quickly as I can. I promise." Lawry took my hand and held it to his smiling lips. "And, as I said, the sooner I get started, the sooner I'll be finished. I have a feeling this week is going to be torture, wanting to see you but having to work."

"We really ought to get downstairs if the cake is finished. You don't have all day, after all."

"You're right, I don't. It's an unfortunate fact. But you had better believe you are the best birthday present I've ever received." He took my hand and led me out of the dormer. "You were well worth the wait, Merit."

NINETEEN

The Letter

"It is easier to perceive error than to find truth...."
—Johann Wolfgang von Goethe

W hen I entered the front hall of Summerton later that afternoon, Fenley immediately presented me with a small white envelope upon his trusty silver tray.

"This came for you today, Miss Meredyth."

"Thank you, Fenley." I took the envelope, but I didn't study it closely. I was still rather preoccupied with the memory of the last, breathless kiss Lawry had given me inside his carriage before walking me to the door for our last good-bye until we met again in Bar Harbor. I couldn't help but smile as I recalled the possessiveness of his hands on my neck, reaching into my hair, and of his lips not leaving mine for the longest time. I was his—at least, I would be soon. And, more amazingly, he would be mine.

The quaint birthday party had been a perfect example of what my future with Lawry would entail, only instead of celebrating with Wynn, Benta, Mrs. Allister, and Dr. Wellesley in the parlor of an inn, we would be sitting around a table with Mrs. Flanagan and Amelia Grendahl and over a dozen scruffy children at an orphanage in Seattle.

On my way up the stairs, I rearranged my handbag and the French book, which Lawry had insisted I keep, to take a better look at the envelope. It was unimportant-looking, with my name and address scrawled sloppily in thick black ink. However, when I flipped it over, my breath caught. Embossed in blood-red wax was the monogram VEX. I couldn't take another step, and I dropped the book and my handbag, sending them tumbling down the stairs.

"Would you like some help, Miss Meredyth?" Fenley stood at the foot of the staircase, a look of fatherly concern on his aged face.

"No, thank you. I simply lost my grip." I stood there for a moment, still stunned, but then I somehow managed to descend the stairs to hurriedly retrieve my items.

With another quick word of thanks to Fenley, I clutched them to my chest and sprinted up the two flights of stairs to my bed-chamber. With my back against the locked door, I finally let out the sob I'd been holding in.

I dreaded what the letter would say—dreaded that the rumors of Vance's being married were somehow false; that, somehow, the freedom I'd thought I'd attained was only a cruel joke, and that Nicholette and Will, and even Estella, had made up the story about Giselle Gerard.

And that I was the greatest fool who ever lived.

God, let it not be true. Let it be nothing....

Sinking onto the edge of my bed, I tore open the seal and unfolded a single sheet of thick, expensive-looking stationery.

Meredyth,

Prepare yourself for some shocking news. My wife, Giselle, is dead, and from what I've heard from Will, it seems you're resisting anyone else's interest and attention. I can only assume it's because you're still set on marrying me, even after all these years. Father says he'll reinstate my inheritance as soon as I marry properly. Who would be more proper for me to marry than you? And now I might as well.

I'm ready to move on from this whole debacle—I'm sure no one in the States will expect me to mourn Giselle. We were hardly married, after all.

We can announce our engagement the week of Will's wedding. I'll be back just in time.

Ever yours,
Vance X. Everstone

I sat there for several minutes, numb to everything but the shock of being so entirely caught off guard, even though I knew very well I shouldn't have been. Had I not always known what my *expected end* would be?

I shot to my feet, suddenly unable to think of anything else but finding that Bible verse Lawry had read about expected ends.

I retrieved the small, thick Bible bound in leather I'd confiscated from the library downstairs and sat again on the edge of my bed. I went through every chapter, searching for the chapter containing the eleventh verse I was seeking. When I reached chapter seventeen, my attention was snagged by the words of verse nine. I swallowed the hard lump in my throat as I took in every word.

I couldn't believe my eyes. There, in print, was the description of my own deceptive heart.

The heart is deceitful above all things, and desperately wicked: who can know it? I the LORD *search the heart, I try the reins, even to give every man according to his ways, and according to the fruit of his doings.*

My search for Lawry's verse stopped as tears flooded my eyes, the truth of the matter registering in my heart. The constricted feeling in my chest told me better than anything else that, despite my best efforts to break free, I had failed. For if I were truly free, I wouldn't have been so positively certain my life was over. I'd been fooling myself, thinking I could have anything with Lawry.

I didn't deserve him, and God didn't want me to have him. That much was clear.

I stretched out on my bed, buried my face in my arms, and cried—as if wailing to God would make Him pay attention to me. Oh, that I could make Him forget all my prayers over the years in which I'd begged for Vance to want to marry me. If only I could replace all those with my most recent ones, pleading for Lawry's heart, instead.

Did Vance's sudden desire to marry me mean that I'd been right for all those years? Had I fooled myself into thinking I could escape God's wrath and somehow deserve as good a man as Lawry Hampton? Was this my punishment for trying so earnestly to have Lawry when I only deserved Vance?

The sickening questions circled unendingly in my mind until it hurt to breathe. Oh, if I could just go back to being numb, the way I'd been for all those years before Lawry had kissed me…back when marrying Vance was all I wanted.

Oh, Lawry.

I didn't know how I would make him understand that I'd been wrong to encourage him, to tell him I loved him. He would likely hate me even more than I hated myself once I told him I wouldn't be marrying him, after all; that I would be marrying Vance Everstone, instead.

Just as I'd always known I would, ever since that day in the cave.

When it was over, Vance had pulled me out of the cave, dragging me by the hand from the shadows into the bright light of day, forcing me to accept the fact that I would have to face the world again at some point.

Damaged and ruined.

And that moment had happened much sooner than anticipated, for there had stood Natalia, pausing in the midst of her daily walk down the coast from her house to mine.

I'd dreaded to wonder how long she had been there.

⟋⟍

"Meredyth?" Natalia's startled green eyes met mine. Had she heard—?

I took a moment to examine my dress but saw no evidence to condemn me. I tried desperately to seem normal. Surely, she couldn't tell what I'd done simply by looking at me!

And yet, somehow, she knew.

Her eyes narrowed on her brother. "Vance!" She uttered the single syllable with such power, such authority. "What have you done?"

I could tell Vance didn't care one way or the other that his sister was confronting him. He kept a strong grip on my hand and continued to drag me across the rocky, uneven coast in the direction of Rockwood.

"Vance!" she repeated, even louder.

"This doesn't concern you," he barked over his shoulder. "Go back to your walk." He turned back to me and pulled at my hand all the more. "Keep walking, Meredyth."

"What are you going to do with her now?" Natalia followed us close behind.

"Go away, Natalia," Vance growled at his sister, not bothering to look her way.

She reached for my arm, stopping us both. "How could you—to Mere?"

She was becoming hysterical, probably appalled at both of us. Who did such evil things? And what were the costs? I had thought earlier that I was in love with him—for years, in fact. But as I dragged my feet across the rocks, following Vance down the coast, I felt something entirely different—something completely opposite of love.

I had no idea what was going on, what I was feeling, what I was going to do. I just needed to find a way to fix what I'd done. There was only one thing I could think of, and Natalia said the words for me just as they formed in my mind.

"Are you going to marry her?" She had her eyes leveled at Vance, her arms crossed over her chest. That she somehow knew exactly what had happened in the cave horrified me to the depths of my soul.

I noticed that she placed absolutely no blame upon me whatsoever, but that didn't change the way I felt about it. I knew I was just as much at fault as Vance. I'd put myself in the situation, after all.

"I don't know," he answered gruffly. "I suppose I will, though I far from meant anything like this to happen with her! It was never my plan to—"

"It was easy, though, wasn't it, Vance?" Natalia said calmly. "It's always easy for you to have whatever you want without thinking how it affects others. It's different this time, wouldn't you agree? You've known Meredyth since the day she was born! She's a respectable girl!"

I could still hear Natalia's questions echoing off the rocks as Vance yanked me away from her. The three of us continued on to Rockwood without exchanging another word. Not that I'd said a thing since leaving the cave.

Once we reached Rockwood, Natalia hurried me through the house to the vacant bedchamber with the blue walls, pretending that I'd injured myself on the rocks—a fitting explanation for the blood on the back hem of my dress, if anyone happened to see it.

As Natalia helped me change out of the dress and ran a hot bath for me, she kept on insisting that Vance would do right by me, that he would surely marry me.

When my bath was finished, and I was dressed in an old dress of Estella's, I watched silently as Natalia burned my soiled dress and underclothes in the hearth of the blue bedchamber. Even as she escorted me home—Vance had promptly disappeared once Natalia took over—I still didn't say one word.

I was too dead inside to speak. Too numb.

If I'd been able to say something, it surely would have been the only word I could summon, the only one I felt certain of.

Ruined.

TWENTY

Rockwood

"A ruffled mind makes a restless pillow."
—Charlotte Brontë, *The Professor*

Mount Desert Island · Bar Harbor, Maine

Despite the fact that my legs were stiff from sitting for hours on end while traveling in the Everstones' private railcar, I was hardly able to wait until the coach halted to open the carriage door and gracelessly climb down without assistance.

Nathan and Amaryllis Everstone stood before the front door of the Everstone family's great limestone mansion called Rockwood.

"Amaryllis!" I hurried as fast as my legs could take me along the gravel path, across the lawn, and up the steps of the sprawling stone veranda, leaving Estella and her father to follow me from the coach. We'd just traveled the last ten miles from Ellsworth, Maine, having stopped only once to drop Claudine and Ainsley up the coast at Truesdale, where Edward and Lizabeth Hampton, Lawry's parents, lived year-round.

Nathan's twin sister, Natalia Livingston, and her husband, George, who also made their permanent home on Mount Desert Island, also stood with Nathan and Amaryllis, waiting to greet me. Natalia, who, I'd learned from Estella, was expecting, was quite unable to hide the fact.

Amaryllis looked the same and was as tiny as ever. I'd fully expected to find her in an extreme state of increasing size due to a baby, as well, since she and Nathan had been married for almost eleven months.

"Oh, Meredyth, it's good to see you again." Amaryllis reached out and gave me a hug. "I've missed you so very much."

Before I could respond, Nathan interjected, "Lawry didn't come up with you?"

I swallowed hard. "He had business he needed to finish in New York."

As Estella and her father came up the steps, I turned to George and asked quietly, "Do you know when Vance is set to arrive?"

It seemed George hadn't heard my question, and so I turned back to Amaryllis. She looked suddenly pale, and her even, dark eyebrows were furrowed with concern.

"Sometime early this week, I believe," Nathan said, his green gaze squared on me.

"Elle!" Natalia walked right past them to greet Estella.

"Talia! Just look at you. You're radiant!" Estella embraced her sister. "When will the baby come?"

"Most likely July or August." Natalia, with her sunny straw-blonde hair and contented smile, glowed with happiness. I couldn't blame her. She'd been married for around ten years and was finally having her first baby. "You're all just in time to have a good rest before dinner," Natalia said, coming up beside me and gently putting an arm about my shoulder. "It's so good to see you."

As far as I knew, Natalia was the only one with knowledge of what had transpired between Vance and me. Now, with her arm around me, she had to sense how embarrassed I was to be near her, even after so many years. Still, she never let on. With a smile, she said, "Elle, would you and Meredyth be dears and take Amaryllis upstairs? She looks rather fatigued."

"Of course," Estella said, and I nodded.

Since my parents weren't coming to Bar Harbor until the day before the wedding, still a week and a half away, I would be staying at Rockwood until they arrived. Ainsley had also insinuated long ago that she wanted me to spend a few nights with her at Truesdale. However, I was set on finding a way to avoid that. I didn't need the added stress of staying at the home of Lawry's parents, wondering when he would show up. No, it was better that I spend most of my time as possible at Rockwood. I needed to be there when Vance arrived.

The sooner everything was settled, the better.

Estella led us up the stairs to a bedchamber that was once Nathan's. It had a large, masculine-looking cherry four-poster bed and two leather wingback chairs facing the tall fieldstone fireplace, which was flanked by floor-to-ceiling windows. Above the mantelpiece was a massive portrait of Amaryllis wearing an old-fashioned cream-colored gown and standing beside a Grecian pedestal displaying a caged white bird.

"I didn't know you had such an affinity for birds," I teased.

Amaryllis grimaced and sank onto the bed. "It's a portrait of my mother...from when she was engaged to Bram Everstone. She does resemble me closely, though, doesn't she?" She sounded—and looked—positively wilted.

"Are you going to make it through dinner?" I pulled back the hunter green jacquard coverlet for her.

Amaryllis immediately lay down, half on top of the folded coverlet, half on top of the cream-colored sheets. She closed her eyes and let out a sigh as her head met the pillow. "Sleep...."

"Do you need your stays to be loosened?"

"They're already loose." Her eyes remained closed, and I wondered if she even knew she was participating in a conversation. "I'm so tired."

I spread the coverlet over her, even though she was still fully dressed and wearing her shoes.

"Amaryllis, are you expecting a baby, as well?" Estella stood beside the bed and fingered Amaryllis's dark hair, now strewn about the pillows.

Amaryllis sighed, but also allowed a small smile. "I am."

"Does Nathan know?" Estella leaned against the bed for a moment but immediately returned to a standing pose.

"Of course." Amaryllis propped herself up on her elbows, her eyes suddenly wide open. "Meredyth, why do you remain so concerned with Vance's whereabouts?"

I stared at her, a little dumbfounded. She and I used to dart around touchy subjects with each other, and I was a little shocked at how straight-forward she'd become.

"I'm going to marry him."

Estella gasped, "You're what?"

Amaryllis narrowed her eyes. "Isn't Vance already married?"

Estella stood stock-still. "Father received a letter Saturday—"

"Vance *was* married, but his wife has died." I turned and walked to the foot of the bed.

Amaryllis's brow was more deeply furrowed now than when I'd first asked about Vance on the front portico. "You're going to marry Vance…and not—"

"Yes, I'm going to marry Vance, and not *anyone* else." I grabbed one of the two thick carved bedposts, hoping neither she nor Estella would notice how I was shaking. There was no going back now. "I've known it for years."

Amaryllis laid her head down and draped her right elbow over her eyes. "Oh." She turned to her side, facing the dark, windowless side of the room.

Estella continued to stare at me. She was likely wondering how I'd become engaged to Vance before anyone in her family had even learned he was a widower.

"I want Nathan," Amaryllis mumbled into the pillow. "Estella, would you get Nathan for me?"

Estella pried my left hand free from the bedpost and guided me across the room. "Yes, I'll get Nathan for you—and we'll leave you to rest. I'm certain Natalia will understand if you would prefer to take your dinner in your room."

Amaryllis didn't answer, but I thought I heard her weeping.

Estella pulled me from the room and asked a servant to summon Nathan for Amaryllis. Then she tugged me down the hall toward her own bedchamber. Her belongings had already been put away, her empty luggage stacked just outside her door, waiting for the footmen to collect them.

Inside the room, Estella almost slammed the door and turned to me sharply. "*You're* the one Vance is planning to marry so quickly?" Her face still showed some of the shock I'd seen when I'd first revealed my plans.

"You knew?"

"We received a letter Saturday, saying he was engaged again, but he didn't say to whom. I hardly believed it of him...not after these last six months." When I didn't answer her right away, she began rearranging the pink and white pillows at the head of her tall four-poster bed.

"We...we've had somewhat of an understanding."

"I never knew we had so much in common, Meredyth." She picked up a pillow embroidered with delicate ribbon and studied it closely, as if it were the subject of our conversation. "In the last few months, I was under the impression you were falling in love with Lawry. You two have always been such close friends; it always surprised me that nothing ever developed between the two of you. But now I can understand why it didn't, if you've been in love with Vance and waiting for him to come home all this time."

It nearly suffocated me to hear her joyful exuberance in regard to my appalling plight. "Estella, it's really not as romantic as all that. Really, I—"

"You don't have to tell me, Meredyth. I know it's not romantic to have to wait for the person you love to want you. I know it's torture." She placed the pillow back on the bed and looked me in the eye. "It is heartening to see everything end well for you and Vance, even if you had to endure the anguish of knowing about his sham marriage to Giselle Gerard. I'm sure it was all a misunderstanding. Just think—God's hand must have been at work all along, making sure you would end up together at just the right—"

"Estella—"

"We're to be sisters now." She came up and looped her arm through mine. "You and Vance, married…I think I will enjoy this."

I let her words hang in the air and tried my best to take comfort in them. For most of my adult life, I'd looked forward to being part of the Everstone family—to have Natalia and Estella as my true sisters. Only now it seemed like a bad dream, keeping me hostage against my will.

All I really wanted was to wake up and run to Lawry.

"When will your wedding be?" she pressed on. "It will have to be small, since you'll be breaking the rules of propriety to be together. Will you be married in the chapel later this summer? It would almost be considered an elopement…like Nathan and Amaryllis, but even more romantic because of the chapel. I always thought I'd be married there, too, but perhaps I won't, after all."

Poor, lonely Estella. My heart went out to her because I knew just how she felt. She wanted Jayson Crawford Castleman just as much as, if not more than, I'd wanted Vance all those years. And while things were actually turning out rather tragically for me, all she saw was the hope of the situation.

I wasn't sure how her own waiting would turn out—not when Jay rejected her every time he came around. After being commissioned by the Boston Inland Mission Society to find any suitable woman to marry and take West with him, he'd ultimately given up the mission in Aberdeen, Washington, in order to escape the obligation to marry anyone so quickly—though he had tried to entice Amaryllis to go with him before she'd fallen in love with Nathan. "We should probably get ready for dinner," Estella said. "Your things are, I believe, in the blue room, just like always. That room practically belongs to you."

As I made my way to my bedchamber, I came upon Natalia. I really didn't feel up to conversing with her. Not when I knew what the discussion would entail.

"Meredyth," she whispered softly, one hand resting upon her round midsection. With the other hand, she touched my elbow. "How have you been?"

She had always been so incredibly gentle, just as I remembered her mother from when we were children. Natalia genuinely cared for me, even though she knew my greatest sin.

I didn't answer beyond the smile I forced my lips to produce.

"I had a letter from Vance the other day. Do you still think he is the best person for you to marry, after everything he's been through in the last six months?"

I nodded, still unable to respond verbally.

I let Natalia lead me by the arm along the hall and down the stairs toward the back of the mansion, to the conservatory. The looming room was vacant, moonlight streaming in through the glass.

I stopped in the middle of the conservatory, next to the elaborate stone water fountain. Natalia came up to stand beside me. I forced myself to concentrate upon the never-ending sound of the rushing water.

Natalia took my hand in hers, and I could see the expression upon her face in the moonlight. She was happy. "I always knew he would eventually do the right thing, and that we would someday be sisters."

"Nearly six years later," I finally said.

"I do believe he would have done this sooner, if it were needed." She grasped my other hand and now held them both. "I, too, wish he had—but you do understand, don't you, Meredyth? You were both very young at the time."

"Yes. Young and foolish."

"You do want this engagement, don't you—despite everything? I guess I've assumed it's what you've been waiting for, turning down all those other suitors over the years...."

"Yes, I want this," I lied. It sounded rather perfunctory. "It's what I've been waiting for."

"You're not in love with someone else, are you? I think it was Nicholette who mentioned you'd been spending much of your time with Lawry lately. She thought that perhaps he—"

"No, Lawry isn't in love," I lied.

"I'm relieved to hear it. Of course, if you had the choice, you would choose Lawry over Vance, if he were at all in love with you. He always did seem to bring out the best in you. But yes, if there's no romantic love there, it's really best not to force the matter."

The air whooshed out of my lungs with what sounded like a whimper, and my knees went weak. I took my hands from Natalia's grasp and leaned against the fountain, pressing my fingers to my temples. "Forgive me, but I think I'm coming down with an awful headache. You wouldn't mind terribly if I made my way up to my room and retired for the remainder of the evening, would you?"

"No, go ahead—you've had such a trying day full of travel and company." Natalia walked me out of the conservatory and down the hall to the elegant staircase of marble and wrought iron at the center of the great hall before joining the rest of her family.

With every hollow tap my slippers made as I slowly ascended the stairs, I could only hear Natalia's words repeat over and over inside my mind—"Of course, you would choose Lawry over Vance, if he were at all in love with you."

TWENTY-ONE

Vance Everstone

"Love is strong as death; jealously is cruel as the grave."
—Song of Solomon 8:6

It wasn't the first time I'd awakened thinking I was engaged to Lawry.

But really, something had to be done to make it the last. I didn't think I could bear the heartbreak of realizing it wasn't true—every single morning for the rest of my life.

It had been about a week since my arrival at Rockwood, and the days had been filled with all kinds of odd jobs delegated by both Daphne and Nicholette. They wanted as much help as they could get to make sure the gardens were pruned to perfection and the ribbons and vases for the outdoor luncheon reception were positioned just right for when the flowers would arrive.

Surprisingly, Nicholette and Daphne got along rather well throughout the extensive planning of their double wedding. Over the months, they had somehow developed an almost sisterly relationship. It made me a little uncomfortable to witness, as I'd never had a sisterly relationship with any woman. I could hardly understand how such a thing was possible—especially between those two.

Early one morning, I made my way out to the chapel Bram Everstone had had built years before in memory of his wife, Grace.

For years, it had been one of my favorite places to visit while at Rockwood, and I'd gone there every morning since arriving, in an effort to forget Lawry. However, this was the first time I'd made it there just as the dawn was breaking.

I walked through the morning mist in the direction of the chapel until it loomed before me. Tracing my fingertips over the rough mortar cementing the stones in place, I strolled around the outer perimeter of the building.

The Everstones were a strange lot, indeed. Bram Everstone could very well have made the chapel a palace of marble if he'd wanted to.

It really wasn't a proper building at all, having only three ivy-covered walls, two of which were filled with spear-shaped windows of leaded glass. And it had no roof whatsoever. Where a fourth wall ought to have been, there was a large opening that faced down to the cliffs and the never quiet, low rocky coast. There were rows and rows of rustic wooden pews on either side of the center aisle.

The aisle that would soon seal my fate.

I would become an Everstone within those three stone walls.

There had never been any kind of service held in the chapel, although it had been erected for the sole purpose of marrying off the five Everstone children. For years, I'd known that the chapel would be the setting where everything I'd done would be *fixed*. I just had not imagined I'd ever come to the point in my life that I'd wish it didn't have to be so.

I made my way down one of the side aisles, staring at the pulpit at the front of the shadow-darkened space. As I stood there, the early morning sun came streaming in through the eastward windows, illuminating the altar with long, bright streaks of light.

I leaned against the jagged wall between two windows.

I had to stop waking to that dream. Having to remind myself that I was engaged to Vance and not Lawry…it just hurt too much.

Would this same dream inflict me for months and years to come? Even after I married Vance? I hoped not. With all my heart.

When I reached the wooden altar, I knelt carefully on the gravel floor.

I'd become quite efficient at not thinking about Lawry—at least while awake—and the fact that he would soon arrive with the rest of the wedding party, and soon after have his heart broken. By me.

No one had heard from him, and I assumed that meant he was still busy taking care of his business in New York City, with plans to join us as quickly as he was able.

If only he would make it to Bar Harbor before Vance, perhaps then I could—

I pressed my fists to my brows with a sigh.

Then I could what? Un-tell Amaryllis, Estella, Natalia, and whoever else might secretly know of my foolish plans already? Could I take back what I'd said? Tell them I'd changed my mind and wanted to marry Lawry instead?

"God, guide me through these days. I need You so much. I need Your strength to help me through this. And…if You could… if You could send Lawry to me first, then perhaps I would dare to believe—"

"Mere'dy?"

I pushed to my feet and spun around. "Wynn?" My heart stammered at the sight of her. Was Lawry there and looking for me?

She ran down the center aisle, the hem of her short white dress clutched in both fists, and I met her halfway. I fell to my knees once again and took her in my arms.

She was crying, and they didn't seem like happy tears.

I pulled back to wipe the dark, wet strands of hair from her face. "Where's Lawry?"

"I don't know." She buried her head in my chest.

"Wynn? Where have you run off—?" Benta Allister whipped around the wall and stood as if paralyzed. "Miss Summercourt."

I stood, keeping hold of Wynn's warm little hand. "Where is Lawry? Why— And how are you here without him?"

"As far as I know, Mr. Hampton is still in New York City, ma'am."

"Why are you suddenly so formal, Bent—?"

"Unfortunately, your ever-faithful Lawry wasn't around when Wynn happened to need him the most." Vance strolled around the end of the chapel wall to stand directly next to Benta.

He was still dressed in his traveling clothes, minus his hat. The chocolate brown of his exquisite suit was perfectly set off by his black hair and black eyes. He looked even better than I remembered— except that he was smoking a cigarette. "I found her at The Olde Ram Boardinghouse a few days ago when I went there to check on her and her mother. And since then, she and Miss Allister here have been telling me the most fascinating stories. Many of them having much to do with you, Mere, and with Lawry Hampton." His voice was the same, deep and rough and always saying the wrong thing.

I stood there, holding Wynn's hand while I faced Vance Everstone's sardonic grin. Where was Lawry? And why had Wynn and Benta been at The Olde Ram?

"What, aren't you glad I'm home, Meredyth?" Vance took another drag from his cigarette and then, with a quick move, discarded the thing on the floor, making a point to crush it into the gravel with the toe of his fine Italian leather shoe. "I thought you'd be happy to see me."

Meeting his dark, intense gaze as he walked toward us, I lied to his face. "I am. But how were Benta and Wynn at The Olde Ram?"

"The Waterhouse Inn burnt down." Wynn spoke into my skirts, her words muffled. She still cowered behind me, still clutching my hand. "And he says he's my papa."

I turned around and caught Wynn's face in my hands. "But is everyone all right?"

"Everyone is perfectly fine, Meredyth." Vance took my hands from Wynn. "No one perished. The poor souls simply had to find new lodgings."

"And Mrs. Allister?"

"She's staying at The Olde Ram. Seems that the owner is her sister, or something of the sort. I don't know. I wasn't interested in details that didn't concern me." Vance pulled Wynn from my skirts, took her by the waist, and lifted her to stand on the pew beside him.

"Does Lawry know?"

Vance swiveled to face me with a scathing look. "Does it really matter? Miss Allister, will you please take Wynn away? Perhaps you would both enjoy exploring the rocks."

"Yes, sir." Benta scurried over from where she'd been standing.

Wynn reached out for me. "I don't want to go to see rocks. I want to stay with Mere'dy."

"Wynn, please," Vance drawled. "Don't call your soon-to-be-mother by such a name."

My mouth dropped open. He meant to keep her. And me.

"Wynn." I took her tiny hands in mine. "I will still be here when you're finished exploring the rocks. Van—Mr. Everstone—I mean, your father and I need to have a talk. I won't be going anywhere. Ever. I promise."

Once Benta led Wynn away, out of the stone structure and a good thirty feet out to the coast, Vance silently walked me to the front of the chapel, stopping in front of the pulpit. I turned to catch a glimpse of Wynn and Benta but instead found Vance's hard, cold eyes on me. He stepped closer, placed a hand on the pulpit behind me, and leaned in close. "Do I not deserve a better welcome than that from my Mere, who has been waiting so faithfully all these years?"

"You were married only weeks ago." Keeping my hands clutched together between us, I fought the urge to run. Knowing Vance, he would make a game of it—and I couldn't stand such games. Not with him.

He gave me a wicked, sneering smile. "And I look forward to being married again. This time to you."

This was not the same Vance Everstone I'd associated with all those years before—back when I used to beg him to consider marrying me.

With his other hand, he reached up to caress my neck, sending cold shivers down my spine.

I closed my eyes, but he didn't kiss me, so I opened them again. He stood close, only inches away, staring down at me. But there was something behind the look in his eyes that told me he was testing me.

I couldn't look away, or he would know—unless he already did. Would he be able to tell I no longer wanted him as I had all those years ago? That would not do. If he suspected anything of the love between Lawry and me, he would make our lives miserable. If Vance found out that Lawry loved me, he would surely flaunt me in his face.

Growing up, there had always been some sort of twisted competition between them, involving almost anything—largely having to do with Nathan. The brother and the best friend. I never understood why they couldn't all three be friends together.

I studied Vance's eyes, searching deeper. There was hunger and scorn, as well as a distinct hardness that told me he didn't quite believe me yet. But he would. No matter what Benta and Wynn might have said regarding Lawry and me.

Placing my hands against his chest, I slid my fingers up the lapels of his jacket. I tried to think back to how I'd felt all those times when I'd yearned for him—when I'd wanted him more than anything. But they were gone. All I had now were empty gestures, acted out in hopes of perfecting a lie.

"You're going to marry me." His words came out without a hitch.

Reaching up, I cradled his face in my hands. I knew I would have to recall his look of disdain at the mention of Lawry. It was the only thing that would be able to keep me focused on the task at hand.

I would make him want me again, trust me again. It would be a fine line I would need to balance, but what better way to revert all my thoughts and attentions away from Lawry than to make Vance Everstone fall in love with me?

"Finally." I lifted to my toes, and he met me halfway, letting me kiss him for the first time since that day in the cave. Vance pressed me against the pulpit, deepening the kiss. I clawed at the lapels of his jacket, clutching him to me, forcing myself to continue, despite the foreign taste of tobacco on his lips.

And forcing myself not to compare him to Lawry...which was when I realized I'd been counting on Vance to make me forget. And that it hadn't worked. Kissing Vance now felt like kissing one of my brothers.

Vance rested his hands chastely at my waist as I took a tiny step away. He held on, and I kept my hands on his chest. I didn't know what else to do with them.

"While in Boston, I went to Summerton, expecting to find you still there with your parents. I've already asked your father for your hand."

"What did he say?"

He cocked a curious glance my way. "His answer was rather cryptic. He said, 'May the best man win her heart.'" Vance grabbed my chin.

"Well, that was silly of him. I'm sure he's known I've been waiting for you all these years. Mother did."

"Have you, indeed? *All* these years?" He continued to hold my chin, forcing me to look him in the eyes.

I was already resolved. "I'm here now, aren't I?"

"Yes. Yes, you are." He let go of me, but it was almost as if he wanted to see how easily I would let go of him.

So I held on.

"Something about being forced to marry Giselle made me realize how much I'd always looked forward to someday coming home to you."

"Looked forward—to me?" I was shocked...and disgusted with myself. "You didn't want Giselle at all?"

"Oh, she was young and beautiful, and I knew her quite well for a little while. But she tricked me. She'd found herself in the family way, and since she couldn't marry the man who'd created the problem in the first place, she chose to compromise me. Quite thoroughly, I might add."

"Giselle compromised *you?*" I could hardly fathom it. Vance Everstone, caught in the clutches of a devising woman. I fought back a smile at the thought of such irony. "But she couldn't have been completely to blame."

"Oh, but she was. Nothing really happened at all, but that wasn't what her father thought. He believed each and every one of her outrageous lies."

"What happened to her?"

"She had some pains in her stomach. They thought it was something to do with the child she carried, but too late they discovered it was actually appendicitis."

"We all thought you'd compromised her." I slid my hand up his chest to his collar, and something about his demeanor changed. He seemed almost sorry.

"Don't you think I might have learned my lesson over the years? Sure, I wanted my freedom, and I wanted to explore Europe, but

I'm not so debased as to have seduced every young maiden I came across in France."

"Why didn't you write to me all that time? You wrote to Olivia Rosselet."

"Ah, yes. Wynn's mother. Lawry told you about all that, did he?"

"Ainsley and I have been volunteering at a girls' school this year. Wynn was a student, near the end."

"And who, may I ask, was paying her tuition to attend this school?"

"Law—"

"Lawry Hampton?" Vance roared the name as he turned away from me and paced down the center aisle. "He probably thinks I purposefully left that girl on the streets. Is that what you thought, as well?" His fingers tunneled through his thick hair, as if he were actually concerned for Wynn. "That I'd let her mother die and forgotten all about my responsibility to her? I wouldn't have let her run the streets if I'd known—"

"How did you not know?"

"I'd set up everything through one of my father's attorneys. All these years, he's been making sure Olivia and Wynn had a roof over their heads and enough money to live on besides. I guess when he learned she was dead, he decided to pocket the cash and go on acting as if he were delivering my letters."

"Why did you keep writing to her and never to me—even secretly?"

He measured me with his eyes. "Olivia didn't have anything. I stole everything from her when I—" Vance sat in the second row pew. "You didn't lose everything because of me. Not the way Olivia did."

I begged to differ, but I knew he was right. At least on some level.

"Why didn't you marry her?"

"I was still at university. I couldn't forget Harvard. No matter how she would have benefitted from my noble actions, I couldn't make myself do it." Vance placed his hands upon the pew in front of him and rested his forehead against his long, lean fingers. "And then the very next summer, right after Wynn was born, I did the same thing to you."

I finally moved away from the pulpit. I seated myself sideways in the front pew, directly before Vance, with my elbow draped over the edge, my fingers grazing his.

"Even when I knew I didn't need to marry you, I still felt that I ought to, eventually. It was already too late for me to do the correct thing in regard to Olivia, but I thought that if I could make it up to you, I would feel better…." He glanced up at me, our faces only inches apart.

"Did she know about me?"

"Yes. She knew I was planning to marry you. And why."

"Didn't she hate you because of it?"

"She already hated me a long time before she knew I was set on marrying you. And she probably hated me all the more if she ever got my letter explaining that I'd been forced to marry Giselle. But from what the lady at the boardinghouse says, Olivia was already dead by the time I would have sent it."

"Yes, I believe she passed away right after Christmas." I rested my forehead in the crook of my elbow, sure that if Vance saw my eyes, he'd be able to tell I no longer wanted him.

"Did you know Lawry planned to adopt the brat right out from under my nose?" Vance scoffed. "What does he want with a daughter, anyway?"

After a few moments, I forced myself to lift my face to his. "I don't know. But I doubt he thought you'd want her. How would you ever explain her to your family? Do you think they will accept—?"

"They will."

"I didn't know you wanted children so badly." I hoped to God that he wouldn't want any *more* children than Wynn, that I wouldn't have the added torture of giving myself so fully to him every night—

"Sure, I want lots of children. I want *your* children. And I want to be married by the end of the summer, right here in this chapel."

"That sounds lovely." I was barely able to say those three words; it was a wonder he even heard them. I wanted to bury my head in my arm again and let my tears fall freely.

"Let's go tell everyone our news, then." Vance stood and offered me his hand. He seemed to have calmed down. Perhaps I'd done a good enough job convincing him I truly wanted him.

He took my hand, and I let him pull me to my feet. "We really ought to wait until after the wedding is finished. Garrett's planning to propose to Ainsley when he arrives, and Father told me he plans to announce their engagement at the reception on Friday. It would be best if we announced ours then, as well."

"Garrett and Ainsley Hampton, huh?" He gave me the handsome, crooked smile that reminded me of the Vance I'd once known. "Did you have any part in that?"

I tried to smile back, but I couldn't produce anything more than a half grimace. "Perhaps."

"I suppose I can wait a few more days. Who knows? Perhaps in that time, it won't seem so scandalous that I'm marrying again, or that I have a daughter...."

I let the rest of his words drift in one ear and out the other. They didn't really matter. Not much did anymore, except that I would somehow have Wynn when all was said and done. But I wasn't sure I could even be truly happy about being her mother.

Not when I knew how much pain it would cause Lawry to lose both of us.

TWENTY-TWO

Burning

"One does not love a place the less for having suffered in it, unless it has been all suffering, nothing but suffering."
—Jane Austen, *Persuasion*

After lunch, the large group staying at Rockwood and the neighboring cottages in preparation for the wedding remained on the veranda and lawn for hours on end, playing or watching lawn tennis, then relaxing and taking in the cool, salty air of the sea breeze. For the entire afternoon, I'd wanted nothing more than to go up to the nursery to see Wynn, but I constantly found Vance's eyes on me. He watched me unendingly, and I knew I wasn't allowed to see her.

In an effort to escape his penetrating gaze, I walked to the edge of the grass where the rocks began protruding from the earth.

I tried not to think—which was useless.

It was a strange trap Wynn and I were caught in. We were to be family—mother and daughter—but would Vance ever allow us to become as close as we had been in those weeks I'd visited her with Lawry at The Waterhouse Inn?

It hurt to think that inn was no more. The attic where Wynn and I had hidden from Lawry so many times was gone forever. I didn't know why we'd called the game we kept playing all those weeks "hide-and-seek." It was a misnomer, since Wynn and I always found ourselves in that same dormer behind the trunks, and Lawry knew just where to find us, every time.

Especially that last time. Yes, that day, a mere week and a half ago, I'd felt found, indeed.

Then, there was the kitchen where I'd heard Lawry pray… where I'd felt nearer to God just by his sitting next to me, holding my hand. And, of course, there was the day of Lawry's birthday party—my last memories of how true happiness felt.

"Lawry sent me a package from New York."

I snapped my attention from the lull of ocean currents to Ainsley, who was standing beside me, holding out an envelope. "But I think this is the real reason he thought to send anything. It's a letter for you."

I stared at the thickly packed parchment envelope. The wax seal barely kept it closed.

"Don't you want it?"

I reached out, but I didn't touch it. Yes, I wanted it. But could I endure reading it?

I quickly scanned the yard for Vance. He was nowhere in sight, and before I realized what I was doing, I clutched the envelope to my chest and started walking to the house.

I hastened to the blue bedchamber, where I knew I was safe from Vance. He could control me all he wanted everywhere else in the world, but he wouldn't have this room—at least for now.

I broke the seal and pulled out a pile of papers. I still wasn't certain if it would be wise to read them. But once they were in hand, I was unable to keep my fingers from unfolding the sheets of paper, bending them back, smoothing them out.

No, reading them wouldn't be wise. I could tell that much. There was already some kind of hope growing in my heart—a hope that perhaps Lawry had written something that would make everything from the last weeks go away. As impossible as it seemed.

Lowering myself to the edge of the bed, I started to read.

My dearest, loveliest Meredyth,

I have something important to give to you, though the proper thing is to wait until Daphne's wedding is completed and everyone is finished congratulating the two most recently wed couples before turning their attention to the next couple eager to make their vows. I don't know how I'll be able to wait that long. I returned to Boston after you left to speak with your father, obtaining his blessing—

I wanted to rip the letter to shreds. For as much as his words thrilled me, there was a dark and overwhelming oppression covering my heart. Despite what I'd hoped earlier that morning, I knew without a doubt that there was nothing Lawry could say in his letter that could ever free me from my destiny of being bound to Vance Everstone.

I forced myself to read on.

You're all I've truly wanted for as long as I can remember. Ever since…do you remember when I finally came home for good from Dartmouth? You'd just graduated finishing school and were about to turn eighteen and make your debut— which was the last thing you wanted to do. You told me so yourself. You wondered why we couldn't all just go on as we'd always done instead of making spectacles of ourselves like puffed-up nincompoops trying to impress all the people who didn't care one lick about who we truly were on the inside. That was exactly what you said. I remember, because that was the moment I realized I was in love with you—my dearest of friends—and I've loved you every single day since.

Which reminds me…have you read all of Vance's letters to Olivia yet? I doubt it; but please, for me and for Wynn, I want you to—

I couldn't read any more. The tears in my eyes prevented me from even seeing the paper in my hands, let alone the now-blurry words upon the pages. There were still two more sheets full of Lawry's elegant handwriting, but I folded them together tightly and stuffed them back inside the envelope.

Lawry was right; I'd never read any of the other letters Vance had written to Wynn's mother, and I'd left them hidden in my room in Boston on purpose. I still didn't see why I needed to read them—it would only add to my torture. Did I not already have enough reasons to hate my life?

I stood and held the stuffed envelope to my chest, trying to decide what to do with Lawry's letter. It wouldn't do to keep it. There was no point in torturing myself with its presence for months and years to come. I had to get rid of it, or it would taunt me for the rest of my life.

Without a second thought, I tossed it into the hearth and crossed the room to gather the matches from my bedside table. After retrieving them, I turned and stopped at the center of the room, stunned by how white the envelope seemed against the dingy backdrop of the dark and dirty hearth, shining bright like hope. Such hope—even from Lawry Hampton—was something I couldn't afford. And it needed to be burned and forgotten. How fitting that it should take place right there in the hearth of the blue bedchamber.

I grabbed Lawry's handkerchief and the ancient French book I'd brought with me to Rockwood, then walked to the fireplace, my eyes focused on the old iron grates and the fire-scorched bricks. There was something inside me that matched the filthy, ash-covered hearth—a darkness in my soul that was forever fighting to have its way.

And this was it. The darkness would win. Because it was what I deserved.

I knelt before the hearth and looked once more at the envelope, marveling at the lovely script Lawry had used to write out my name, and the time he'd spent putting his heart down on paper.

I covered the envelope with Lawry's handkerchief, then opened the book and set it on top, pages down. I stared at the pile of mementos. I might as well have been burning my own heart.

I lit the match and watched for a second as the flame burned the tiny wooden stick. Then I reached it into the hearth and held the fire to a corner of the envelope. I quickly pulled it back to blow it out before it had a chance to burn me, as well. And then I watched the thick envelope filled with Lawry's love for me slowly burn.

Then the handkerchief.

Then the pages of the book.

I flicked the charred match into the hearth as the flames grew, as they consumed everything.

"Good-bye, Lawry." That was when I realized my tears had stopped. I hadn't cried since kneeling on that familiar hearth and hardening my heart.

I continued to sit there when the fire died away, staring dry-eyed at the empty hearth—empty, save for the ashes I'd created.

TWENTY-THREE

Lawry

"Absence diminishes mediocre passions and increases great ones, as the wind extinguishes candles and fans fires."
—François de la Rochefoucauld

Later that evening, after dinner, I went up to the nursery, resolved to find Wynn and Benta.

A large room situated on the top floor of the east wing of Rockwood, the nursery hadn't been in use for over a decade—ever since Mrs. Everstone died in the shipwreck and Estella, Will, and Vance were shipped off to boarding school. It was around the same time that Natalia had married Dr. George Livingston and Nathan had begun at Dartmouth with Lawry.

There had been no babies in all the years since.

Once I reached the third floor, I stood outside the door a moment before knocking. I was going against Vance's wishes in seeing Wynn, but I didn't care. Lawry could arrive at any moment, and I needed to explain some things before he did.

I stuffed my irrational anxiety down into the same place where I'd stuffed my every thought of Lawry and gently knocked on the door. "Wynn? Benta?"

The door opened. Benta held it wide for me to enter. "Miss Summercourt," she whispered. "I didn't think we were allowed to—"

"Never mind what Mr. Everstone said." I entered the high-ceilinged room and was immediately reminded of the attic at the inn—the attic that held so many torturous memories. Instead of dormers, though, there were two round turret towers built onto the corners of the room facing the ocean, just as there were two larger ones built onto the attic over the main part of the house.

I turned to Benta once more. "You are my friends. Mr. Everstone has no right to tell us we aren't to see each other."

"But Miss Summercourt—"

"Where's Wynn?" It didn't surprise me that Benta insisted upon using my formal name, even when we were alone. She never had taken to heart my request that she call me Meredyth.

"She's sleeping on the window seat of that tower, passed out from crying for hours on end." She jerked her thumb toward the far corner of the room. "The poor little thing is so worn out and distraught, mostly about not being able to see you and wondering where Law—Mr. Hampton is. But her seeing Mr. Everstone and what he says to her hasn't helped none."

"Do you know what he's said to her?" I touched Benta's shoulder and led her to the corner of the room farthest from where Wynn slept.

"He said he was her father—and I don't doubt it, seeing them together. They look just the same." Benta stood before me, wringing her hands. "He also said he was going to marry you."

I closed my eyes. How would I ever explain?

"It's true." I opened my eyes and took Benta's hands in mine. "I was never officially engaged to him, but there was a mutual understanding. However, this past spring, Mr. Everstone was married… only to become a widower soon after."

Her eyes were downcast.

"Benta, look at me." I shook her hands, and she looked up, meeting my gaze. I realized it was the first time I was daring to speak of such things to anyone—and it struck me as odd that my confidante was Benta Allister. "I didn't know his wife had died. I thought I was free."

She just stood there, still awkwardly letting me hold her hands. "I'm sorry," she whispered.

Tears sprang to my eyes. "Your aunt is staying with her sister at The Olde Ram, right? What will she do?"

"There's nothing left of The Waterhouse Inn but charred walls of brick, and she doesn't want to rebuild. She saw this arrangement—my caring for Wynn, at Mr. Everstone's request—as an answer to her prayers, since things aren't working out exactly the way Law—I mean, Mr. Hampton thought."

"You can call him Lawry with me, Benta. And you can call me Meredyth, as well. Please. At least when no one else is around. Lawry didn't know about the fire when you left Boston, did he?"

"I wanted to send a telegram, Miss Summercourt—anything—but Mr. Everstone came to the boardinghouse, looking for Wynn and her mum, within an hour of when we walked in the door. He completely took over, and no one ever had the chance to even try to notify Lawry—not that we had a way. All we knew was that he was in New York, and that he would find out soon enough when he returned and found the inn burnt to the ground. There really wasn't anything he could do, anyway. Not with Mr. Everstone's claim to Wynn and his offering me the job."

"Mere'dy! You come!"

Benta and I both turned sharply at the high-pitched squeal.

I hardly took one step before Wynn ran to me, tears spilling down her cheeks, and buried her face against my thigh, clutching my skirts. I fell to my knees and wrapped my arms around her narrow shoulders. The sound of her breathless sobs against my neck broke my heart.

"I want Lawry."

I stood and swiveled to face Benta again. "Benta, you can have the rest of the night off—do whatever you want. Just don't let Mr.

Everstone see you without Wynn. I'm taking her to my room for the remainder of the evening."

⌒

Wynn was asleep again, this time in my bed. After I'd snuck her to my room, she'd refused to say anything more than what she'd already said in the nursery. *"I want Lawry."*

And every time she did, it only echoed every beat of my heart.

I had opened the windows in my bedchamber to let in the salty evening breeze, and also so I would hear if Lawry happened to arrive. I could hear the voices of the Everstone family on the veranda below, enjoying the cool night air.

For a good hour, I tried to sleep—something that had become somewhat of an escape for me over the past week. But with Wynn lying next to me, it was impossible. I lay there in my nightgown, staring at the shadows of the chandelier cast by moonlight, thinking of one thing:

The heart is deceitful above all things, and desperately wicked: who can know it? I the LORD search the heart...to give every man according to his ways, and according to the fruit of his doings.

Those words were to be my constant reminder.

I wanted mercy. And I wanted freedom. But how?

Through the open windows, I heard the hoofbeats of an approaching horse. Then some of the men called out Lawry's name.

I swung my legs over the edge of the bed and scrambled across the room. I grabbed my wrap off the chair and pulled it on before nearing one window from the side. In the darkness of my bedchamber, I would be unnoticed from below, but I wanted to be sure.

I peeked through the lace curtains into the hazy dusk and saw Lawry quickly dismount from his horse. I watched in awe as his tall, muscular frame stomped up the gravel path to the veranda. My heart thundered in my chest at the sight of him—he seemed so angry! Did he already know?

I wrung my hair nervously in my hands. Had one of the servants heard and spread the rumor of my engagement all the way to Truesdale already?

Lawry wasn't looking at the house. His attention was focused upon one thing: Vance Everstone, who stood at the convergence of the stone steps, the gravel path, and the grass.

They were directly below me, and I heard Vance mutter, "Well, well, well. If it isn't Lawry Hampton."

Instead of answering Vance as he drew closer, Lawry wound up his right arm and slammed his fist into Vance's face.

"What the—?" Vance staggered, holding his nose.

"That was for Wynn and Olivia," Lawry growled as he stepped forward again, towering over Vance, and reared to punch him yet again. "And this one is for—"

"Lawry! What are you doing?" Will came to stand between them, holding Lawry back from Vance, who had come to his senses enough to want to fight back. "Vance, stop! What's the meaning of this?"

By then, all the men had gathered around them, as had Natalia and Estella.

Nathan stepped in to restrain Vance, who fought against his hold. "He's the one who—"

"Where's Meredyth?" I heard Lawry's strained voice ask in the same instance. "Is she here?" He glanced at the faces of the crowd.

Natalia answered, "She's upstairs."

Lawry broke free from Will's hold and headed through the crowd for the door leading into the house.

I wheeled around to find Wynn still sound asleep, despite the ruckus outside. I didn't know what I was doing as I crossed the room and flung the door open. I raced down the hall toward the stairs as if something were pushing me—or pulling me. All I could think of was seeing Lawry again.

Not that I knew what I would say to him.

When I reached the foot of the stairs in the dimly lit great hall, I saw him coming. The determination in his eyes took my breath away. He didn't appear to be angry anymore. He also didn't act as if he were going to stop.

And he didn't stop until his arms were around me and his lips were on mine, one hand possessively pressed against the small of my back, the other cradling the nape of my neck.

When the kiss ended, my tears began. "Lawry...."

"Meredyth." He grabbed my hand and pulled me down the hall to one of the parlors. The door was ajar, and a lamp was lit inside, but the room was empty. Once he slid the door closed behind us, he reached into his breast pocket and dropped to his knee.

"You can't—"

"Will you marry me?" He held up his aunt Claudine's square-cut diamond ring. In the following silence, his beautiful blue eyes kept asking, confident of my answer. And why wouldn't he be?

The pocket door opened. "You cannot be serious."

I turned at the sound of Vance's sneering voice. He stood just inside the room. "Mere can't marry both of us, and she's already agreed—"

"Oh!" Amaryllis was right behind Vance, her bright eyes wide with shock. She quickly slammed the massive pocket door closed with a loud clap, obviously intent on keeping anyone else from following Vance inside.

"You're already married," Lawry grumbled at Vance, though his eyes remained focused on me.

"Oh, have you not heard?" Vance stepped closer. I could see that his nose was swollen and that he had bruises already forming around both eyes. "I've recently had the good fortune of being widowed."

Lawry's anger was back—only it was somewhat different now. His even eyebrows pushed together into a line, and his gaze was directed to the floor for a moment before darting back to me. "And what does he mean by saying you've already agreed?" He still knelt before me, the impressive ring now positioned on the tip of his pointer finger as his hand rested upon his knee.

I stood stone still. I couldn't move. The questions, the confusion on Lawry's face, paralyzed me. My tears were the only thing moving freely.

"For Pete's sake, Lawry, get off the floor."

"What does he mean, Meredyth?"

"It means, Lawry, that you have absolutely no right to ask Meredyth to marry you, because she's already engaged to me." Vance pulled at one of the ruffles of my wrap. Chills swept down my back at the intimate touch. "She's mine."

Lawry stood to his feet. "Is this true?" His face suddenly looked haggard, his eyebrows low over his blue eyes. They were filled with even more questions, only it seemed he couldn't find the resolve to voice them.

"I—" There was nothing I could say. Nothing made any sense.

"Tell him, Meredyth," Vance baited me. "Tell him how you've been begging me to marry you for years, how you've wanted me all this time. How you've always been mine for the asking."

I'd known these mocking taunts would come, but somehow, hearing them, while watching Vance's arrogant face, was more than I could bear.

Yet there was nothing I could do but agree. "I'm going to marry Vance."

Lawry didn't seem to have anything to say to that. He stared at me as if unable to comprehend my words. And then he looked as if he'd been struck in the stomach.

Vance grabbed my arm and walked me to the other side of the room, toward the door that led out to the garden.

"Meredyth." Lawry found his voice as we were walking away.

I wrenched my elbow from Vance's grip and twisted around, my heart beating wildly in my chest. "Lawry, there's nothing I can—"

"So, I'll be going back to Washington alone," Lawry interrupted, "without Wynn...and without you?"

Vance came up behind me and rested his arm over my shoulders. "And what right would you have to take my daughter to Washington?" He was enjoying this entirely too much. Oh, how would I survive being married to such a vile man?

"Wynn belongs with Lawry, Vance. She adores him." I tried to wriggle free from his hold, but he moved his arm from my shoulders to grasp my waist, turning me to face him.

"Come on, Mere. Admit it—you adore him, too. I can see it in your eyes. But you're still choosing me. You and Wynn belong with me." Vance tightened his grip on my waist. There was no escaping him, even if I thought I had a chance. "Consider dear Wynn Rosselet an early wedding present. A happy family of three from the start."

"You're—you're just going to let him win?" Lawry questioned. "When all he's done is wrong you, and when I've— When you—"

"That about sums it up." Vance swiveled around, making certain to keep me from facing Lawry again. "Now, Lawry, if you wouldn't mind giving us some time alone, I'd like to have a word with my fiancée in private."

Vance ushered me forcefully across the room, opened the sturdy wood door, and urged me outside, slamming the door behind us.

Once outside, Vance turned and pushed me back against the closed door. His long fingers grasped my jaw, forcing me to look him in the eyes. "I believe that you and I need to take a little walk."

"I don't think I'm dressed appropriately for a—"

"Come on, Mere. If everyone knew what we've already done together, it would hardly matter what you were wearing while merely *speaking* with me."

He propelled me past the high hedges and flower beds next to the house and around to where the lawn met the rocks along the shore. The veranda was deserted, but the lanterns still blazed. I didn't know where everyone could have gone, only that Amaryllis must have made it clear to them that Lawry, Vance, and I needed some privacy to work things out between us.

Vance led me to a stone bench at the edge of the grass and sat me down but didn't join me.

The tears I'd cried earlier in front of Lawry had dried. They'd stopped the moment Vance had grabbed my arm and pulled me away.

"Do you want to tell me what that was all about?" Thankfully, the sound of the waves lapping the rocks diminished the perceived volume of his heated tone. "Why is Lawry Hampton charging in here like a bull, taking all of his aggression out on me?"

"I don't know why he felt the need to box you—"

"And what about the need to propose marriage to you the first moment he saw you? Do you know anything about that?" Vance paced before me, his nostrils flaring as he huffed out the words. "Have you been encouraging his affections in my absence?"

"In fact, Vance, I've fought rather tirelessly against him all spring, but it hardly mattered. Not when it came to Lawry's determination to...." Trying desperately to keep a steady composure, I held the ruffled white collar of my wrap to my neck.

"Yes, it's rather obvious that Lawry's still carrying his heart on his sleeve for you, even after all these years. I would have expected him to give up on you by now, being as he's been in Washington for so many years. Unless...." Vance circled around the bench to face me. "I never would have thought it of straightlaced Lawry. How far did he get?"

I jumped to my feet. "He would never—"

"No, I suppose he wouldn't, would he? Not someone like Lawry Hampton. But he did something, I'm guessing, or you wouldn't be so torn up about that disastrous proposal I just witnessed."

"Lawry is the best friend I've ever had." I forced Vance to look me in the eye. "Why do you hate him so?"

Vance shook his fists at the star-studded sky and grumbled, "Because he's always done everything right."

He turned quickly and took me by the shoulders. His grasp was strong, his fingers digging into the backs of my arms, as he jerked me forward. As he held me tight against his chest, the sharp scent of the tobacco clinging to his jacket overwhelmed my senses.

"But he can't take you from me now. It's too late. I won't let him." His words created a sudden and unmistakable void within me, and I struggled against his hold. But he wouldn't let me go.

His lips moved against my ear as he whispered, "He can't have you. You have a place, and it's with me. It's the only way—"

"I know." It seemed like a strange thing to say—but appropriate. I had no choice. I was going to be Vance's wife and not Lawry's. I had to accept it. I lifted my arms from my sides and smoothed my hands around to his back. Then I pressed my face to his neck and wept. "I know."

TWENTY-FOUR

The Hunt

"*Beware the fury of a patient man.*"
—John Dryden, *Absalom and Achitophel*

The next morning, Nicholette stood at the top of the steps of the wide front portico of Rockwood alongside her fiancé, Will Everstone, and clapped her hands in an effort to gain the attention of the attendants of her wedding party. We were all gathered in the yard, facing the ocean, awaiting our orders. However, the small group continued to talk excitedly, not really paying any mind to Nicholette.

Will cleared his throat and bellowed in his deep voice, "Nicholette is ready to speak her mind. Now, if you would kindly give her your undivided attention."

I watched as Nicholette breathed in and glared at Will. But then, the quick glance quickly changed to something that looked more like playful encouragement. Will gave her that deceptively handsome Everstone smile...and seemed to be immediately forgiven.

"Yes, attention, everyone," Nicholette finally said. "It's time for the surprise that Will and I—as well as Roderick and Daphne—have been coordinating very diligently over the last few days, perfecting just for you. It's a scavenger hunt."

I'd tucked myself between Vance and Amaryllis behind the wide, gnarly trunk of a century-old oak tree close to the front porch. I wasn't sure where Lawry was. I purposefully didn't search for him. I hadn't seen him since the night before, but I knew he had to be there. He was part of the wedding party, after all.

Daphne stepped out the front door of Rockwood to join Will and Nicholette. She carried two small baskets—one black and one white—and dragged Captain Parker with her other hand. "We have the names."

"Great." Nicholette didn't waste any time in reaching for the black basket. "I'll pull the gentlemen's names from this basket, and it will be their job to choose a name from the white basket. Gentlemen, whomever you choose, she will be your partner for the scavenger hunt, as well as the lady you will escort down the aisle at the ceremony tomorrow."

My stomach roiled. I still hadn't seen Lawry anywhere. Nathan stood next to Amaryllis, and there was Vance, of course, and the three unknown gentlemen of the wedding party, whom I'd met the day before. For the life of me, I couldn't remember a single one of their names.

Nicholette rustled her fingers through the six names in the basket and pulled out a tightly folded piece of paper. Her eyes glanced over the name, and she smiled. "Lawry Hampton will be the first to choose his partner." No one moved. Was Lawry even there? "Lawry, come up and make your choice."

I peeked around the tree and immediately felt Vance grip my arm, not allowing me to move any farther away from him. I didn't see Lawry until he stood next to his sister at the top of the steps. She held the white basket before him.

He looked tired and miserable, as if he would rather have been anywhere else in the world than standing there, his broken heart on display for all his friends to see.

I moved closer to Vance so that the tree blocked my view of Lawry.

There were six names in the white basket. What were the chances of his picking mine?

"Mere—" Lawry's voice cracked. After the minutest of pauses, he continued with more fortitude, speaking rather quickly, albeit with absolutely no excitement at all. "Meredyth Summercourt."

Was this some kind of joke? Surely, everyone there knew we did not wish to speak to each other, let alone form any kind of alliance for a scavenger hunt, and then to have to walk down the aisle together at the wedding.

"Meredyth, where are you?" Daphne called out. "Come up here and join Lawry."

I pulled away from Vance's grasp—and he had to let go. I circled around the tree, staring at the ground and then at the steps as I slowly made my way to Lawry's side. Once I faced the small gathering, I paid special attention to both Vance and Amaryllis, whom I could see still standing on opposite sides of the large tree.

Amaryllis, of course, seemed concerned—and Vance looked like he wanted to kill someone. But what was I to do? Tell Daphne I couldn't partner with her brother because he was in love with me, and I had broken his heart into a million pieces the night before?

Will pulled a stack of folded papers from his breast pocket and handed one to me. "Don't look at this yet. No cheating."

I wished, for about the hundredth time, that everything between Lawry, Vance, and me had not culminated right before the wedding of no escape.

"You can wait over there." Will pointed to a bench at the end of the long limestone portico.

I followed Lawry, and we both sat. I watched as Nathan came up the steps, and then Amaryllis. I didn't pay heed to what was going on with the rest of our friends after that. My thoughts were clogged in my mind, and my eyes were focused on one thing: the folded paper in my hand. It reminded me of the paper tucked inside the pocket of my dress. Vance's letter.

I wouldn't allow myself to think of Lawry silently sitting a few feet away from me. There was an insurmountable wall between us now. Even if I couldn't see it, I could feel it. It reached to the heavens, and there was no getting around it.

Even after Nathan and Amaryllis and all the rest of the couples were situated on the porch, no one came near us. They had to know what kind of torture it was for us to be paired together. Even if the only ones who knew I planned to marry Vance were Estella, Natalia, Amaryllis, and Lawry, everyone else knew Lawry had been racing to find me the moment he'd arrived. And even if no one had seen him kiss me—or propose—everybody knew enough.

Out of the corner of my eye, I could see Lawry sitting beside me with his elbows resting on his knees, his hands clutched tightly together between them.

Vance stood at the other end of the veranda next to one of Lawry's beautiful blonde cousins who were also part of the wedding party, but he stared at me. I jerked my gaze back to the piece of paper in my hand.

From the yard, Nicholette announced, "Go ahead and look at your clues now. And when you find your last clue, meet back here, and we will read them all together."

I unfolded the clue and began reading aloud. "Team One, your first clue of three: Look near a place made of stones, and there you might find some peace for your groans." I refolded the paper, already knowing the answer to the simple riddle. "The chapel."

I stood and moved toward the steps. Everyone else had already dispersed to find the answer to their first clue. Since we were alone again, I dared a glance at Lawry.

He hadn't followed me but had remained seated, still with his elbows resting on his knees, only now his head was lowered as he raked his fingers through his sandy brown hair. I really didn't know why I'd expected him to follow me anywhere. Not after—

He straightened and stood. "The evangelist Charles Spurgeon once said, 'Groans that words cannot express are often prayers that God cannot refuse.'"

I quickly took the steps down to the grass, leaving Lawry on the portico. This time, he followed, although I wished more than anything to simply give up the game, go to my room, and hide until the wedding.

Fortunately, the end of the torturous week was near—even if it meant the beginning of the rest of my life...without Lawry.

I walked across the lawn to where the rocks began to protrude out of the grass, and I kept going until they completely took over and the lawn disappeared. There was a good twenty feet of dark brown and rust-red boulders making up the outline of the coast where the chapel was nestled at the edge of the pine tree forest.

I didn't know how I was supposed to find a clue hidden somewhere in the rugged stone walls, not when I didn't want to go inside ever again.

Lawry came to stand beside me. As if he didn't hate me. "Are you familiar with the verse in Romans that says, '*For we know not what we should pray for as we ought: but the Spirit itself maketh intercession for us with groanings which cannot be uttered*'? That's what Charles Spurgeon was referring to."

"I don't recall ever reading that." I took a few steps closer to the chapel. "But it makes sense."

Lawry followed, right beside me.

"Do you think God wants to punish you?" he asked over the sound of the crashing waves.

I turned sharply at his words. His blue gaze held mine for just a moment before I continued to scan the rocks for our clue, ignoring his question. "I think I see it." I pointed to a white jar positioned on one of the small ledges about twenty feet below—the very ledges I used to sit upon with Lawry for hours on end when we were younger.

"Don't worry. I'll get it for you." His kindness to me was almost unbearable. Why wasn't he angry with me? Why didn't he hate me?

I watched as he climbed down the uneven coast. He'd always been quick on his feet, always having to help me up and around the constantly changing elevation of the rocks because of my short dresses—and then, later, my long ones. The giant boulders running along the coast were essentially a never-ending staircase going nowhere, up and down, over and over, nowhere and everywhere all at once.

When he returned to me, he handed me the jar. I unscrewed the lid, pulled out the piece of paper inside, and read aloud: "Look for a place, coated from the start, where you just might find the desire of your heart."

"The coat closet of Rockwood."

"Is where the heart's desires are found?" I asked skeptically.

"The secret passageways." Lawry turned away from me and gestured to the massive stone mansion. "I know they seemed as if they were built for our amusement when we were children, but I'm afraid their purposes were for more than merely supplying a place to play hide-and-seek. Who knows how many foolish young couples have found the 'desires of their heart' within those hidden corridors over the years?"

He didn't turn to me before starting up the hill. As I followed him in silence, I couldn't help but study the squareness of his shoulders, the way he still carried himself with such confidence.

There were other teams of couples scattered about the yard and in the house. Many of them had a small white jar just like ours, and all of them seemed wholly focused on their latest clue. No one seemed to think it at all strange, or even notice, that Lawry and I were intent on entering the coat closet.

It had been years since I'd entered the hidden corridors of Rockwood, and I knew it really wasn't a good idea for me to go exploring them with Lawry. Being near him wasn't a good idea, not when all I wanted to do was throw myself at his neck and beg for his forgiveness.

It was fortunate he would soon be leaving for Washington. Faced with that knowledge, my hardness of heart was still intact—my self-preservation was strong whenever it came to what the future held. It was only how I felt in Lawry's presence that I had the most difficult time mastering.

I stood in the doorway as Lawry searched the pockets of all the coats, jackets, and capes hanging along the wall. Then he turned his back to me, fingering the dark wood trim of the small room. After a few moments, he found the trick piece, which was actually a lever that opened a secret door.

Holding the wood panel aside, he reached down and picked up another white jar. "Here it is." He closed the door and leaned against it, obviously just as hesitant about the hidden staircase behind the wall as I was. After unscrewing the tin lid, he pulled out the clue and handed the jar to me so that he could unfold the paper.

"Look for a place which will give your eyes much pleasure; there it will be, what you seek—such a treasure." Lawry read in such a subdued manner, it hardly sounded like his voice.

He handed me the clue, and I forced myself to look into his clear blue eyes. "The turrets."

This game grew worse and worse with every added clue. The last thing I needed was to follow Lawry Hampton up the secret staircase to the attic of Rockwood.

Without answering me, he turned and opened the secret door once again. "Come with me."

For some reason, I knew his command had absolutely nothing to do with completing the scavenger hunt. And yet, for some reason, I obeyed.

I followed him through the narrow opening into the cramped little room that had space enough for only a tightly spiraled staircase. The high Gothic windows at the top of the stairs offered just enough illumination to see the stairs.

Lawry closed the door behind us. I knew being there with him was not the best thing for me, but I still trusted him more than anyone else. Somehow, I knew he just needed to speak with me one last time, away from everyone.

Lawry took my hand and started up the narrow staircase. We ascended three stories to the turret we were supposedly in search of. I had no doubt he knew exactly where each and every one of the secret doors led; he and Nathan had drawn up and memorized a map of the entire system of secret tunnels when we were children.

Light flooded the stuffy tower-like room. With his back to me, Lawry opened the latches to the ancient glass encasements to let a breeze waft through. A tiny brown glass apothecary bottle waited for us on the windowsill. He grabbed it and immediately placed it in his pocket. Neither of us seemed that interested in finding out what our so-called treasure entailed. What did we care about a stupid game when our hearts were being torn apart?

Lawry came back to the top of the stairs and sat on the floor, sprawling his long legs toward me. I backed farther down the steps, shrouded in shadows, still clutching the white jars we'd collected.

He pulled his hands slowly down his face. "Meredyth, you can't just let Vance win like this." His every word, I could tell, had been well thought out. It was the exact thing he'd said the previous day, just before Vance had taken me away.

"You don't know what kind of game he's playing, or what kind of hold he has on…."

He quickly lifted off the stairs, taking a few steps down to meet me where I stood. "Is that it? You still think I don't know about— Did you not receive my letter?"

"Yes, I received your letter!" Tears blurred my eyes, and I hurled the glass jars down the stairs, smashing them into a thousand tiny white shards with a sharp, tinkling crash. I hated that he forced me to keep breaking his heart. How much was he willing to take? Why couldn't he just hate me? "And, yes, I read it—most of it. And then I burned it."

"You burned it?" Disbelief masked his every feature.

"It didn't matter anymore. I have a letter from Vance. It trumps everything."

"May I read this 'trumping' letter?"

I reached into my pocket, pulled out the tightly folded paper, and handed it to him. Only after I released it did I remember the Bible verse about my own deceitful heart I'd written on the reverse side.

Lawry took the letter and spread it out to read by the sunlight streaming into the little stairwell. After a few moments, he took several deep breaths. "'And now I might as well.' These are the words that so easily dissuade your heart from clinging to mine? I thought you might have at least been deceived into thinking Vance loved you a little." He started refolding the thick paper and noticed my handwriting on the back. He read the verse. "What does this mean?"

"Nothing." I snatched the letter from his hand, crumpling it against my chest. "You wouldn't understand."

"Perhaps I'd like to try." He was being very logical, in true Lawry fashion. "Those verses don't describe you or your heart—"

"Vance and I, we need to make up for...something we did." I wasn't ready to tell him the truth, even if it seemed to be the only way of making him hate me. "You wouldn't understand, unless you knew how we—"

"I already know, Meredyth." He spoke the words so slowly, so articulately. "I know everything."

"You—you can't…or you wouldn't…." I took a step back, down the stairs. Away.

"Did you ever read Vance's letters to Olivia?"

"No, I— Just one." I had Vance's letter clutched in my hand.

"Vance wrote to Olivia about what he did to you. And I've known for—"

"Stop, please!" I couldn't breathe—I could only stare at him. I didn't know how to comprehend his words; they were unfathomable. Lawry couldn't have known for all those weeks. Even when he'd told me Vance was Wynn's father, he'd known what Vance had done? What *I* had done?

"Don't you see, Mere? I want you, and I love you—still." With his right hand, he reached out to me, trying to pry my fingers from Vance's letter. "It doesn't matter what you've done; I still love you." His dear, sweet blue eyes held mine as he caressed my hands with his thumbs. "Because that's what love is."

I slipped my hands from his and backed away. "But don't *you* see? I told Vance I would wait for him, and now he's come home to marry me—just like I've wanted him to, for years. This is what God wants me to do." I turned and stepped down the twisted stairs. "Marrying him is the only way I can make things right. I never meant to love you, Lawry, and I certainly don't deserve you—"

Lawry thundered down the wooden steps and caught up with me on the landing of the third-floor attic. His fingers gripped my arms. In the dim light, I could just make out the panic in his eyes. "Do I have no say in whether you deserve me or not? It's my future you're determining with these reckless decisions, as well as your own."

"You'll be better off without—"

"Then take me out of the equation entirely, Mere. If I didn't matter at all—if I didn't exist—you would still be tying yourself to someone who will, in all honesty, only make you more miserable than you already are. Is that what you want—to punish yourself for the rest of your life? Is that what you think God wants?" Lawry held on to me, waiting for my answer.

And I didn't have one.

"You're a Christian, Meredyth. You're already free from the bondages of sin. All you have to do is claim your freedom." He let go of my arms and ran his fingers through his hair. "Good grief, you're not tied to Vance against your will! I want you to come with me to Washington as my wife. I don't care what you did with him years ago. I don't care if he is finally willing to marry you now. And I don't care if you think God is holding it over your head until you do so. It isn't true. Marrying Vance Everstone will not free you from the guilt you obviously still carry. It will absolve nothing."

I hurried past him up the stairs to get away. "We left the window open," I offered as an excuse.

Lawry came after me, took my hand, and pulled me down to the landing of the second floor. He stopped suddenly, causing me to collide into his broad back. He immediately turned and took me in his arms, pressed his lips to my ear, and whispered, "What would you do if you'd let the same thing happen with me? Would you marry me then? Or would you still insist on marrying the rake who happened to have first rights, even though you love me?"

"But you would never— I know you would never—" As I stood so close to him, able to see only the outline of his head and shoulders in the shadows, the full understanding of what he was explaining made me wonder if he wasn't right. What if there had been another time, another person, whom I had—? How would I fix that on my own? Maybe it was foolish to think Vance and I could fix anything by marrying.

"No, I would never do such a thing. And you know that, don't you?" He stood back, creating a little more space between us, and then took my hands, as well as Vance's letter, clutching them in his strong grasp. "I wouldn't hurt you for the world."

I looked down at his hands holding mine around Vance's awful, crumpled letter and recalled Vance the night before, rationalizing that marrying me was his best chance at attaining any kind of redemption.

Vance understood.

Lawry was so good. What could he see in me that made him believe our souls were alike in any way? Even if Jesus had died to make me free, I still felt guilty. The only freedom I would ever attain would come with heaven. In life, it seemed impossible.

I pulled myself from Lawry's grasp and turned to face the wall.

Lawry reached around me and unlatched the secret panel door, but instead of moving to open it, he leaned in behind me. "You do love me."

More uncontrollable tears suddenly spilled down my face. He had me surrounded with his hands resting against the wall, barricading me in.

I closed my eyes. I knew full well it was likely going to be the last thing I said to him, but I didn't care. I knew those stolen moments were all I would have of the truest kind of love for the rest of my life.

And I had to tell him the truth. "I do."

"But it doesn't matter, does it?" he said under his breath, the hardness of steel in his voice. He knew now. Vance *had* won. Vance had me first. Vance would have me forever.

Lawry pushed open the panel door, and light gleamed into the dark stairwell. I realized that this door led directly into my bedchamber. I turned my back to the glaring brightness and caught a glimpse of the dejected expression on Lawry's face.

"Does it?" The words came out hoarse.

I simply shook my head. I couldn't speak.

"Very well, then." Reaching into his pocket, he pulled out the apothecary bottle with the last clue inside. "Here, you'll want this. I don't plan on seeing anyone for the rest of the day, if I can help it."

And with that, Lawry clambered down the stairs, crunching the shards of white glass under his feet, as if he couldn't get away fast enough. I heard the door to the coat closet slam shut one floor below. He might as well have told me he never wanted to see me again. That was what it had sounded like.

TWENTY-FIVE

Upheaval

"We loved with a love that was more than love...."
—Edgar Allan Poe, *Annabel Lee*

A little later, as I made my way down the hall to the nursery, I heard Lawry's gentle, soothing voice from inside, as well as heartbreaking sobs from Wynn.

"And Meredyth loves you so very much—"

"But I want to go with you."

"She'll be a wonderful mother, I've always known that. And you do love her—"

"But don't you, too?"

Lawry didn't respond.

"I don't want her," she cried. "I just want to be with you."

I crept closer to the door as silently as possible and peeked in through the crack. Lawry sat upon a small bed, his profile to me. Wynn was seated in his lap, her face pressed to his chest, her little fingers clinging to his jacket.

"Do you remember the pocket watch I gave you a few weeks ago?" Lawry caressed the dark curls falling down her back. "That was your father's. He has a rightful claim to you—"

"Why does he get Mere'dy, too?"

Again, Lawry didn't answer for some time. "I don't know. But you'll be together, and that's what matters."

"Don't you want us anymore?" she sobbed against his neck.

Lawry's arms tightened around Wynn, and he bent his head low. Was he crying, as well?

"I do want you—" His voice faltered. "I want both of you, but part of life, Wynn, is learning that you can't always have what you want." Lawry stood, cradling Wynn's slight frame in his arms. "You'll be happy, though. You'll be with Meredyth, and she loves you."

As he took a step forward from the bed, I backed away from the door and collided with Benta, who'd been quietly standing directly behind me. She gently took hold of my shoulders as if she were going to hug me. A jolt of fear raced through my veins at the thought of facing Lawry again, and I jerked away from her.

"Please don't tell him I'm here," I whispered, then sprinted down the hall and around the corner to hide. I stood there with my back to the wall, and my labored breaths nearly masked the sound of the nursery door opening. Wynn's sobs nearly forced me from my hiding place.

"Here, let me take the little dear," Benta gently fussed.

"I don't want Mere'dy, I want you." Wynn screeched, presumably as Lawry attempted to hand her to Benta. "I want to go with you!"

"I've tried to explain to her—"

"Wynn, we'll see Lawry again someday," Benta assured her. "I'm certain we will. Don't you fear. And you'll be happy once more until then, I promise."

"Benta, you'll—you'll take good care of them, won't you?"

"Of course I will. Now, Wynn…shh, it'll be all right. Shh."

Wynn immediately quieted down. Benta was so good with children. She always managed to get Wynn to do what she wanted.

"I wish things had turned out differently," Benta said to Lawry. "I would have much preferred going to work at the orphanage in Washington State with you and Miss Summercourt than nannying the poor little dear for that mean Mr. Everstone."

There was a long pause, and I was certain I would never be able to take another breath without remembering how difficult it was to inhale and exhale while listening to such a heartrending exchange.

"I know, Benta…I know."

I heard Lawry's footsteps on the rough wood floor until they disappeared down the stairs at the other end of the hall. But even then, I didn't move. What was I supposed to do? Comfort Wynn with the knowledge that we would be trapped together in an unpleasant life of belonging to Vance Everstone? How would I face her every day without remembering Lawry?

I waited a few minutes before I finally gathered my resolve and marched down the hall into the nursery, ready to face whatever I would have to do in order to be everything Wynn needed.

Benta had her arm around Wynn's tiny shoulders as they sat upon the cushioned window seat of the small tower-like room that faced the woods off the side yard. They gazed quietly out the window. I walked up and sat next to Benta just in time to see Lawry cross the yard and mount his horse. Nathan and his father stood nearby, and Lawry said something briefly before he tore down the gravel path leading to Truesdale.

As the three of us sat in silence, a carriage came up the drive—my parents' carriage.

"Oh no." I would soon have to explain everything—my engagement to Vance, my connection to Wynn, and my severed relationship with Lawry. And I had a feeling they weren't going to understand any of it.

"Who is it?" Wynn asked, her voice ragged and filled with tears.

"My parents."

"More relatives, Wynn—your grandparents," Benta said with a smile, as if that were a good thing. But then, to Wynn, it would be. Yet would they even matter when all she wanted was Lawry?

"Are they nice?" Wynn asked sadly, her nose pressed to the rounded window. Tears still streamed down her face, but at least she wasn't asking for Lawry any longer.

"Well, yes, they're very nice people. Actually, you'll like them a lot. They've been waiting too many years for grandchildren, and they'll be overjoyed to meet you."

"Oh, but we're not allowed to go down," Benta whispered. "Mr. Everstone said we were to stay up here until he came for us."

"And I'm sure he made it clear to Law—" I suddenly thought better of mentioning Lawry in front of Wynn. "I'm certain Mr. Everstone made it clear that no one was to come up here to see you. But I'm going to take you with me to Summerhouse. There is no reason he should object to that."

"Do you mind if we wait up here until you get his permission?" How interesting that Benta already knew what to expect from Vance Everstone after knowing him all of a few short days.

"That's fine, Benta, if that's what you'd prefer. But know that I'll do everything in my power to take the two of you from this nursery-prison he's confined you to." I looked at Wynn, who still silently stared out the window in the direction of the woods into which Lawry had disappeared, and took her hand. Surprisingly, she let me hold it. "I love you, Wynn, and I do look forward to being your mother."

She nodded only slightly, keeping her eyes glued to the horse trail at the edge of the trees. As if she could make him come back.

But I knew he wouldn't be coming back for either one of us. In some way or another, Vance and I had made it so he had no other choice.

A little while later, Ainsley met me on the second-floor landing of the main white marble staircase. "Meredyth, where have you been? Your parents just arrived with Garrett, and he asked me to marry him, right in front of everyone!" She clearly thought I would be surprised by such news, or perhaps for me to be exuberantly happy for them. "Nicholette isn't very pleased with you and Lawry for ruining the end of the scavenger hunt. We were all supposed to read our 'treasures' aloud and in order. I guess the one you and Lawry were to find was the first and most important sentence to some poem. Do you have it? There might still be time. Lawry left so suddenly. He said he had something urgent to take care of that he'd forgotten about. But, really, that doesn't sound like Lawry at all—"

"Yes, well, Lawry hasn't quite seemed much like himself today." I reached into my pocket and pulled out the brown glass apothecary bottle Lawry had handed to me after I'd smashed all the others.

"Oh, you do have it. We all thought...well, never mind what we thought. Let's see if Nicholette will forgive you for taking your sweet time." She took my hand and led me down the marble stairs.

Before we could join the wedding party on the lawn, Vance walked in through the front door and intercepted us. I stuffed the bottle with the tightly furled message back into my pocket.

Ainsley continued on out to the portico, and I called after her, "I'll be out in a little while."

"I gather your heart-to-heart with Lawry went well," Vance said under his breath as he closed the door behind Ainsley.

I ignored his comment. "My parents have arrived, have they?"

He came up beside me and took my arm. "Visiting with all their long-lost friends, yes." He walked me slowly through the empty hall. I glanced up to better, yet discreetly, examine his eyes—the tender skin around them had begun turning an awful bluish-purple.

"And so I'll be losing my one object of stimulating diversion to her dear mama and papa today?"

"What do you mean?"

"I mean, I'd planned to make a special trek through the hidden passages tonight to come see you," he said quietly. "You don't know how awful it was for me this morning to find out you've been stay-ing in the blue room, so easily accessible by the east hidden stair-case. Last night could have been so much more eventful...and enjoyable...if I had only known."

I knew very well what he was getting at and was suddenly overjoyed by the arrival of my parents. "I've always stayed in the blue room while visiting your family. If you'd been around in the last few years, perhaps you would have known as much." Not that I was sad he'd missed out on his opportunity. "And anyhow, we're not married."

"What should that matter to you? We will be soon; and like I said last night, it's not as if I haven't already had everything you have to offer. You're already mine because you've already *been* mine." Such bone-chilling words—but they were the truth. The only truth I'd ever known.

"You're going to have to wait. I'm not the same naive girl I used to be. I didn't know what I was doing."

"You just need a bit of practice."

"After the wedding."

"Of course. Now that you'll be moving in with your family, I've lost my chance."

I tried to slip my hand from the crook of his arm, but he caught it with his other hand and held it fast.

"I'm taking Wynn and Benta with me to Summerhouse."

"So the three of you can run off with Lawry tonight?"

"No—"

"You know he would take you back, regardless of whatever you said to him today to make him fly off like the devil. He's just the kind who will continue to hope against all hope. He'll likely be waiting for you fifty years from now, when I'm dead."

"You really believe that?" Personally, I didn't expect such for-giveness from Lawry. Not after what I'd said and done. I fully expected him to hate me for the rest of his life.

"Unfortunately for him, yes." Vance said this just as we reached the back door, and it opened to reveal Natalia Livingston escorting my parents into the house.

I freed my hand from Vance's stiff, controlling arm and reached for Mother's proffered embrace.

"Merie, darling, you look absolutely overwrought. Are you feeling unwell?"

I clung to her perhaps a moment too long, collecting the courage I would need to tell her and Father my news. "Mother, Father." I took Father's hand in both of mine. He stood next to Mother, his stern, steely eyes leveled at Vance. "We have some news to share."

Father's eyes moved to me. "You're not telling me you've accepted Vance Everstone?"

"Well, it's about time!" Mother's hands sought mine, stealing them from Father's clasp; she held them tightly.

"And what about—"

"You did give Vance your blessing," I stated before Father had the chance to name names.

"Yes, but I thought you'd...." Father wiped a hand down his face, as if considering for the very first time that I would actually accept Vance Everstone's proposal. "I suppose congratulations are in order." He shook Vance's hand. "Welcome to the family."

Mother embraced Natalia affectionately. "Oh, I knew this day would come. I knew our families would be joined one day."

"But that isn't all the news." Vance stepped forward again, his sights set on me, daring me to stop him. "If you haven't heard already, I have a child—a six-year-old daughter I would like Meredyth to adopt as her own."

"A daughter? But how—" Mother pressed her hand to her frail, narrow chest. "Oh! She must be your late wife's daughter, then. I did not realize she'd been a widow."

No one corrected her. No one said a word until I replied, "She's the sweetest little girl, Mother. And her name is Wynn. Wynn Everstone."

⌒

Vance didn't end up letting me take Wynn and Benta with me to Summerhouse. He wouldn't even allow me to bring her down to meet her soon-to-be grandparents, claiming that he knew for a fact she was napping. It was strange to me how he barred her away. Was he ashamed of her? I could hardly believe that notion—not from Vance Everstone, who never cared what anyone thought.

He still didn't trust me, which was surprising, considering I did all he asked without complaint. He wanted me, so he had me. What more did he want?

He accompanied me and my parents to Summerhouse, taking his rightful place beside me as my future husband. He and my father discussed the idea of announcing our engagement near the end of the open house luncheon reception at Truesdale after the wedding. My mother was so overjoyed at our news and so welcoming of the idea of having a six-year-old granddaughter—no matter who had borne her—that it seemed all was well. Garrett was engaged to Ainsley Hampton, and I was engaged to Vance Everstone. Everything was perfect.

Garrett joined us at Summerhouse after spending the afternoon at Truesdale with Ainsley and her family, doing very similar things that my parents, Vance, and I had done for those very same hours—discussing wedding plans and other aspects of our future together.

Garrett had, no doubt, seen Lawry while at Truesdale and had somehow heard all about my impending engagement. When he walked into the room, I could see the anger burning from his eyes as he looked at Vance, reclining next to me on the sofa. "I'd like to have a private word with my family, if you don't mind waiting outside."

"No, of course not. I'm certain there is much you need to discuss." Vance stood and made his exit.

Garrett closed the pocket doors, then turned around slowly. "What is this I hear about Meredyth being engaged to that coxcomb?"

"Garrett, don't use such vulgar language!" Mother cried. "Meredyth has been waiting all these years—"

"And he was married to someone else in the meantime…only months ago."

"But Vance is the one Merie wants. We've all known that for years." Mother fanned herself more rapidly but seemed to remain calm.

Garrett turned to me sharply. "Is that true, Meredyth? Is Vance the only one you've wanted? What about Lawry? I just came from Truesdale—he looks like death. Did you know he's planning to move to Washington permanently now? He can't wait to leave."

"I didn't mean for him to—"

"You have no idea what you've meant—to him or otherwise." Garrett paced between me and where Father sat, silent, in his favorite leather chair.

"Garrett, if Merie wanted Lawry, she could have had him," Mother reasoned. "He asked for her hand just days before Vance did, but she's been holding out for—"

"That she would choose Vance over him!" Garrett interrupted her unceremoniously. "I'm sorry, Mother, but everyone knows she's been stringing Lawry along for the last few months—probably years, if we really sat down to analyze the facts!" He stopped to face me where I sat, taking in every truthful word, unable to look anyone in the eye. "You don't deserve him."

Finally I stood. "I know that all too well, Garrett. What do you think has kept me from having him?"

The three of them simply stared at me—my father still silently considering every explosive word; my mother still fanning herself, though much more rigorously now; and Garrett looking half ashamed for making me admit such a thing.

I tore open the pocket doors and hastened from the room, hoping that Vance hadn't made it too far. He could very well have started back to Rockwood in the time he'd had.

But he hadn't. He was waiting in the hall. The one person I wished would forget I was alive was the only person I had left to run to. He wasn't safe, and he didn't love me; but he was there. He needed to be there. He took my hand, as if he knew he'd just won some battle.

Vance stopped me near the intricate carved-wood staircase, gently pushing me back against the wall. "While everyone was waiting for you to finish up your part of the scavenger hunt, I managed to convince Nicholette that you should walk down the aisle with me instead of Lawry tomorrow. After witnessing the way you two were associating with each other earlier today, it was plain, even to her, that it was the best arrangement."

At the mention of Nicholette, I realized I'd never returned the bottle containing the opening sentence to her poem.

"That's probably true. Thank you." I wouldn't allow myself to back down from him. I reached into my pocket, pulled out the short brown bottle. Vance took it from my hand, uncorked it, and scooped up the tiny scroll with his pinkie finger.

"What's this?"

"My treasure from the scavenger hunt. Ainsley said it's the opening line to a poem Nicholette wanted us all to read together or something."

Vance unfurled it awkwardly with his lean, muscular fingers. Once he read the words, he let out a low, menacing laugh.

"What does it say?"

"Nothing that could be more ironic. Read it yourself." Vance crumpled the thin strip of paper with his fingers and shoved it into my outstretched hand.

I took the wadded scroll and pulled at the ends to smooth it out so I could see the entire sentence.

Bright star! would I were steadfast as thou art....

TWENTY-SIX

The Wedding

> *"For what thou art is mine:*
> *Our state cannot be sever'd; we are one,*
> *One flesh; to lose thee were to lose myself."*
> —John Milton, *Paradise Lost*

Well, if it isn't Crawford walking up the drive. It's about time he showed up." Garrett stood beside me as I filled my plate from the breakfast buffet in the dining room the next morning. He stared out the beveled window above the buffet, his plate of food balanced in one hand.

I looked around his shoulder and out the window. Sure enough, there was Jay. He'd always been good friends with Garrett, although that hadn't stopped him from remaining a complete mystery to the rest of us. I didn't think anyone truly knew Jayson Crawford Castleman, and that seemed to be just the way he wanted it.

When Jay was shown into the dining room, he took a seat at the table beside me, as if he hadn't been missing from our company for almost the entire last year. He smiled at me, which was greeting enough from Jay.

"Where have you been?" I asked while Garrett busily piled his breakfast into his mouth. No doubt, he desired to be on his way to accompany Ainsley from Truesdale to Rockwood.

"Everston. I was under the impression that Estella knew that, at least, and that everyone would find out."

"She did mention something," I reflected.

He smiled, his brown eyes brightening. "Of course, she did."

"Yes, well, someone had to tell us." I remained coolly disinterested. I wasn't sure if Estella knew Jay would be attending the wedding, but surely Jay knew that Estella would be part of the wedding party. What was he going to do when he saw her again? And what would he say if I asked? I slowly shuffled my eggs and bacon around my plate with my fork.

"So, you are, indeed, practicing medicine...at a mountain resort?"

"I'm doing more than that, but I don't need to get into the details." His unwillingness to share didn't shock me. That was usually how Jay was.

"Interesting." And the conversation was finished.

After an awkward silence, Garrett asked, "Have you heard the news...that I'm going to marry Ainsley?"

"I did. You have my hearty congratulations—"

"And our complete sympathy," my eldest brother, Alex, interrupted from the entryway to the hall. Clyde stood beside him, both of them looking like older versions of Garrett and younger versions of Father, all red hair and flashy grins. It was strange that they'd always been so popular, having such peculiar looks. But, like Garrett, most of their appeal was probably due to their charm and irresistible charisma.

Jay stood to greet Alex and Clyde, who had arrived from New York City the night before. They probably hadn't seen him in at least five years. While they all got reacquainted, I tried my best to eat something from my plate, though I had no appetite. It was going to be a long, trying day. I prayed that my own, awful news wouldn't come up as a topic of conversation.

But when my mother breezed into the room a few minutes later, all hope of that disappeared. The first thing out of her mouth was: "Have you heard our fortunate news, Jay? Two engagements in a week! Any mother's dream."

"Two engagements? That truly is...amazing." He glanced about the room, his puzzled gaze traveling over every face until it finally landed upon mine. "Who—"

"Why, my sweet little Meredyth is going to finally marry Vance Everstone," Mother added happily.

Clyde whistled. "And down she goes, the spoiled little sister who once considered herself too good for anyone, caught in the snares of one the most vicious players of all...."

"Clyde, really—what are you saying?" Mother asked, completely befuddled.

"Nothing at all, Mother," Alex responded in Clyde's place.

"That truly is...fortunate." Jay struggled to get the words out, and I was certain that he, too, knew of Lawry's long, relentless love for me. But what was it to him? Of everyone in my acquaintance, Jay knew best what it was like to string someone along. At least I hadn't known what I was doing to Lawry. At least it hadn't been intentional for all those years.

"Her father was concerned that she ought to choose Lawry Hampton, instead...both Vance and Lawry asked for her hand within a matter of days, you know. But he's convinced now that she must be utterly in love with Vance to have refused Lawry as she has. I guess Lawry's been in love with her all these years, but I certainly didn't know it. He always was her dearest friend, and I'm sure Merie hadn't a clue." Mother fluttered about the room, too distracted by her immense good fortune to even make a straight line to the buffet.

"Is that right?" Jay asked, turning a sharp glance my way.

"Now, I know as well as anyone else that Merie has had her fair share of attention from gentlemen over the years," Mother replied, "but never any two as worthy as Vance Everstone and Lawry Hampton!"

"How did you ever choose between them?" Jay's question was directed specifically at me; however, I refused to take part in the conversation. Everyone else was saying quite enough without my input.

I noticed our butler standing outside the entrance of the dining room. "Quincy, is my carriage ready?" Never in my life had I been so eager to escape Summerhouse, even if my journey would take me to Rockwood, and Vance… and probably to see Lawry, too.

"Yes, Miss Summercourt, it's all set to take you to Rockwood. Your gown has been sent ahead, as planned."

I stood from my place at the table, never having eaten a bite. "Thank you, Quincy. I am quite ready. If you'll all excuse my departure, I really must hurry off."

"We'll be right behind you, dearest," Mother said as she put her plate down to give me a small hug. "Have fun with all your friends beforehand. Being a member of the party is so exciting. There's nothing like a wedding day."

⌣⟋

The wedding was planned for eleven in the morning. When I was delivered to Rockwood, Vance met me on the front steps. Wynn stood solemnly beside him, dressed as if it were just another ordinary day to be cooped up in the nursery. Vance was already wearing his tuxedo, and, save for the jealous gleam in his bruised eyes, he looked rather exceptional.

He pushed Wynn's shoulder in an effort to make her move forward. "I told her she could help you prepare yourself for the wedding with the women upstairs. But when it's time for the ceremony, I want her back up in the nursery with Miss Allister for the rest of the day."

I didn't answer him, other than to give a curt nod, as I silently took Wynn's hand and headed inside. It was probably best that Wynn not be present that day, for I certainly didn't need to witness another scene like the one I'd eavesdropped on the day before.

The mansion seemed utterly empty as our footsteps echoed up the marble stairs to the vaulted ceiling of the great hall. I'd never been a member of a wedding party before, and I really expected there to be much more commotion involved. But then again, perhaps most of it was already taking place at the chapel. Where were the men readying themselves? Or were they already finished, as Vance was?

As we approached Estella's bedchamber, one of the Hampton cousins rushed from the room, her hand covering her mouth. She was already dressed in the ocean-blue gown Daphne and Nicholette had chosen for us to wear.

I stopped and eyed her worriedly. "Is something wrong?"

"Oh, I think I might be sick, as well, if I don't get away from that wretched sound!" She raced past us and continued down the stairs.

I guided Wynn into Estella's room and closed the door. Immediately, we heard someone emptying her stomach behind the wall of the attached bathroom.

Natalia came through the open doorway and smiled. "You've made it! Hurry, we have just half an hour. Oh, and you've brought Wynn! I don't know why I didn't think of that. Of course, she would enjoy this." She turned around suddenly and covered her mouth with her fingers as she looked into the smaller room, her attention obviously taken by whoever was ill. "Amaryllis isn't quite feeling all that well."

Wynn tightened her grip on my hand as she took in her surroundings with troubled black eyes. The rest of the party, minus Amaryllis and the girl who'd flown out of the room, were scattered about, all in various stages of dress.

Nicholette and Daphne stood apart from the small crowd of young ladies and spoke quietly to each other, looking like perfection on display in their flowing gowns. Since Daphne had been married once before and widowed, she wore an ivory-colored two-piece gown of ribbed silk, while Nicholette was dressed in an exquisite, tight-waisted creation of white patterned silk with a high ridged collar edged with chiffon that flared open in the front.

My maid, Hilda, had taken my dress to Rockwood and had been preparing it in the room as she'd waited for me to arrive. Wynn had to let go of my hand, which I could tell she didn't want to do. As Hilda helped me undress, I paid close attention to Wynn as she sat upon a chair near one of the windows, peeping through the curtains. She still hadn't said a word to me all morning, and I wondered if she was too busy thinking of a way to somehow see Lawry. As much as she wanted to see him, I didn't want to, and yet it was inevitable. Even though I no longer had to endure the prospect of walking down the aisle with him, I would see him at the front of the chapel. And I didn't know how my heart would react.

After Hilda pulled my dress over my head and began positioning it about me, I glanced over to the window where Wynn had been sitting. She was no longer there.

As soon as I was properly dressed, I hurried down the marble steps, knowing that I had little time to find Wynn before the wedding began. I made it down to the front lawn and found most of the groomsmen gathered there—all but Vance and Lawry—awaiting the bridesmaids.

My stomach dropped to my toes. After taking a steadying breath, I charged ahead, hoping I wouldn't find all three of them together. I looked down the drive, past the massive line of closed carriages ready to escort the wedding guests from the chapel to Truesdale following the ceremony. As my gaze traveled the distance, searching for a glimpse of Wynn, Vance appeared between two of the coaches, dragging her by the hand toward the house. She fought him every step until he stopped and lifted her into his arms. She continued to kick, scream, and pound at his arms with her tiny fists, but nothing deterred him. He took her into the house through the back door and reappeared within a minute, his black eyes blazing when he reached me.

I couldn't help but frown as I stepped aside from the crowd of bridesmaids now gathered about me. "She was looking for Lawry, wasn't she?"

He closed his bruised eyelids, reaching up slowly to smooth his fingers over his dark brows. "She found him, too."

"What is he doing at the chapel already?"

"Avoiding having to see you, I suppose."

That Vance had figured everything out between Lawry and me was humbling. Would he hold it over my head for the rest of my life that I'd given my heart to someone he loathed instead of waiting for him with the steadfastness I'd promised long ago? And could he really blame me? He'd never given me a reason to sustain any hope about a relationship with him; it had been all me and my own determination to see things through.

And suddenly, there we were, with everything all backward and flipped around so that I could hardly recognize what I was doing, or why.

Natalia urged us all in the direction of the chapel. It really wasn't that great of a distance, and we were there in a matter of minutes, lined up with our designated partner to wait beyond the side wall of the chapel.

I didn't see Lawry—at least until Vance grabbed my elbow and turned me around in preparation for our walk down the aisle.

Lawry stood in the procession line, right in front of me, next to his cousin—the one who had burst from the bedchamber when Amaryllis had gotten sick. I didn't know how long he'd been there, ignoring me. At the sight of him, I had to fight tears. Vance held on to my arm—his usual stance over the past few days—as if to remind me just how bound to him I was.

And that he wasn't ever going to let me go.

As the orchestra began playing the melodious strands of Nicholette's favorite piece, Pachelbel's *Canon in D*, I watched as Lawry started down the aisle, away from me. I watched until he turned the corner around the stone wall into the opened back of the chapel, which was our signal to follow.

Vance and I rounded the corner and were met with a sea of faces turned to the middle aisle, all watching us. All these people would soon be at a wedding just like this one—a wedding at the end of the summer, at which I would forever affix myself to Vance. And everyone would know about it by the end of the day.

When I finally gathered the nerve to look down to the end of the aisle, I caught Lawry staring in our direction, disappointment etching his rigid face. His penetrating blue eyes immediately flitted to Vance, and there was no mistaking the anger, and even hatred, I saw directed at my would-be husband. I found it odd that these emotions were not directed at me, as well. They should have been. I deserved Lawry's hatred more than Vance, considering all I'd done and said in previous weeks.

Through the entire ceremony, I struggled to pay no mind to the fact that Lawry, after the initial shock of seeing Vance and me walking down the aisle together, ignored my presence completely. If I could have one more look from him, maybe it would result in some change. Perhaps it would trigger the release of whatever kept me forever out of his reach. But even as I dwelled upon those treacherous thoughts, I knew there was nothing to be done. Even if Lawry looked my way once more, it would only serve to make me want him to look again...and again. What I wanted was for him to never give up on me—but how could I even ask that of him when I was the one constantly insisting he do so? Oh, how selfish I was when it came to his love.

At the conclusion of the ceremony, the wedding party filed out of the chapel in the opposite order of how we'd entered, and that was the only time I was certain Lawry's gaze was on me. He was directly behind me, and I knew. Even as Vance guided me twenty feet across the green lawn, I felt his stare.

Vance and I stood near the carriages, my hand on his arm, my gaze focused on the ground. I couldn't allow myself to search for Lawry.

The two pairs of newlyweds greeted all the guests as they came down the aisle together, showered with a flurry of dried lavender blossoms. My deceitful gaze strayed from the couples to find Lawry leaning against the end of one of the stone walls, staring blankly at the crowd. I knew then that he would keep himself from me, staying lost in the crowds, for the remainder of the day.

To reach Truesdale, I rode with Vance, Nathan, and Amaryllis in the last carriage of the wedding party. As we rolled down the gravel drive, I asked Vance, "Would it not have been fun to let Wynn attend the wedding, if not the reception?"

He took my hand in his, drawing my attention from the thick forest of pine trees passing outside the open window. The breeze kept snatching strands of my hair from my pins.

"I thought it best to keep her at Rockwood for the duration of the day." He squeezed my hand. "You know she would just seek out Lawry. It isn't healthy, the way she clings to him. What on earth did he do to make her so attached to him?"

Tears threatened to spill from my eyes, but I refused to let Vance see them.

"He loved her," I choked out as I turned back to the window.

TWENTY-SEVEN

Truesdale

*"Groans that words cannot express are often
prayers that God cannot refuse."*
—Charles H. Spurgeon

When our carriage came to a halt in front of Truesdale, Vance quickly opened the door and alighted. After a moment, he turned back to take my arm. "Soon, this will all be for us," he breathed. "Very soon, I hope—"

A gunshot pierced the air.

"William!" Nicholette screamed from nearby. "Oh, William!"

Vance let go of my arm and took a few steps away from the carriage, as if searching for something...or someone.

Nathan caught hold of the door, latched it, and slammed Amaryllis and me to the floor, throwing himself on top of us.

Another gunshot thundered.

I pushed up against Nathan. "Vance?" I called through the open window. "Vance, are you still there?"

"Meredyth, stay down!" Amaryllis grasped me tightly at the waist.

A light moan sounded just outside the coach just before more shots were fired in the distance.

Long minutes later, we heard footsteps hurry up the gravel path and skid to a stop next to our carriage.

"The gunman has been stopped, but hurry, help me—Vance has been shot." The voice belonged to Nathan's friend Henry Goodenough, who rapped loudly on the carriage door before opening it.

Nathan scrambled out of the carriage, and I carefully climbed off of Amaryllis, turned, and peeked outside.

Henry was crouched next to Vance, who lay on his back about ten feet from the carriage. His right hand was pressed against the muscle between his neck and left shoulder; his eyes were closed, and the ground was covered with bright red blood.

I hurried from the coach and dropped beside him. "Vance, open your eyes. Look at me." I hardly knew what I was saying, what I was doing. I hardly realized my hands were at his shoulder, pressing against his hot, sticky wound—as if I could stop the bleeding. Vance had given up applying any pressure himself. He looked pale, his skin pasty white, except for the purple bruises around his eyes.

Henry whispered something in Nathan's ear...something about Will's having been shot, as well.

Vance's dark eyelashes fluttered. A second later, his black eyes opened. His focus wasn't upon me but down the drive. I followed his gaze and watched as his father, Bram, and Daphne's new husband, Captain Parker, carried William's limp body into the house, a massive, bleeding wound in the center of his chest. My heart constricted at the implications and at Nicholette's mournful wailing as she followed close behind them, with Natalia and Estella at her sides.

"Vance, he'll—" Moving my hand from Vance's wound, I traced his jaw with the back of my fingers, bringing his attention back to me. "I'm sure he'll be fine."

"Save Will," Vance whispered before his eyes drifted closed again.

"He'll be all right, Vance, I'm sure," I said again. "Just as you will be."

Amaryllis appeared beside Nathan, clutching a handful of petticoat ruffles. Nathan and I got out of her way as she pressed the wad of white material to Vance's shoulder with all her weight, resolve beaming in her bluish-green gaze.

Vance opened his pain-filled eyes once more and stared at Amaryllis. His lips crooked into the tiniest of smiles. "Don't bother with me. Go. Save your care for Will." A tear slid out of the corner of his eye. "I saw—"

"He'll be fine." Tears coursed down my cheeks at his concern for his brother. I went to brush them away, but my hands were bloodstained—even wiping them on my dress didn't help.

Vance stifled a groan as he tried to sit up. "Go see how Will is. I'll be in...I can take care of myself."

"Yes, go," I urged Amaryllis and Nathan. "I'll stay with him."

As the two of them hastened toward Truesdale, Vance let me help him sit up. His gaze remained on the house.

"Shall I try to help you inside?" I tried to heft him from the ground, but he refused to budge. "Come now, Vance. Everything will be fine."

I kept telling myself that—kept telling him it would all be fine. But really, deep down, I wasn't so sure. Will had looked anything but fine; and if a flesh wound to a shoulder bled this much, I could only imagine the scene inside the house.

The yard seemed eerily empty. Everyone was bent on saving the younger brother, the newly married, the more promising son who would take over an empire. I alone remained by Vance's side.

Vance simply sat in silence, holding the ruffles of Amaryllis's petticoat to his shoulder, staring off in a daze. "This is my fault."

"No, Vance—"

"Meredyth, you don't know the half of it."

"Then tell me."

"I saw who shot Will...and the confusion on his face right before he took his shot at me." Vance choked back a sob. "The man Henry shot was Giselle's brother, Pierre. He mistook Will for me. I should be the one in there dying."

A cloud of confusion blanketed my mind. "Why would Giselle's brother want to kill you?"

"When Giselle told her family I'd seduced her, they believed her, of course. I tried to explain to her brothers that my days of dallying with innocents were over, that I had plans to come home this summer for Will's wedding, and that I was already as good as engaged to you."

"And they still forced you to marry her?"

Vance grimaced—whether at the pain or at the memories, I wasn't certain.

"Giselle's family is very powerful and crooked, the kind of people no one should mess with. Had I known just how divisive they were, I never would have kept up my acquaintance with Giselle."

"And after they forced you into marriage with her, she died, and her death appeared...."

"Yes. A little too convenient."

From the far side of the house, I heard a line of carriages drive up.

The wedding guests.

The Hamptons' butler appeared at the front door, as if standing guard. Before I turned back to Vance, I heard rushed footsteps pounding the gravel behind me.

"Meredyth, are you hurt?" Garrett was beside me in an instant, Jay at his side. My brother grabbed my arms and pulled me to my feet. My gaze followed his as he took in the smears of blood covering my hands and gown.

"It's Vance—he was shot. So was Will. They've taken him into the house."

Jay helped Vance to his feet. Not that Vance looked as if he wanted to stand or go anywhere. He still had a blank expression on his face, sick with guilt over his brother's death before it was even confirmed.

"Let's get you inside." Jay held Vance around the waist, as if guiding a blind man.

"I don't want to go in," Vance said stubbornly, fighting him. "I can't face them."

More wedding guests exited their carriages and stared at us, as if unsure of what to do. A multitude of tables had been set up in the garden for the open house reception, but who would want to stay and celebrate after such a tragedy?

Standing beside me, Garrett addressed the mass of people gathered before us. "I'm sorry, but it seems the wedding celebrations have been put to a stop. Please, if you have no immediate connection to the family, it's best that you be on your way. There's been a terrible accident, and the last thing we need is people shuffling about...."

I clung to Garrett in such a haze of uncertainty, I hardly realized he was leading me into the house until I heard the front door close behind me. I didn't want to be in Truesdale. I didn't want to face the grief of everyone close to me—the Everstones, the Hamptons, and especially Nicholette.

Her repetitious weeping of Will's name carried from the dining room as I was guided through the foyer. Everyone stood silently, lining the walls, bearing the heavy sadness of such a distressful sound. Captain Parker held Daphne in the corner near the stairs, and as Jay led Vance into one of the parlors, Natalia, Estella, Bram, and Madame Boutilier solemnly followed. I heard Nathan instruct Jay to lower Vance onto the long sofa at the center of the room.

Ainsley appeared at the landing of the stairs, and Garrett quickly released my arm. He met her halfway. "Is it true? Will is... dead?"

She nodded her head and buried her face in his chest.

And I stood alone.

Where was Lawry? He was there somewhere, wasn't he? He had to be.

Still in a haze, I stepped toward the partially open pocket doors to the dining room and looked inside. Nicholette was hunched over, heaving wretched sobs upon Will's lifeless body. The dark crimson stain of his blood covered the table, the floor, and, from what I could tell, the entire front of her white wedding dress. She didn't look up from her station at Will's side, her face pressed to his neck, one hand holding his, and the other covering his eyes. With a sudden stab, I became aware of just how much Nicholette had gained and lost within only a few short hours.

I forced my gaze from the tragic picture and searched again for Lawry, but the only other people in the room were Natalia and her doctor husband, George, holding each other in the far corner, weeping.

I turned around and made my way back out to the foyer, through the front door, past the butler, and into the waiting arms of my father.

Mother soon stepped between us and pressed a hand to my wet cheek. "Merie, you're covered in blood! We heard that Vance has been shot. And Will, too! Are they going to be all right?"

"Will's been killed." I stared blankly. "But Vance will be fine."

"Oh, you poor dear! And poor Nicholette! Have her parents even arrived yet?"

"I don't know."

Releasing me, Mother hurried into the house along with the butler, leaving the door wide open. Father remained beside me with one arm about my shoulders. I was sure he could feel my chest heaving with the sobs I refused to release.

"There, there, my sweet Meredyth," he said gently into my hair. "You just said Vance would be fine, did you not?"

"Meredyth." Jay spoke from the doorway. "Vance is asking for you."

"See, dearest? He'll be fine." Father's soothing words only cut deeper into my heart.

No, nothing would really be fine ever again.

I tore myself from Father's hold, backing toward the steps that led down to the flagstone path.

"He said he has something important he needs to tell you." Jay turned and headed back inside. He must have believed I'd follow him. Instead, I looked at my father, who stood quietly, watching me.

"No." I shook my head. "I don't want to see Vance. I don't want him. I want—" The truth of my thoughtlessly spoken words hung in the air as I turned and raced down the steps.

Out of the corner of my eye, I saw Father leaning over the handrail, staring at me. "Merie, you won't find him."

His words paralyzed me. How did he know my heart so well?

I slowly turned and looked at him. Unabashed tears trickled down my cheeks, and I wiped them away with the backs of my bloodstained hands. The ache in my chest expanded with every passing moment Lawry remained missing. "Where is he?" My words escaped with a sob.

Father glanced away, tears in his eyes. He reached down and lifted his pocket watch, clicked it open, then quickly shut it. "I'd say he's on his way from Ellsworth to Bangor by now." He dropped the watch back inside the pocket of his waistcoat. "On his way to Washington."

I'd thought I would be strong enough. But I'd been terribly wrong. How could I live with my heart still in Lawry's hands—with him living on the other side of the country?

"Did he tell you?" I asked.

"Tell me what? That you'd as good as told him you'd marry him and move with him to Washington by the end of the summer, only to decide you had other plans?"

"I did have other plans. I just thought that…."

He pushed off the rail and slowly descended the steps. I'd never seen my father so serious—as if I'd never done anything so horrible as to reject Lawry Hampton's suit. "You thought you'd marry Vance Everstone instead, whom you don't want—your almost-fiancé, who is inside, bleeding from a gunshot wound, while you're out here searching for Lawry Hampton…."

His words rang with a truth I couldn't deny.

Father gently took my hand. "In your unwise treatment of him during the last few days, you've convinced him quite thoroughly that it's best for him to live without you." He paused until I looked at him. "Is that indeed what you want?"

It wasn't, but it was best for Lawry. And for me. Wasn't it?

"Sweetest Merie, is that truly what you think is the best outcome for you and Lawry—your being torn apart for the sake of… what? Vance Everstone? Do you really believe that's what God wants for His beloved?"

His beloved. Yes, if His beloved was Lawry. "Yes."

What God wanted for me surely couldn't be the same as what I truly, selfishly wanted for myself…could it?

"Merie, come inside at once!" Mother rushed out the front door and hurried halfway down the stone steps, past Father. "Vance wants to speak with you. Why must you keep the poor man waiting? He's in there, wounded and bleeding without you."

I shook my head. "I can't go back in there. Not with everyone crying and grieving…and on Will's wedding day…." I couldn't stand the thought of seeing Nicholette again—or the rest of Vance's family.

"But Vance is your fiancé. It's your obligation, your duty, to be at his side."

Yes, my obligation. How easily I forgot.

"Let her go, Anna," Father interjected. "Merie needs some time alone, away from all that is happening in Truesdale right now."

He took her hand, and at his touch, Mother immediately seemed to calm—so like the effect Lawry had upon me, when I let him. I turned away from the sight, my heart swelling in my chest.

"Would you like to take the carriage back to Summerhouse, Mere?" Father asked.

"No, I don't want the carriage," I answered flatly. What I wanted was a train, a very fast train that could somehow catch up to Lawry Hampton.

Oh, my treacherously deceitful and desperately, desperately wicked heart!

I stalked across the lawn without another word. I needed to be alone, and I suddenly knew just where to go.

TWENTY-EIGHT

Freedom

"And I will be found of you, saith the LORD:
and I will turn away your captivity."
—Jeremiah 29:14

Lawry was gone.

Had I not been prepared for this? Had I not been telling myself for months that it was best?

"It doesn't matter what I want." Although the words escaped my lips only once, as a mutter, they repeated over and over in my mind, an ever-growing thump of a drum behind my temples. The words stayed with me as I climbed all the way down to the rocky shore and made it around the bend of the cove down the cliffs from the trail between Truesdale and Summerhouse. Finally, at the sight of the cave, the air in my lungs constricted. I stopped in my tracks, but only for a moment.

The nearest I'd been to the caves in all those years had been when Lawry had dragged me down to the beach at my family's Cove Party the summer before. I didn't know why I'd let him. Perhaps it had been some secret wish of my heart even back then, a buried hope, that he could tear me away from that which I'd been bound to for so long. It had been right there in front of the cave, where my life had changed so drastically, that I'd learned Vance probably wasn't ever coming home from Europe for me...

and where I'd begun to give up hope of ever marrying him. Or anyone.

My knees grew gradually weaker as I approached the cavern. My feet stumbled over the rocks, and the cracks in the deep boulders prevented me from running as I wished to. I was impatient to see it again—this place I'd been bound to for so long.

Despite the strange urgency rushing through my veins, my feet stopped just outside the cave at the edge of the incoming tide. The waters were inching closer, but I had to go in. I needed to.

I stared into the blackness. I'd hoped that Lawry could rescue me—could save me from this expected end of mine. But such hopes—as I'd known from the start—had been in vain. Nothing could stop the course of events that needed to take place now.

Nothing had worked.

I stepped into the cave, into what had always seemed like utter blackness from the uneven shore. However, once inside, it never was all that dark during the daytime hours. My eyes adjusted quickly, and I immediately recognized the specific spot where I'd lost everything.

My heart lurched in my chest, and I crashed onto my knees, my face pressed into the crook of my elbow, buried in shame.

I don't know how long I wept there before I cried out, "Oh God, if I could erase one day of my existence...."

It wouldn't be enough.

No, nothing would ever be enough.

I am enough.

I stilled, searching the darkness. Could it be? My heart thudded in my chest. Oh, how I wanted to believe it. "Then be enough for me," I choked out with a whisper, every fiber of my being wishing, hoping, it was true. "Be enough. All I want is freedom from this—" At the weight of *this*, my deepest desire, I dropped my head back to the cool stone as sobs ripped from my chest. "Oh God, it's not just Lawry I desire; it's You. Please, please free me...." As I cried out, the cavern grew brighter with one smooth shift of shadowless light, and I lifted my head as it filtered around me, through me. I stood and backed against the rough wall, unable to comprehend the light. And that was when I realized that the heaviness I had known so well, for so long, was gone.

The chains, the ropes, the binds to this place—they were all gone.

The light suddenly shifted away, and I found myself standing in a new blackness—much darker than before. All I could see were the incoming waves of the tide outside.

Follow Me, beloved, out of this cave and through the coming water. Come out of the darkness, once and for all. I have so much more for you. And I love you—still.

My feet moved as if something in me were being pulled to the light, which now shone from outside the cave. I walked toward it, despite the waters that had begun to creep slowly in.

It was the only way out.

Stepping into the water, soaking my slippers and the bottom half of my gown, I stumbled out, forgetting all else but the fulfillment of the freedom I had so desperately longed for. I would not stay in that cave for one moment longer.

Just as I neared the higher embankment down the cove, I tripped in the water. I collapsed and fell on my hands and elbows, immersing the entire front of my bloodstained dress.

I rolled over to sit at the water's edge and investigated my scrapes. I turned my hands over and studied my palms. Vance's dried blood, which had been caked into every crevice of my skin and nails, now streaked down my arms, washing away.

I pushed my hands under the water again, scrubbing the rest of the stains off.

You, my beloved, are washed white as snow.

With clean hands, I touched my face, drenched with saltwater and with thankful tears as I realized what I'd been given.

A clean heart.

Tenderness filled my soul, followed by an overwhelming sense of gratitude for my freedom. "Thank You, Lord." I stood, the heaviness of my saturated gown pulling me down. Yet even that could not stifle the lightness I felt in my soul. After a moment of walking, I stopped.

Lawry.

It was too late. "Oh God, what am I supposed to do now?" I asked, sounding absolutely ridiculous to myself.

Until I felt the answer.

Follow after him...to Seattle.

TWENTY-NINE

The Funeral

"Humanity is never so beautiful as when praying for forgiveness,
or else forgiving another."
—Jean Paul Richter

M erie, go stand with Vance. He needs you."

I glanced from Mother to Vance, across the room in the front parlor of Rockwood. He still stood at the foot of his brother's casket. His hand hadn't moved from the corner of the smooth wood coffin in all the hours we'd been there. His sad eyes—still bruised from when Lawry had punched him days before—never left Will's pale, lifeless face. Nicholette had also staked a spot next to the casket, nearest to Will, her small hands clutching the edge of the casket. Her mother lingered beside her, in spite of Nicholette's repeated requests to be left alone.

I remained wedged between my parents and Garrett and Ainsley. Vance and I hadn't spoken since our conversation directly after the shootings, but I could tell he still carried the guilt of Will's death. He wouldn't speak to anyone. I'd watched his family try to reason with him time and again, for hours.

I certainly didn't know what Mother thought I might say to comfort him. The only thing I wanted to tell him was that I wouldn't be marrying him. And I wasn't sure he was up to hearing that in his present state. I would tell him eventually, though. It was all I could think about doing. I still felt something tying me to him, but now it was very small and insignificant, compared with the debilitating binds I'd suffocated under for six years.

A day later, I still marveled at the lightness in my soul because of the grace and mercy of God. It had taken my going back to the hardest place in the world for me to face in order to realize that it was the freedom found only in Christ that I needed most. Of course, Lawry Hampton hadn't been able to save me from the prison my sin had created, but it was unfortunate that it had taken my loving and losing him to finally realize *Who* I needed most of all.

And He wanted me to follow after Lawry...to Seattle.

Somehow.

It had turned out to be fortunate that Vance had kept Benta and Wynn at Rockwood the day of the wedding. They'd learned what had happened, and also that Lawry had already left for Washington. Wynn hadn't taken the news well. Honestly, neither had Benta.

"Dearest, just look at him," Mother reiterated, since her first nudge in Vance's direction hadn't worked. "He's absolutely miserable. What he must think of you! Go hold your fiancé's hand. No one will mind at a time like this." When all else failed, she took hold of my arm and guided me straight across the congested room to stand next to Vance. And then she left me there.

But I wasn't about to hold his hand. I simply stood beside him at the foot of the casket.

Taking special effort not to look at Nicholette, I noticed that half the crowd seemed to be watching my every move. Hopefully, the rumors I'd started about our engagement hadn't gone far, and everyone would understand that it had all been a terrible misunderstanding. Could they really expect Vance Everstone to marry so soon after losing both a wife and a brother in a matter of months?

Of course not. Of course, they would understand. Hopefully.

Vance had the same blank expression upon his face as he'd had the day before, and he wouldn't look at me. What had he wanted to tell me yesterday at Truesdale when I'd hurried away to the cave? Had he simply desired my presence? Instead, what had I done? Run away, and essentially resolved to tear myself from his grasp forever.

Only, Vance's grasp didn't seem so tight now.

"Meredyth," Vance whispered. He stepped closer and removed his right hand from Will's casket for the first time all morning. His left arm was in a sling, pressed flat against his stomach, and his bruises from Lawry's fist were still evident. "Come, walk with me." With his good arm, he took hold of my elbow and guided me through the mass of people into the great hall and then out the front door. We walked until we reached the edge of the lawn, where the low tide had bared the rocks and gravel of the beach before us. He was silent for some moments before he said, "I can't marry you."

My eyes flew to his gaze, and yes, he was looking down at me, speaking those words in earnest. I could hardly comprehend how it was possible.

"I can't imagine marrying anyone after yesterday...can't imagine having a wife and children to protect from people like the Gerards for the rest of my life. You'll take Wynn, won't you? Having any connection with me would only endanger your lives."

"You—" The rest of my intended words stuck in my throat.

"It was selfish of me to hold you to your forgotten promises. Anyone can tell who it is you love." One corner of his mouth cocked up in a subtle smirk. "It certainly isn't me. And he deserves you far more than I do." His glance darted away, in the direction of the caves. "It was despicable of me, what I did that summer—when I could tell he was already in love with you."

"I was willingly led, Vance, and I didn't know how he felt—"

"But I used you. I didn't think it would go so far as it did; I only wanted to hurt him—and I used you to do it. And made sure he knew all about it, too."

My stomach lurched, and I thought I was going to retch. Lawry had known all along? "You told him?" I was barely able to breathe.

"It was spiteful, but yes. I told him you were so sick in love with me that you'd let me—" Vance took hold of one of my hands, gripping it tightly, gazing down at me again. "When it was obvious it didn't matter to you whether Lawry loved you or not, I decided I could leave the country and trust that you would wait for me. I didn't want to be married yet, and I assumed I could have my fun while you awaited my return. I never dreamed Lawry would prove to be so steadfast."

My hand felt numb in his; he wouldn't let go, no matter how I pulled. I resisted the tears gathering behind my eyelids as much as I could, but it was useless. I simply closed my eyes, but the tears escaped nonetheless and fell down my face. Snapshots of things Lawry had done and said in the last six years flashed through my mind: his perseverance, his running to Washington, his coming back, that first kiss, and everything since.

And he'd known all along.

"Will you forgive me, Mere?"

An odd tingle coursed through me, something like mercy—and it flooded my soul. "I...yes, Vance, I forgive you." The words were out of my mouth before I knew what I was saying, but they were words I understood—words I myself had discovered only yesterday and now could freely give.

Vance loosened his grip on my hand, a reluctant smile on his lips. "You don't hate me?"

"Hardly." I stared blankly into his face, as if finally seeing him. Even with as much as he'd just confessed and opened up to me, he was still a brick wall, his black eyes letting everyone see only what he wanted them to see.

"I hear he's on his way back to Seattle already. What are you going to do?"

"He left as soon as the wedding was finished, with good reason," I answered, ignoring the question. I pulled my hand free, thinking that if Vance looked too closely, he might see exactly how apprehensive I suddenly was to face Lawry Hampton again.

"He still loves you."

I turned to face the house. "I'm sure he must hate me by now."

"I saw him before he left yesterday. I saw him watching you. He doesn't hate you."

"I'm sure he never wants to see me again."

Vance grabbed my shoulder with his good hand and spun me to face him. "There's only one way to find out."

"Right." I walked a little ways toward the house, thinking he would follow. When I didn't hear his footsteps, I glanced back. He still stood facing the ocean, his good arm crossed over his torso, cradling his injured one.

"Have Nathan and Amaryllis take you back with them to Washington. I'm sure they'll understand."

I hadn't even thought of that. But I'd hardly thought of anything besides the fact that I had no idea how I would attain enough courage to ever face Lawry again.

Vance's gaze seemed concentrated upon the low waves, as if he'd already forgotten I was there.

"What are you going to do now?"

"I'm going to take Will's place in Father's company," he answered rather decidedly, still searching the expanse of ocean. "And, of course, stay on my toes, considering Giselle's family will likely want to see me pay for what happened to Giselle, and now Pierre."

"I'll pray for your safety always, Vance." I took a step in the opposite direction, and he did likewise. Already, we were taking our separate paths.

"I appreciate that, Mere." He turned back one last time. "And I will covet those prayers every day. I have a feeling I'm going to need them."

THIRTY

Seattle

> "And his heart was going like mad and yes I said yes I will Yes."
> —James Joyce, *Ulysses*

July 4, 1891 · Seattle, Washington

The carriage halted, and I grabbed the leather handle at my
side.

I looked up.

There, embedded in the side of the massive hill the carriage
had just climbed, tucked quaintly along the steep road and surrounded by tall, thick trees and bushes, was Lawry's house. The
wide porch from the photo I'd seen was actually half hidden by the
hill. It was an older, two-story Queen Anne house with a square-
shaped turret at the front that towered two levels over the rest of
the roofline, like a beacon.

It was unexplainable, the rush of contentment that settled
over my bones as Nathan helped me from the carriage. My eyes
didn't leave the house as I moved forward somewhat in a trance,
in love with this house, this orphanage, the children...and Lawry.

The more I stared, the more I saw, the more I knew that this
was my home. Where God wanted me to be.

My expected end.

Before Benta and Wynn had exited the carriage, I raced up the walk to the front porch. I could hear the voices of children coming from inside the house.

I knocked on the door. When it creaked open, I held my breath.

The woman standing there was not one I recognized—not Mrs. Flanagan or Amelia Grendahl. Older and very round, she hadn't been in any of Lawry's photographs, as far as I could recall.

"Who are you?" I asked, still a little out of breath.

"I'm Mrs. Trombley...." Her eyes narrowed, and she closed the door a fraction of an inch. "And now it's my turn to be asking the very same thing. Who are you?"

Before I could answer, Nathan came up behind me. "Ah, Mrs. Trombley. Did Lawry not tell you about her, Meredyth? While in Boston, he was always looking for more workers. He had Mrs. Flanagan hire Mrs. Trombley in February."

"Meredyth? As in, Meredyth Summercourt?" Mrs. Trombley asked with a huff.

"Is Lawry here?" I would not be deterred. I had a fire blazing within me, ready to charge forward to wherever he was.

"No, he's not here." Mrs. Trombley crossed her big arms high over her chest. But then, at the sight of Wynn, Benta, and Amaryllis walking up the path, her eyes brightened, and she smiled. "Could that be the dear little Wynn we've heard so much about?"

Before anyone could answer, Wynn plowed through the group, past Mrs. Trombley, and stopped just inside the door. "Where's Lawry?"

"Why, he's with Amelia and Mrs. Flanagan at the church, of course, being as the wedding's today."

My heart stopped. "The wedding? What church? Where is it?" The questions tumbled out. I couldn't breathe. I'd broken his heart, and he'd turned to Amelia Grendahl.

"The Swedish Christian Mission at the corner of Stewart and Ninth. I'm sure you know the one, Mr. Everstone."

"Yes, I do." Nathan was already headed back to the carriage, with Amaryllis in tow, obviously concerned by the news of Lawry marrying Amelia so quickly.

I followed close behind them, my heart racing out of control. If Lawry married Amelia, I didn't know what I was going to do.

"Benta, stay here with Wynn," Nathan called over his shoulder. "We'll be back soon."

The three of us traveled in silence, Nathan having instructed the hired groom to travel as quickly as possible through town—to wherever Stewart and Ninth was. The burning fire and the contentment I'd felt when I first saw the house had diminished—it wasn't to be mine. Lawry wouldn't be mine, unless I somehow reached this wedding in time and was able to stop it from taking place.

It took forever to travel the mile or so to the church; we pretty much retraced the same route we'd taken to Lawry's house. With every bump in the road, all I could think of was seeing Lawry again. Facing him again would be humbling—it would strip me of all my pride. Surely, he would know why I'd come all the way across the country...and he would take me back. Hopefully, he would still love me.

At least, if I made it there before he said his vows to Amelia Grendahl.

For the first time, I regretted not telling Lawry that we were coming. I hadn't thought about Mrs. Flanagan or Amelia Grendahl, but now the image of that blonde beauty working side by side with Lawry at the orphanage took the wind from my chest. Had he turned to her with his broken heart? Had she been ready and waiting to put her claws in him?

Lawry couldn't have reached Seattle more than a week before us...but apparently, one week was enough time to become engaged and plan a wedding.

What if all God really meant for me to do in Seattle was deliver Wynn? What would I do then?

I would return home to Boston and help Ainsley plan her wedding to my brother. And I would continue teaching at the school… and end up just like Claudine Abernathy, after all.

I understood now why she'd never married. She was still too in love with her Eliot, and she wouldn't—no, couldn't—marry anyone else. I knew there would be a similar hole in my life to the one Eliot had left in Claudine. I knew I would never marry—not if I couldn't have Lawry Hampton.

Yes, God had filled my heart, taken my life—and I trusted Him that whatever did happen in the next few minutes would be in accordance with His will. If it was indeed His will that I lose my chance with Lawry, then I would be all right with that. Somehow. I didn't like the thought of having to accept such a thing, but I would, if God willed it, and I would pray every day that my heart would survive.

When the carriage stopped on the steep incline of the crowded street, I was ready. I jumped out and ran up to the front of a white church with a set of double doors at each of the front corners of the building closest to the street. I took the steps to the nearer one and tried the handle. Finding the door unlocked, I threw it open and hurried inside, to another set of smaller double doors in the corner of the vestibule. A sliver of bluish-tinted light sifted through the crack between them.

When I heard a male voice ask, "Who gives this woman—" I wrenched open the doors. I didn't care if I was rudely interrupting or if Nathan and Amaryllis were behind me. When I saw Lawry, dressed in a gray suit, standing at the altar, I rushed forward, down one of the two aisles that met at the front of the sanctuary. Everyone in the pews on either side of the aisle stared coldly at me.

"Have you come to the part where we're asked to speak now or forever hold our peace?" My voice echoed above me off the vaulted ceiling.

Lawry didn't immediately turn around. And as I walked toward him, I noticed his shoulders stiffen as he took a deep breath.

Amelia Grendahl—a young woman I'd never met—faced me with an expression akin to shock. And then, for some odd reason, she smiled—first at me, then at Lawry. She stood on tiptoe to whisper something in his ear.

"Young lady, do you have something you'd like to say?" the pastor asked from the altar.

I must not have missed my chance. "I don't believe this wedding should take—"

Before I realized what was going on, Lawry gripped me by the arm and propelled me to the back of the sanctuary, pushing past the same doors I'd just come through. He stopped in the vestibule and held my arms down at my sides—his hands were so strong, holding on to my elbows so tightly. He stood stone-still, showing not an ounce of emotion.

"Meredyth, I'm not marrying Amelia."

A flash of relief swept through me, but I shook it off. "What do you mean? I just saw—"

"You just interrupted my giving Amelia away at *her* wedding. Not mine."

"Oh." He was telling the truth. I could see it in his eyes. He wasn't getting married. "Good."

"So, if you'll excuse me, I need to get back in there." He just barely smiled. "Wait for me right here." He let go of me and disappeared back through the sanctuary doors.

I sank against the wall.

What had just happened?

I waited for what seemed like an hour—which was probably more like ten minutes—watching through the crack as Lawry gave his friend Amelia away to be married, and then as the pastor brought forth Amelia and her groom to be joined together. I didn't know what had happened to Nathan and Amaryllis until the wedding concluded, and they opened the door I'd been peeking through.

"Pity you had to miss such a touching ceremony, Mere." Nathan propped the door open.

"Lawry told me to wait in here."

"Was he happy to see you?" Amaryllis asked.

"I think so." Really, I wasn't all that certain. Behind Nathan, the wedding guests exited the sanctuary down the other aisle into the vestibule on the other side of the church. "Where is he?"

"He's coming," Nathan answered.

Lawry appeared around the open door and cleared his throat.

As if on cue, Amaryllis and Nathan turned around and disappeared into the sanctuary, closing the doors behind them. Lawry leaned against the door frame, his arms crossed at his chest, a frown marring his perfect, gorgeous face.

"Meredyth." He didn't smile. He hardly seemed like he wanted to see me.

"Lawry." I backed against the wall. What was I supposed to say?

"What are you doing here?" Still, no emotion whatsoever.

I pushed off the wall. I would do this. No matter how he appeared, no matter how irritated he seemed with me. Only, I still didn't know what words to use.

"Did you bring Wynn?" he asked.

I nodded. "And Benta. We're all here."

He arched an eyebrow and stood perfectly still for some moments. Would he not speak to me? Finally, "You're no longer engaged to Vance?"

I swallowed the lump in my throat. "No, I'm not. I'm not going to marry Vance."

"Why not?"

"Because you were right." I took a step forward. "For years, I thought I needed to be the one to make up for what we'd done."

My face burned with shame, remembering that Lawry knew…that he'd known for all those years. "But after you left, I went back there. I went to the cave where I—where we…." I couldn't go on. It was impossible. I could hardly find the words to describe how my soul twisted and groaned inside, just thinking of what I'd done and how undeserving I was of love and mercy, from him and from God. "I don't deserve you, but I don't deserve God's love and forgiveness, either. And yet, somehow, I have them…in abundance."

Lawry's arms fell to his sides. His deep blue eyes glanced up and held my gaze—and finally, what I'd been looking for, hoping to see, for weeks glimmered through, piercing me to my very depths.

I took another step forward. He met me with one long stride of his own and wrapped his arms tightly around me, holding me close; as if afraid I might disappear.

Somehow, I hadn't shed a tear until that moment, but they all broke loose the instant I pressed my cheek to his jaw and put my arms around his waist. I breathed in his peppermint scent and choked past my tears. "You still want me?"

Lawry took my face in his hands, forcing me to look him in the eye. "I would have waited, Meredyth. I would have wanted you forever. And I would have waited my whole life for you."

"Well, I'm glad it didn't come to that." I grinned through my tears.

"I love you…so very much." He didn't smile; rather, his look made it seem as if those few words still weighed heavily upon his soul, as if no earthly thing meant more to him than me.

"I love you, too, Lawry. Don't doubt it for a moment. Despite how it's seemed, I never stopped loving you. Not for one torturous minute."

Finally, he smiled again. "Nevertheless, I don't think I'm going to let you out of my sight." He reached into his coat pocket and produced a small leather box. "And before you have a chance to change your mind again…will you marry me?" He popped it open with one hand, revealing Claudine's square-cut diamond ring. His other hand still held my face, as if he couldn't stop touching me for fear I'd prove to be only an illusion. "Marry me today?"

I nodded as I released his waist and splayed my hands over his chest. I couldn't stop touching him, either, it seemed. He slipped the ring onto my left hand.

"There. Right where it belongs."

My arms again went around his waist. It was difficult to believe—difficult to understand how he could love me so, for so long, and through everything.

"You really don't mind, Merit, do you...getting married today?" he asked. "Nathan and Amaryllis are in there waiting with the pastor, as are Amelia, her new husband, and Mrs. Flanagan. They're all waiting for us at the altar."

"Are they really?" My heart suddenly sounded in my ears, thumping wildly at the thought of settling everything so quickly. But really, what would be the point of waiting one day more?

"I told you, I'm serious." His voice now sounded rough with pent-up emotion. "I don't want to be separated from you ever again."

I nodded and whispered, "I don't, either."

"Then it's agreed?"

"Agreed."

Lawry grabbed me by the hand, and together we pulled the doors open wide. He marched me straight down the aisle to where the pastor, Nathan, Amaryllis, and the rest of Lawry's Seattle friends waited for us at the altar.

"We'll have time for more lengthy introductions once we're back at the house," Lawry told the group. "All you need to know right now is that this is my lovely bride, Meredyth, who is ready and willing in her dress of white...with a pretty blue sash." He cut me a glance and smiled dashingly. "If you don't mind, I'd rather properly introduce her to you in just a little while as Mrs. Lawrence Hampton."

A Preview of

The Captive Imposter

Book Three, The Everstone Chronicles
Coming Spring 2015

About the Author

Agraduate of Taylor University with a degree in Christian education, and a former bookseller at Barnes & Noble, Dawn Crandall didn't begin writing until 2010, when her husband found out about her long-buried dream of writing a book. Without a doubt that she would someday be published, he encouraged her to quit her job in 2010 in order to focus on writing *The Hesitant Heiress* (book one in The Everstone Chronicles). It didn't take her long to realize that writing books was what she was made to do.

Apart from writing books, Dawn is also a first-time mom to a precious little boy (born March 2014) and serves with her husband in a premarital mentorship program at their local church in Fort Wayne, Indiana.

Dawn is a member of the American Christian Fiction Writers, the secretary for the Indiana ACFW Chapter (Hoosier Ink), and an associate member of the Great Lakes ACFW Chapter. She is represented by Joyce Hart of Hartline Literary Agency.

The Everstone Chronicles is Dawn Crandall's first series. All three books composing the series were semifinalists in ACFW's prestigious Genesis Writing Contest for pre-published authors, the third book going on to become a finalist in 2013.